TWISTS AND TURNS

TWISTS AND TURNS

TALES OF MYSTERY, ADVENTURE, CRIME, AND HUMOR BY BERNARD CAPES

COACHWHIP PUBLICATIONS

Landisville, Pennsylvania

Twists and Turns: Tales of Mystery, Adventure, Crime, and Humor by
  Bernard Capes
Copyright © 2011 Coachwhip Publications
No claim made on public domain material.

Bernard Capes (1854-1918)

ISBN 1-61646-094-6
ISBN-13 978-1-61646-094-5

CoachwhipBooks.com

CONTENTS

A Lazy Romance

I had slept but two nights at King's Cobb, when I saw distinctly that the novel with which I was to revolutionize society and my own fortunes, and with the purpose of writing which in an unvexed seclusion I had buried myself in this expedient hamlet on the South Coast, was withered in the bud beyond redemption. To this lamentable canker of a seedling hope the eternal harmony of the sea was a principal contributor; but Miss Whiffle confirmed the blight. I had fled from the jangle of a city, and the worries incidental to a life of threepenny sociabilities; and the result was—

I had rooms on the Parade—a suggestive mouthful. But then the Parade is such a modest little affair. The town itself is flung down a steep hill, at the mouth of a verdurous gorge; and lies pitched so far as the very waterside, a picturesque jumble of wall and roof. Its banked edges bristle and stand up in the bight of a vaster bay, with a crooked breakwater, like a bent finger, beckoning passing sails to its harbourage—an invitation which most are coy of accepting. For the attractions of King's Cobb are—comparatively—limited, and its nearest station is a full six miles distant along a switchback road.

Possibly this last fact may have militated against the popularity of King's Cobb as a holiday resort. If so, all the better; and may enterprise for ever languish in the matter. For vulgarity can claim no commoner purpose with fashion than is shown in that destruction of ancient landmarks and double gilding of new which follows the "opening out" of some unsophisticated colony of simple souls.

7

King's Cobb, if "remote and unfriended," is neither "melancholy" nor "slow"; but it is small, and all its fine little history—for it has had a stirring one—has ruffled itself out on a liliputian platform.

Than this, its insignificance, I desired nothing better. I wished to feel the comparative importance of the individual, which one cannot do in crowded colonies. I coveted surroundings that should be primitive—an atmosphere in which my thoughts could speak to me coherent. I would be as one in a cave, looking forth on sea, and sky, and the buoyant glory of Nature; unvexed of conventions; untrammelled by social observances; building up my enchanted palace of the imagination against such a background as only the unsullied majesty of sky and ocean could present. For the result was to crown with my name an epoch in literature; and hither in future ages should the pilgrim stand at gaze, murmuring to himself, "And here he wrote it!"

I laid my head on my pillow, that first night of my stay, with a brimming brain and a heart of high resolve. The two little windows, under a thatched roof, of my sleeping place (*that* lay over my sitting-room, and both looked oceanwards) were open to the inpour of sweet hot air; and only the regular wash of the sea below broke the close stillness of the night. I say this was all; and, with the memory upon me, I could easily, at any time, break the second commandment.

I had thought myself fortunate in my lodgings. They were in a most charming old-world cottage—as I have said on the Parade—and at high tide I could have thrown a biscuit into the sea with merely a lazy jerk. My sitting-room put forth a semi-circular window—like a lighthouse lantern—upon the very pathway, and it had been soothing during the afternoon to look from out this upon the little world of sea and sky and striding cliff that was temporarily mine. From the Parade four feet of stone wall dipped to a second narrow terrace, and this, in its turn, was but a step above a slope of shingle that ran down to the water.

Veritably had I pitched my tent on the wide littoral of rest. So I thought with a smile, as I composed myself for slumber.

I slept, and I woke, and I lay awake for hours. Every vext problem of my life and of the hereafter presented itself to me, and had to be argued out and puzzled over with maddening reiteration. The reason for this was evident and flagrant. It had woven itself into the tissue of my brief unconsciousness, and was now recognised as, ineradicably, part of myself.

The tide was incoming, that was all, and the waves currycombed the beach with a swishing monotony that would have dehumanized an ostler.

This rings like the undue inflation of a little theme. I ask no pity for it, nor do I make apology for my weakness. Men there may be, no doubt, to whom the unceasing recurrent thump and scream of a coasting tide on shingle speaks, even in sleep, of the bountiful rhythm of Nature. I am not one of them—at least, since I visited King's Cobb. The noise of the waters got into my brain and stayed there. It turned everything else out—sleep, thought, faith, hope, and charity. From that first awakening my skull was a mere globe of stagnant fluid, for any disease germs that listed to propagate in.

Perhaps I was too near the coast-line. The highest appreciations of Nature's thunderous forces are conceived, I believe, in the muffled seclusion of the study. I had heard of still-rooms. I did not quite know what they were; but they seemed to me an indispensable part of seaside lodgings, and for the rest of that night I ardently and almost tearfully longed to be in one.

I came down in the morning jaded and utterly unrefreshed. It was patent that I was in no state to so much as outline the preliminaries of my great undertaking. "Use shall accustom me," I groaned. "I shall scarcely notice it to-night."

And it was at this point that Miss Whiffle walked like a banshee into the disturbed chambers of my life, and completed my demoralization.

I must premise that I am an exquisitely nervous man—one who would accept almost ridiculous impositions if the alternative were a "scene." Strangers, I fancy, are quick to detect the signs of this weakness in me; but none before had ever ventured to take such outrageous advantage of it as did Miss Whiffle, with the completest success.

This lady had secured me for a month. My rights extended over the lantern-windowed sitting-room and the bedroom above it. They were to include, moreover, board of a select quality.

"Select" represented Miss Whiffle's brazen mean of morality; and, indeed, it is an elastic and accommodating word. One, for instance, may select an aged gander for its wisdom, knowing that the youthful gosling is proverbially "green." Miss Whiffle selected the aged gander for me, and I gnawed its sinewy limbs without a protest. On a similar principle she appeared to ransack the town shops for prehistoric joints (the locality was rich in fossils), and vegetables that, like eggs, only grew harder the more they were boiled.

I submitted, of course; and should have done no less by a landlady not so obstreperously constituted. But this terrible person gauged and took me in hand from the very morning following my arrival.

She came to receive my *orders* after breakfast (tepid chicory and an omelette like a fragment of scorched blanket) with her head wrapped up in a towel. Thus habited she had the effrontery to trust the meal had been to my liking. I gave myself away at once by weakly answering, "Oh, certainly!"

"As to dinner, sir," she said faintly, "it is agreed, no kitching fire in the hevening. That is understood."

I said, "Oh, certainly!" again.

"What I should recommend," she said—and she winced obtrusively at every sixth word— "is an 'arty meal at one, and a light supper at height."

"That will suit me admirably," I said.

She tapped her fingers together indulgently.

"So I thought," she murmured. "Now, what do you fancy, sir?"

"Dear me!" I exclaimed, for her face was horribly contorted. "Are you in pain?"

"Agonies!" said Miss Whiffle.

"Toothache?"

"Neuralgia, sir, for my sins."

"Is there—is there no remedy?"

She was taken with a sharp spasm of laughter, mirthless, but consciously expressive of all the familiar processes of self-effacement under torture.

"I arks nothing but my duty, sir," she said. "That is the myrrh and balsam to a racking 'ed. Not but what I owns to a shrinking like unto death over the thought of what lays before me this very morning. Rest and quiet is needful, but it's little I shall get of either out of a kitching fire in the dog days. And what would you fancy for your dinner, sir?"

"I am sorry," I murmured, "that you should suffer on my account. I suppose there is nothing cold—"

"Not enough, sir, in all the 'ouse to bait a mousetrap. Nor would I inconvenience you, if not for your own kind suggestion. But potted meats is 'andy and ever sweet, and if I might make bold to propose a tin—"

"Very well. Get me what you like, Miss Whiffle."

"I must arks your pardin, sir. But to walk out in this 'eat, and every rolling pebble under my foot a knife through my 'ed—no, sir. I make bold to claim that consideration for myself."

"Leave it to me, then. I will do my own catering this morning."

Then I added, in the forlorn hope of justifying my moral ineptitude to myself, "If you take my advice, you will lie down."

"And where, sir?" she answered, with a particularly patient smile. "The beds is unmade as yet, sir," she went on, in a suffering decline, "and rumpled sheets is thorns to a bursting brain."

Then she looked meaningly at the sitting-room sofa.

"I made bold to think, if you 'ad 'appened to been a-going to bathe, the only quiet place in the 'ouse—" she murmured, in semi-detached sentences, and put her hand to her brow.

Five minutes later (I fear no one will credit it) I was outside the house, and Miss Whiffle was installed, towel and all, upon my sofa.

For a moment I really think the outrageous absurdity of the situation did goad me to the tottering point of rebellion. I had not the courage, however, to let myself go, and, as usual, succumbed to the tyranny of circumstances.

It was a blazing morning. The flat sea lay panting on its coasts, as if, for all its liquid sparkle, it were athirst; and the town, under the oven of its hills, burned red-hot, like pottery in a kiln.

I went and bought my tinned meat (a form of preserve quite odious to me) and strolled back disconsolately to the Parade. Occasionally, flitting past the lantern window, I would steal a side glance into the cool luminosity of my own inaccessible parlour; and there always, reclining at her ease upon my sofa, was the in-eradicable presentment of Miss Whiffle.

At one o'clock I ventured to reclaim my own, and sat me down at table, a scorched and glutinous wreck, too overcome with lassi-tude to tackle the obnoxious meal of my own providing. And to the sofa, already made familiar of that dishonoured towel, I was fain presently to confide the empty problem of my own aching head.

All this was but the forerunner and earnest of a month's long martyrdom. That night the sea had me by the nerves again, and for many nights after; and, although I grew in time to a certain tolerance of the booming monotony, it was the tolerance of a dully resigned, not an indifferent, brain.

When it came to the second morning, not only the novel, but the mere idea of my ever having contemplated writing one, was a thing with me to feebly marvel over. And from that time I set my-self down to exist and broil only, doling out a languid interest to the locality, the shimmer of whose baking hill-sides made all life a quivering, glaring phantom of itself.

Miss Whiffle tyrannized over me more or less according to her mood; but she did not usurp my sitting-room again. I used to sit by the hour at the lantern window, in a sort of greasy blankness, like a meat pudding, and vacantly scrutinize the loiterers who passed by on the hot asphalt of the Parade. Screened by the win-dow curtains, I could see and hear without endangering my own privacy; and many were the odd interchanges of speech that fell from strangers unconscious of a listener.

One particularly festering day after dinner I had the excitement of quite a pretty little quarrel for dessert. Miss Whiffle had stuffed me with suet, in meat and pudding, to a point of stupefaction that stopped short only of absolute insensibility; and in this state I took up my usual post at the window, awaiting in swollen vacuity the possibilities of the afternoon.

On the horizon violet-hot sea and sky showed scarce a line of demarcation between them. Nearer in the waves snored stertorously from exhausted lungs, as if the very tide were in extremis. Not a breath of air fanned the pitiless Parade, and the sole accent on life came from a droning, monotonous voice pitched from somewhere in querulous complaint.

"Frarsty!" it wailed, "Frarsty! I warnt thee!" and again, "I warnt thee, Frarsty! Frarsty! Frar—r—r—rsty!" drawn out in an inconceivable passionlessness of desire again and again, till I felt myself absorbing the ridiculous yearning for an absurd person and inclined to weep hysterical tears at his unresponsiveness.

Then through the suffocating miasma thridded another sound— the whine of a loafing tramp slowly pleading along the house fronts—vainly, too, as it appeared.

"Friends," went his formula, nasal and forcibly spasmodic in the best gull-catcher style, "p'raps you will ask why I, a able-bodied man, are asking for ass—ist—ance in your town. Friends, I answer, becorse I cannot get work and becorse I cannot starve. Any honest work I would be thankful for; but no one will give it to me."

Then followed an elaborate presentation, in singsong verse, of his own undeserved indigence and the brutality of employers, and so the recitation again:—

"Friends, the least ass—ist—ance would be welcome. I am a honest British workman, and employ—ment I cannot ob—tain. You sit in your com—for—ta—ble 'ouses, and I ask you to ass—ist a fellow creature, driven to this for no fault of his own—for many can 'elp one where one cannot 'elp many."

Then he hove into sight—a gastropodous tub of a fellow, with a rascally red eye; and I shrank behind my curtains, for I never court parley with such gentlemen.

He spotted me, of course,—rogues of his feather have a hawk's eye for timid quarry,—and his bloated face appeared at the window.

"Sir—friend," he said, in a confidential, hoarse whisper, "won't you 'elp a starvin' British workman?"

I gave him sixpence, cursing inwardly this my concession to pure timorousness, and the bestial mask of depravity vanished with a grin.

After that I was left to myself, heat and haze alone reigning without; and presently, I think, I must have fallen into a suetty doze, for I was semi-conscious of voices raised in dispute for a length of time, before I roused to the fact that two people were quarrelling just outside my window.

They were a young man—almost a boy—and a girl of about his own age; and both evidently belonged to the labouring classes.

She was, I took occasion to notice, aggressively pretty in that hot red and black style that finds its warmest admirers in a class cultivated above that to which she belonged; and she was scorning and flouting her slow, perplexed swain with that over-measure of vehemence characteristic of a sex devoid of the sense of proportion.

"Aw!" she was saying, as I came into focus of their dispute. "That's the moral of a mahn, it is. Yer ter work when ye like an' ter play when ye like, and the girls hahs ter sit and dangle their heels fer yer honours' convenience."

"I doan't arlays get my likes, Jenny, or I shud a' met you yester-day."

"Ay, as yer promused."

"We worked ower late pulling the lias, I tell yer. 'Twould 'a' meant half a day's wages garn if I'd com', and theer, my dear, 'ud been reason for another delay in oor getting spliced."

"You're fine and vulgar, upon my word! A little free, too, and a little mistook. I've no mind ter get spliced, as yer carls it, wi' a chap as cannot see's way ter keep tryst."

"Yer doan't mean thart?"

"Doan't I? Yer'll answer fer me in everything, 't seems. But yer've got enough ter answer fer yerself, Jack Curtice. I'm none of the sort ter go or stay at anny mahn's pleasure. There's kerps and dabs in the sea yet, Jack Curtice; and fatter ones ter fish fer, too."

"But yer doan't understand."

"I understand my own vally; and that isn't ter be kep' drarging my toes on the Parade half an a'rtenoon fer a chap as thinks he be better engaged summer else."

"And yer gone ter break wi' me fer thart?"

"Good-bye, Mr. Curtice," she said, and jerked her nose high and walked off.

Now here was an inconsistent jade, and I felt sorry and relieved for the sake of the young fellow.

He stood, after the manner of his kind, amazed and speechless. Man's saving faculty of logic was in him, but tongue-tied; and he could not express his intuitive recognition of the self-contradictory. Such natures frequently make reason articulate through a blow—a rough way of knocking her into shape, but commonly effectual. Jack, however, was evidently a large gentle swain of the dumb-suffering type—one of those unresisting leviathans of good-humour, upon whom a woman loves to vent that passion of the illogical which an antipathetic sex has vainly tried to laugh her out of conceit with.

I peered a little longer, and presently saw Mr. Curtice walk off in a state compound of bewilderment and abject depression.

This was the beginning to me of an interest apart from that which had brought me to King's Cobb. A real nutshell drama had usurped the place of that fictitious one that had as yet failed to mark an epoch by so much as a scratch. I accepted the former as some solace for the intolerable wrong inflicted upon me by the sea and Miss Whiffle.

I happened across my unconscious friends fairly frequently after that my first introduction to them; so often, indeed, that, judged by what followed, it would almost seem as if Fate, desiring record of an incident in the lives of these two, had intentionally worked to discomfit me from a task more engrossing.

Apart, and judged on their natural merits, I took Jack for a good stolid fellow, innately and a little aggravatingly virtuous, and perhaps a trifle more just than generous.

Jenny, I felt, had the spurious brilliancy of that division of her sex that claims as intuition an inability to master the processes of thought, and attributes to this faculty all fortunate conclusions, but none that is faulty. I thought, with some commiseration for him, that at bottom her manner showed some real leaning towards the lover she had discarded—that she felt the need of a pincushion, as it were, into which to stick the little points of her malevolence. I think I was inclined to be hard on her. I have felt the same antagonism many times towards beauty that was unattainable by me. For she was richly pretty, without doubt.

When in the neighbourhood of one another, however, they were wont to assume an elaborate artificiality of speech and manner in communion with their friends, that was designed with each to point the moral of a complete indifference and forgetfulness. But the girl was by far the better actor; and not only did she play her own part convincingly, but she generally managed to show up in her rival that sense of mortification that it was his fond hope he was effectually concealing.

A fortnight passed; and, lo! there came the end of the lovers' quarrel in all dramatic appropriateness.

By that time the doings of Jack and Jenny had come to be my mind's only refuge from such a vacancy of outlook as I had never before experienced. "All down the coast," that summer, "the languid air did swoon." The earth broiled, and very thought perspired; and Miss Whiffle's voice was like a steam-whistle.

One day, as I was exhaustedly trifling with my meridian meal, and balancing the gratification against the trouble of eating lumpy tapioca pudding, a muffled, rolling thud broke upon my ears, making the window and floor vibrate slightly. It seemed so distant and unimportant that I took no notice of it; and it was only when, ten minutes later, I became aware that certain excited townsfolk were scurrying past outside that I roused slowly to the thought that here was something unusual toward. Then, indeed, a sort of insane *abandon* flashed into life in me, and I leapt to my feet with maniac eyes. Something stirring in King's Cobb! I should have thought nothing less than the last trump could have pricked it out of its accustomed grooves; and that even then it would have slipped back into them with a sluggish sense of grievance after the first flourish.

I left my congealing dish, snatched up my hat, and joined the attenuated chase. It was making in one direction—a point, apparently, to the east of the town. As I sped excited through the narrow and tortuous streets, a great bulge of acrid dust bellied upon me suddenly at a corner; and, turning the latter, I plunged into a perfect fog of the same gritty smoke. In this, phantom figures moved, appeared, and vanished; hoarse cries resounded, and a general air of wild confusion and alarm prevailed. For the moment, I felt as if some history of the town's past were re-enacting, as if a sudden swoop of Frank or Dutchman upon the coast had called forth all the defensive ardour of its people. There was nothing of gunpowder in the stringent opacity, however; but, rather, a strong suggestion of ancient and disintegrated mortar.

A shape sped by me in the fog, and I managed to stay and question it.

"What is it all?" I asked.

"House fell down," was the breathless answer; "and a poor chap left aloft on the ruins."

Then I grew as insane as the rest of the company. I strode aimlessly to and fro, striving at every coign to pierce with my eyesight the white drift. I pushed back my hat; I gnawed my knuckles; I felt that I could not stay still, yet knew not for what point to make. Almost I felt that in another moment I should screech out—when a breath of sea air caught the skirt of the cloud, and rolled the bulk of it up and away over the house-tops.

Then, at once, was revealed to me the cause and object of all this gaggle, and confusion, and outcry. It was revealed to the crowd, too, that stood about me, and, in the revelation, the noise of its mouthing went off and faded, till a tense silence reigned and the murmur of one's breathing seemed a sacrilege.

I saw before me a ruinous space—a great ragged gap in a lofty block of brick and mortar. This block had evidently, at one time, consisted of two high semi-detached houses, and of these, one lay a monstrous heap of tumbled and shattered *débris*. A ruin, but not quite; for, as the course of a landslip will often tower with great spires and pinnacles of rock and ragged earth that have withstood the pull and onset of the moving hill-side, so here a high sheet of shattered wall, crowned with a cluster of toppling chimneys, stood up stark in the midst of the general overthrow. And there aloft, clinging to the crumbling stack, that might at any moment part, and fling and crush him into the savage ruin below, stood the figure of a solitary man. And the man was my friend of the Parade, Jack Curtice.

I could see and recognise him plainly—even the frantic clutch of his hands and the deadly pallor of his face.

The block—an ancient one—had been, as I afterwards learned, in course of demolition when the catastrophe took place. At the moment the poor fellow had been alone at his work, and now his destruction seemed a mere matter of seconds.

White dust rose from the heap, like smoke from an extinguished fire; and ever, as we looked, spars and splinters of brick tore away from the high fragment yet standing, and plunged with a thud into the wrack underneath.

It was glaringly evident that not long could elapse before wall and man would come down with a hideous, shattering run. A slip, a wilder clutch at his frail support, might in an instant precipitate the calamity.

Then from the upturned faces of the women cries of pity and anguish broke forth, and men nipped one another's arms and gasped, and knew not what counsel to offer.

"Do summut! do summut!" cried the women; and their mates only shook off their pleadings with a peevish show of callousness, that was merely the dumb anguish of undemonstrativeness. For, while their throats were thick, their practical brains were busy.

Some one suggested a ladder, and in a moment there was an aimless scurrying and turning amongst the women.

"Why don't 'ee stir theeself and hunt for un, Jarge?" panted one that stood near me, twisting hysterically upon a slow youth at her side.

"Shut up, 'Liza!" he answered gruffly; then, with a sort of indrawn gasp— "Look art the wall, lass—look art the wall!"

It was obvious to the least knowing what he meant. To lean so much as a broomstick, it seemed, against that tottering ruin would infallibly complete its destruction.

One foot of the clinging figure high up was seen to move slightly, and a little bomb of mortar span out into the air and burst into dust on a projecting brick. A long shrill sigh broke from the crowd.

Then the male wiseheads came together, and, desperate to snap the chord of impotent suspense, mooted and rejected plan after plan that their sane judgment knew from the first to be impracticable.

At the outset it was plainly impossible for a soul to approach the ruins. Apart from the almost certain mangling such a venture would entail upon the explorer, the least stirring or shifting of the great heap of rubbish flung about the base of the wall would certainly risk the immediate collapse of the latter.

Success, it was evident, must come, if at all, from a distance—but how?

One suggested slinging a rope from window to window of adjacent houses across the path of the broken chimney-stack—a good method of rescue had circumstances lent themselves to it. They did not. On the ruin side a wide space intervened; on the other, the sister house to that which had fallen, and which was also included in the order of demolition, was itself affected by the loss of its support, and leaned in a sinister manner, its party walls bulged and rent towards the scene of devastation.

Nothing short of the great Roc itself could, it seemed, snatch the poor fellow from his death perch.

There came suddenly an ominous silence. Then strode out in front of his fellows—and he moved so close to the ruin that the women whimpered and held one another—an old, rough-bearded chap in stained corduroy.

"Whart's he gone to do?" gasped the sibilant voices.

He hollowed his hands to his mouth, he cleared his hoarse throat two or three times. Only a little trailing screech came from it at first. Then he cursed his weakness, and pulled himself together.

"Jark! Jark Curtus!" he hailed, in an explosive voice.

"Hullo!"

The weak, small response floated down.

"My lard! my poor lard! we've thought oor best, arnd we can do nothun fower 'ee."

Instantly a shrill protest of horror went up from the women. This was not what they had expected.

"What! leave the mis'rable boy to his fate!"

There followed a storm of hisses from them—absolutely unreasonable, of course. The old fellow turned to retire, with hanging head.

At the moment a girl, flushed, blowzed, breathless, broke through the skirt of the mob and barred his retreat.

"Oh!" she panted, shaking her jet-black noddle at him— "here's a parcel o' gor-crows for discussin' help to a Christian marn! What! a score o' wiselings, and not one to hit oot the means and the way?"

She had only just heard, and had run a mile to the rescue of her old lad.

The women caught her enthusiasm, and jeered and cheered formlessly, as their manner is; for each desired for her own voice a separate recognition.

Jenny pushed rudely past the abashed gaffer. She was hatless, and her hair had tumbled abroad. She raised her face, with the eyes shining.

"Jack!" she cried, in a shrill voice— "Jack!"

The little weak response wailed down again.

"Jenny! I'm anigh done."

"Hold on a bit longer, Jack!" she screamed. "Don't move till I tell 'ee. I'm agone to save thee, Jack!"

Again from the women a rapturous cry broke out. What incompetent noodles appeared their masters in juxtaposition with this fearless, defiant creature.

The man up aloft seemed to shiver in the shock of the outcry; and once more some fragments of mortar rolled from under his feet and bounded into the depths. The girl rounded upon the voicers.

"Hold thee blazing tongues!" she cried in fury. "D'ee warnt to shake un from his perch?"

She turned to the foremost group of men.

"A couple o' long scaffold poles fro' yonder!" she cried hurriedly, "and twenty fathom o' rope!"

Her quick eyes and intelligence had found what she wanted in a builder's yard no great distance away.

"Follow, a dozen o' you!" she cried; and sped off in the direction she had indicated.

Just twelve men, and no more, obeyed her. She was mistress of the situation, and the crowd felt it. They made room for the dominant intellect, and awaited developments, watching, in suppressed excitement and trepidation, the figure—whom exhaustion was slowly mastering—high up above them.

Suddenly a sort of huge L-shaped structure moved down the street, until it stood opposite the ruined house. Then, twisting and rearing itself aloft, it took to itself the form of a lofty, slender gallows.

It was formed of a couple of forty-foot scaffolding poles, stoutly bound and corded together, the base of one to the top of the other, so that they stood at right angles. Five or six feet of the butt of the horizontal one was projected beyond its lashings, and to this three lengths of rope were fastened, and trailed long ends in the dust as the structure was held aloft and pushed and dragged into position.

"Now!" shrieked the girl, red-hot, reliant, never still for a moment; "as marny as can hold to each end there, and swing the blessed boom out towards him!"

Fifty may have responded. They swarmed like ants about the upraised pole, and she drove them into position—a black knot of men hauling on the triple cordage—left, right, and middle, like the ribs of a tent.

They saw her meaning and fell into place with a shout. To hold the projecting pole levered up at that height was a test of weight and muscle, even without their man on the end of it; but there were plenty more to help pull, did their united force waver.

"Jack!" screamed the girl again, in a wildness of excitement.
"Only a second longer, Jack! Hold on by your eyelids, and snatch
the stick the moment it comes agen thee!"

The horizontal spar pointed down the street. Slowly the men
worked round with the ropes, and slowly the point of the pole
turned in the direction of the chimney-stack and its forlorn burden. There was room and to spare for the process in the wide gap
made by the tumbled house.

The crowd held its breath. Here and there a strangled sob was
rent from overstrained lungs; here and there the wailing voice of a
baby whined up and subsided.

The pole swung round with the toiling men—neared him on the
ruin. He turned his head and saw, shifted his position and staggered. Jenny gave a piercing screech. The men, thinking something
was wrong, paused a moment.

On the instant there came a crackling, tearing sound—a heav-
ing roll—a splintering crash and uproar. The man aloft was seen
to make a flying leap—or was it only a hurled fragment of the falling chimney?—and white dust rose in a fog once more and blotted
out all the tragedy that might be enacting behind it.

A horrible silence succeeded, then a single woman yelled, and
her cry was echoed by fifty hoarse voices.

The noise came from those at the ropes. They were straining
and tugging, and some of them bobbed up and down like peas on a
drum.

"More on ye! more on ye! We've hooked un, and he's got the
pull of a sea sarpint!"

The ropes became thick with striving men. The whole street
resounded with a medley of cries.

Then the point of the boom swung slowly out of the fog, and
there was the rescued man swinging and swaying at the end of it.

They lowered him gradually into the street. But the strain upon
them was awful, and he came down with a run the last few yards.

Then they let the angle of the gallows wheel over as it listed,
and stood and mopped their hot foreheads, while the crowd rushed
for the poor shaky subject of all its turmoil.

I could not get within fifty feet of him; or, I think, I should have given him and Jenny then and there all my fortune.

Later, I made their acquaintance in a casual way, and compromised with my conscience by presenting them with a very pretty tea-service to help them set up house with.

Black Venn

"George," said Plancine.

"Please say it again," said George.

She dimpled at him and obeyed, with the soft suggestion of accent that was like a tender confidence. Her feet were sunk in Devonshire grass; her name was on the birth register of a little Devonshire sea-town; yet the sun of France was in her veins as surely as his caress was on her lips.

Therefore she said "George" with a sweet dragging sound that greatly fluttered the sensibilities of the person addressed, and not infrequently led them to alight, like Prince Dummling's queen bee, on the very mouth of that honeyed flower of speech.

Now Plancine put her cheek on her George's rough sleeve, and said she,—

"I have a confession to make—about something a little silly. Consequently I have postponed it till now, when it is too dark for you to see my face."

"Never!" he murmured fervently. "A double cataract could not deprive me of that vision. It is printed here, Plancine."

He smacked his chest hard on the left side.

"Yet it sounds hollow, George?"

"Yes," he said. "It is a sandwich-box, an empty one. I would not consign your image to such a deplorable casket. My heart was what I meant. How I hate sandwiches—misers shivering between sheets—a vile gastronomic economy!"

24

"Poor boy! I will make you little dough-cakes when you go apainting."

"Plancine! Your image here, yes. But your dough-cakes—!"

"Then keep to your sandwiches, sir."

"I must. But the person who invented them was no gentleman!"

"Papa would like to hear you say that."

"Say what?"

"Admit the possibility of any social distinction."

"It is only a question of sandwiches."

"George, *must* you be a Chartist and believe in Feargus O'Connor?"

"My soul, I cannot go back on my principles, for all that the violets of your eyes have sprouted under the shadow of a venerable family-tree."

"That is very prettily said. You may kiss my thumb-nail with the white spot in it for luck. No, sir. That is presuming. Now I am snug, and you may talk."

"Plancine, I am a son of the people. I hold by my own. No doubt, if I had blue blood to boast of, I should keep a vial of it in a prominent place on the drawing-room mantelpiece. As it is, I confess my desire is to carve for myself a name in art that shall be independent of all adventitious support; to answer to my vocation straight, upright, and manly."

"That is better than nobility—though I have pride in my own. I wish papa thought so. Yet he has both himself."

"The fine soul! For fifty years he has stood square to adversity with a smile on his face. Could I ever achieve that? Already I cry out on poverty; because I want an unencumbered field for work, and—yes, one other trifle."

"One other trifle, George?"

He took Plancine's face between his hands and looked very lovingly into her eyes.

"I think I did the old man too much honour," he said. "You nestling of eighteen—what credit to scout misfortune with such a bird at one's side!"

"Ah! but papa is sixty-nine and the bird but eighteen."

"And eighteen years of heaven are a good education in happiness."

So they coo'd, these two. The June scents of the little garden were wafted all about them. The moon had come up out of the sea, and, finding a trellis of branches over their heads, hung their young brows with coronals of shadowy leaves, like the old dame she was, rummaging in her trinket box for something for her favourites.

In the dimly-luminous parlour (that smelt of folios and warm coffee) of the little dark house in the background, the figure of papa, poring at the table over geological maps, was visible.

Fifty years ago an *émigré*, denounced, proscribed, and escaped from the ruin of a shattered society: here, in '49, a stately, large-boned man, placidly enjoying the consciousness of a serene dignity maintained at the expense of much and prolonged self-efface-ment—this was papa.

Grey hair, thinning but slightly near the temples; grey moustache and beard pointed *de bouc*; flowered dressing-gown girdled about a heart as simple as a child's—this was papa, papa who grubbed over his ordnance surveys while the young folks outside whispered of the stars.

Right beneath them—the latter—a broad gully of the hills went plunging precipitously, all rolled with leaf and flower, to the undercliff of soft blue lias and the very roof ridges of King's Cobb, whose walls and chimneys, now snowed with light, fretted a scallop of the striding bay that swept the land here like a scythe.

Plancine's village, a lofty appanage or suburb of this little seaboard town at the hill-foot, seemed rather the parent stock from which the other had emancipated itself. For all down the steep slope that fled from Upper to King's Cobb was flung a *débris* of houses that, like the ice-fall of a glacier, would appear to have broken from the main body and gone careering into the valley below.

It was in point of fact, however, but a subordinate hamlet—a hanging garden for the jaded tourist in the dog days, when his soul stifled in the oven of the sea-level cliffs—an eyrie for Plancine, and for George, the earnest painter, a Paradise before the fall.

And now says George, "We have talked all round your confession, and still I wait to give you absolution."

"I will confess. I read it in one of papa's books that is called the *Talmud*."

"Gracious me! you should be careful. What did you read?"

"That whoever wants to see the souls of the dead—"

"Plancine!"

"—must take finely sifted ashes, and strew them round his bed; and in the morning he will see their foot-tracks, as a cock's. I did it."

"You did?"

"Last night, yes. And what a business I had afterwards sweeping them up!"

"And did you see anything?"

"Something—yes—I think so. But it might have been mice. There are plenty up there."

"Now you are an odd Plancine! What did you want with the ghosts of the dead?"

"I will tell you, you tall man; and you will not abuse my confidence. George, for all your gay independence, you must allow me a little family pride and a little pathetic interest in the fortunes of the dead and gone De Jussacs."

"It is Mademoiselle De Jussac that speaks."

"It is Plancine, who knows so little:—that 'The Terror' would have guillotined her father, a boy of fourteen: that he escaped to Prussia, to Belgium, to England; for six years always a wanderer and a fugitive: that he was wrecked on this dear coast and, penniless, started life anew here on his little accomplishments: that he made out a meagre existence, and late in the order of years (he was fifty) married an expatriated countrywoman, who died— George, my mother died when I was seventeen months old—and that is where I stop. My good, big father—so lonely, so poor, and so silent! He tells me little. He speaks scantily of the past. But he was a Vicomte and is the last of his line; and I wanted the ghosts to explain to me so much that I have never learned."

The moonlight fell upon her sweet, pale, uplifted face. There were tears in her eyes that glittered like frost.

But George, for all his love, showed a little masculine impatience.

"Reserve is very good," he said; "but we can't all be Lord Burleighs by holding our tongues. There is a sort of silence that is pregnant with nothing."

"George, you cannot mean to insult my father?"

"No, dear. But why does he make such a mystery of his past? I would have mine as clear as a window, for all to look through. Why does he treat me with such suave and courteous opposition—permitting my suit, yet withholding his consent?"

"If you could be less democratic, dear—"

"It is a religion with me—not a brutal indulgence."

"Perhaps he cannot dissociate the two. Then, he admires your genius and commends your courage; but your poor purse hungers, my lover, and he desires riches for his Plancine."

"And Plancine?"

"She will die a grey-haired maid for thee, 'O Richard! O my king!'"

"My sweet—my bird—my wife! Oh, that you could be that now and kiss me on to fortune! I should be double-souled and inspired. A few months, and Madame la Vicomtesse should 'walk in silk attire.' I flame at the picture. Why will your father not yield you gracefully, instead of plying us with that eternal enigma of Black Venn?"

"Because enthusiasm alone may not command wealth," said a deep voice near them.

Papa had come upon them unobserved. The young man wheeled and charged while his blood was hot.

"Mr. De Jussac, it is a shame to hold me in this unending suspense."

"Is it not better than decided rejection?"

"I have served like Jacob. You cannot doubt my single-hearted devotion?"

"I doubt nothing, my George" (about *his* accent there was no tender compromise)— "I doubt nothing, but that the balance at your bankers' is excessive."

"You would not value Plancine at so much bullion?"

"But yes, my friend; for bullion is the algebraic formula that represents comfort. When Black Venn slips his apron—"

George made a gesture of impatience.

"When Black Venn slips his apron," repeated the father quietly, "I shall be in a position to consider your suit."

"That is tantamount to putting me off altogether. It is ungenerous. It is preposterous. You may or may not be right; but it is simply farcical (Plancine cried, "George!"—but he went on warmly, nevertheless) to make our happiness contingent on the possible tumbling down of a bit of old cliff—an accident that, after all, may never happen."

"Ah!" the quiet, strong voice went on; and in the old eyes turned moonwards one might have fancied one could read a certain pathos of abnegation, or approaching self-sacrifice; "but it will, and shortly, for I prophesy. It was no idle cruelty of mine that first suggested this condition, but a natural reluctance to sign myself back to utter loneliness."

Plancine cried, "Papa! papa!" and sprang into his arms.

"A little patience," said De Jussac, pressing his moustache to the round head, "and you will honour this weary prophet, I think. I was up on the cliff to-day. The great crack is ever widening. A bowling wind, a loud thunderstorm, and that apron of the hill will tear from its bondage and sink sweltering down the slopes."

In the moment of speaking a tremor seized all his limbs, his eyes glared maniacal, his outstretched arm pointed seawards.

"The guillotine!" he shrieked, "the guillotine!"

In the offing of the bay was a vessel making for the unseen harbour below. It stood up black against the moonlight, its sails and yards presenting some fantastic resemblance to that engine of blood.

George stepped back and hung his head embarrassed. He had more than once been witness of a like seizure. It was the guillotine fright—the fright that had smitten the boy of fourteen, and had pursued the man ever since with periodic attacks of illusion. Anything—a branch, a door-post, a window, would suggest the hateful form during those periods—happily brief—when the poor mind was temporarily unhinged. No doubt, in earlier years, the fits had occurred frequently. Now they were rare, and generally, it seemed, attributable to some strong excitement or emotion.

Plancine knew how to act. She put her hand over the frantic eyes, and led the old man stumbling up the garden path. She was going to sing to him from the little sweet folk-ballads of the old gay France before the trouble came—

"The king would wed his daughter
        Over the English sea;
    But never across the water
        Shall a husband come to me."

Love floated on the freshet of her voice straight into the heart of the young man who stood without.

II

Perhaps at first it had not been the least of the bitterness in M. De Jussac's cup of calamity that his mere pride of name must adjust itself to its altered conditions. That the Vicomte De Jussac should have been expatriated because he declined when called upon to contribute his heart's blood to the red conduit in the Faubourg St. Antoine was certainly an infamy, but one of which the very essence was that unquestioning acknowledgment of his rank. That the land of his adoption should have dubbed him Mr. Jussuks—in stolid unconsciousness, too, of the solecism—was an outrage of a totally different order—an outrage only to be condoned on the score that an impenetrable insular *gaucherie*, and not a malicious impertinence, was responsible for it.

Mr. Jussuks had, however, outlived his sense of the injurious appellation; had outlived much prejudice, the wear of poverty, his memory of many things, and, very early, his scorn of the plebeian processes that to the impecunious are a condition of living at all. He was certainly a man of courageous independence, inasmuch as from the hour of his setting foot in England—and that was at the outset of the century—he had controlled his own little fortunes without a hand to help him over the deep places.

Of his first struggles little is known but this—that for years, turning to account some small knowledge of draughtsmanship he had acquired, he found employment in ladies' academies, of which there was a plenitude at that date in King's Cobb.

That, however, which brought him eventually into a modest prominence—not only in that same beautiful but indifferently known watering-place (upon which he had happened, it would appear, fortuitously), but elsewhere and amongst men of a certain mark—was a discovery—or the practical application of one—which in its result procured him a definite object in life, together with the means to pursue it.

Ammonites, and such small geological fry, were to be found by the thousand in the petrified mud beds of the Cobb region; but it was left to the ingenuity, aided by good fortune, of the foreigner to unearth from the flaking and perishing cliffs of lias some of the earliest and finest specimens of the ichthyo- and plesio-saurus that a past world has yielded to the naturalists.

Out of these the *émigré* made money, and so was enabled to pursue and enlarge upon his researches. Presently he prospered into a competence, married (poor Mademoiselle Belleville, of the Silver Street Academy, who died of typhoid at the end of a couple of summers), and so grew into the kindly old age of the absorbed and gentle naturalist, with his Plancine budding at his side.

What in all these fifty years had he forgotten? His name, his rank, his very origin? Much, no doubt. But that there was one haunting memory that had dwelt with him throughout, his child and her lover were to learn—one memory, and that dreadful recurring illusion of the guillotine.

"When Black Venn slips his apron, I shall be in a position to consider your suit."

Surely that was an odd and enigmatical condition, entirely remote from the subject at issue? Yet from the moment of the first impassioned pleadings of the stricken George, De Jussac had insisted upon it as one from which there should be no appeal.

Now the Black Venn referred to was a great mound of lias that rolled up and inland, in the far sweep of the bay, from the giddy margin of the lower ruin of cliffs. These—mere compressed mountains of mud, blown by the winds and battered by the sea—were in

a constant state of yawn and collapse. Yard by yard they yielded to
the scourge of Time, and landslides were of common occurrence.

All along the middle slope of Black Venn itself, a wide, deep
fissure, dark and impenetrable, had stretched from ages unrecorded. But the eventual opening-out of this crevasse, and the
consequent subsidence of the incline, or apron, below it, had been
foretold by Mr. De Jussac; and this, in fact, was the condition to
which he had alluded.

III

"Mr. De Jussac! do you hear me?"

"I am coming, my friend."

The light shining steadily through a front window of the cottage flickered and shifted. The young man in the rain and storm
outside danced with impatience.

Suddenly the door opened, and Plancine's father stood there,
candle in hand.

"What is it, my George?"

"The hill, sir—the hill! It's fallen! You were right. You must
stand by your word. Black Venn has slipped his apron!"

"My God, no!"

There were despair and exultation in his voice.

"My God, no!" he whispered again, and dived into a cupboard
under the stair.

Thence he reappeared with a horn lantern and his old blue cloak.

"Come, then!" he cried. "My hour is upon me!"

"Mr. De Jussac, it will wait till the morning."

"No, no, no! Do you trifle with your destiny? It has happened
opportunely, while all are within doors and we have a clear field.
How do you know? have you seen? Is it possible to descend to it
from above?"

"I passed there less than an hour ago. It is possible, I am sure."

They set off hurriedly through the rain-beaten night. Not a word
passed between them as they left the village and struck into the
high-valley road that ran past, at a moderate distance, the head of

the bay. De Jussac strode rapidly in advance of his companion. His long cloak whirled in the blast; it flogged his gaunt limbs all set to intense action. He seemed uplifted, translated—like one in whom the very article of a life-long faith, or monomania, is about to be justified.

Toiling onward, like driven cattle, they swerved from the road presently and breasted a sharp incline. Their boots squelched on the sodden turf; the wind bore on them heavily.

George saw the dancing lanthorn go up the slope in front of him like a will-o'-the-wisp—stop, and swing steady, heard the loud cry of jubilation that issued from the withered throat.

"It is true! The moment is realized!"

They stood together on the verge of the upper lip of the fissure. It was a cliff now, twenty, thirty feet to its base. The lower ground had fallen like a dead jaw; had slipped—none so great a distance—down the slope leading to the under-cliff, and lay a billowing mass subsided upon itself.

De Jussac would stand not an instant.

"We must climb down—somehow, anyhow!" he cried feverishly. "We must search all along what was once the bottom of the cleft."

"It is a risk, sir. Why not wait till the morning?"

"No, no! now! My God! I demand it. Others may forestall us if we delay. See, my friend, I wish but my own; and what proof of right have I if another should snatch the treasure?"

"The treasure?"

"It is our fortune that lies there—yours, and mine, and the little Plancine's. Do I know what I say? Hurry, hurry, hurry! while my heart does not burst."

He forced the lanthorn into the young man's hands. He was panting and sobbing like a child. Before the other realized his intention, he had flung himself upon his hands and knees, had slipped over the edge, and was scrambling down the broken wall of lias.

There was nothing for George but to take his own life in hand and humour his venerated elder. He followed with the lanthorn, thinking of Plancine a little, and hoping he should fall on a soft place.

But they got down in safety, breathing hard and extremely dirty. Caution, it is true, reacts very commonly upon itself.

The moment his companion's feet touched bottom, De Jussac snatched the light from his hand, roughly enough to send him off his balance, and went scurrying to and fro along the face of the cliff like a mad thing.

"I cannot find it!" he cried, rushing back after an interval—nervous, in an agony of restlessness—a very pitiable old man.

George spoke up from the ground.

"Find what?" said he, feeling all sopped and dazed.

"The box—the casket! It could never perish. It was of sheet-iron. Look, look, my friend! Your eyes are younger than mine—a box, a foot long, of hard iron!"

"I am sitting upon something hard," said George.

He sprang to his feet and took the lanthorn.

"Bones," said he, peering down. "Some old mastodon, I expect. Is this your treasure?"

De Jussac was glaring. His head drooped lower and lower. His lips were parted, and the line of strong white teeth showed between them. His voice, when he spoke, was quite fearful in its low intensity.

"Bones—yes, and human. Where they lie, the other must be near. Ah, Lacombe, Lacombe; you will yield me my own at last!"

He was shaking a slow finger at the poor remnants—a rib or two, the half of a yellow skull.

Suddenly he was down on his knees, tearing at the black, thick soil, diving into it, tossing it hither and thither.

A pause, a rending exclamation, and he was on his feet again with a scream of ecstasy. An oblong casket, rusty, corroded, but unbroken, was in his hand.

"Now," he whispered, sibilant through the wind, controlling himself, though he was shaking from head to foot, "now to return as we have come. Not a word, not a word till we have this safe in the cottage!"

They found, after some search, a difficult way up. By-and-by they stood once more on the lip of the fall, and paused for breath.

It was at this very instant that De Jussac dropped the box beside him and threw up his hands.

"The guillotine!" he shrieked, and fell headlong into the pit he had just issued from.

IV

The poor bandaged figure; the approaching death; the dog whining softly in the yard.

"I am dying, my little Plancine?"

The girl's forehead was bowed on the homely quilt.

"Nay, cry not, little one! I go very happy. That (he indicated by a motion of his eyelids the fatal box, which, yet unopened, lay on a table by the sunny window) shall repay thee for thy long devotion, for thy poverty, and for thy brave sweetness with the old papa."

"No, no, no!"

"But they are diamonds, Plancine—such diamonds, my bird. They have flashed at Versailles, at the little Trianon. They were honoured to lie on the breast of a beautiful and courageous woman—thine aunt, Plancine; the most noble the Comtesse de la Morne. She gave her wealth, almost her life, for her king—all but her diamonds. It was at Brussels, whither I had escaped from The Terror—I, a weak and desolate boy of but fourteen. I lived with her, in her common, cheap lodging. For five years we made out our friendless and deserted existence in company. In truth, we were an embarrassment, and they looked at us askance. Long after her mind failed her, the memory of her own former beauty dwelt with her; yet she could not comprehend but that it was still a talisman to conjure with. Even to the end she would deck herself and coquet to her glass. But she was good and faithful, Plancine; and, at the last, when she was dying, she gave me this box. 'It contains all that is left to me of my former condition,' she said. 'It shall make thy fortune for thee in England, my nephew, whither thou must journey when poor Dorine is underground.' By that I knew it was her cherished diamonds she bequeathed me. 'They do not want thee here,' she said. 'Thou must take boat for England when I am gone.'

"But George, my friend!"

The young man was standing sorrowful by the open window. He could have seen the sailing-boats in the bay, the sailing clouds in the sky placidly floating over a world of serene and verdurous loveliness. But his vision was all inward, of the piteous calm, following storm and disaster, in which the dying voice from the bed was like the lapping of little waves.

He came at once and stood over Plancine, not daring to touch her.

"It was not wilfulness, but my great love," said the broken, gentle voice, "that made the condition. All of you I cannot extol, knowing what I have known. But you are an honest gentleman and a true, my brave; and you shall make this dearest a noble husband."

Waveringly George stole his hand towards the bowed head and let it rest there.

From the battered face a smile broke like flowers from a blasted soil.

"Withholding my countenance only as I foresaw the means to enrich you both were approaching my grasp, I waited for the hill to break away that I might recover my casket. It was there—it is here; and now my Plancine shall never know poverty more, or her husband restrict the scope of his so admirable art on the score of necessity."

He saw the eyes questioning what the lips would not ask.

"But how I lost it?" he said. "I took the box; I obeyed her behests. The moment was acute; the times peremptory. I sailed for England, hurriedly and secretly, never to this day having feasted my eyes on what lies within there. With me went Lacombe, Madame's 'runner' in the old days—a stolid Berrichon, who had lived upon her bounty to the end. The rogue! the ingrate! We were wrecked upon this coast; we plunged and came ashore. I know not who were lost or saved; but Lacombe and I clung together and were thrown upon the land, the box still in my grasp. We climbed the cliffs where a stair had been cut; we broke eastwards from the upper slopes and staggered on through the blown darkness. Suddenly Lacombe stopped. The day was faint then on the watery horizon; and in the ghostly light I saw his face and read the murder in it. We were standing on the verge of the cleft under Black Venn. 'No further!' he whispered. 'You must go down there!' He snatched the box from my hand. In the instant of his doing so, stricken by the death terror, the affection to which I was then much subject seized me. I screamed, 'My God! the guillotine!' Taken by surprise, he started back, staggered, and went down crashing to the fate he had designed for me. I seemed to lie prostrate for hours, while his moans came up fainter and fainter till they ceased. Then I rose and faced life, lonely, friendless, and a beggar."

The restless wandering of his eyes travelled over his daughter's head to the rusty casket by the window.

"It was very well," he whispered. "I thank my God that He has permitted me at the perfect moment to realize my investment in that dead rascal's dishonesty. Have I ever desired wealth save for my little *pouponne* here? And I have sorely tried thee, my George. But the old naturalist had such faith in his prediction. Now—"

His vision was glazing; the muscles of his face were quietly settling to the repose that death only can command.

"Now, I would see the fruit of my prophecy; would see it all hung on the neck, in the hair of my child, that I may die rejoicing. Canst thou force the casket, George?"

The young man turned with a stifled groan. Some tools lay on a shelf hard by. He grasped a chisel and went to his task with shaking hands.

The box was all eaten and corroded. It was a matter of but a few seconds to prise it open. The lid fell back on the table with a rusty clang.

"Ah!" cried the dying man. "What now? Dost thou see them? Quick! quick! to glorify this little head! Are they not exquisite?"

George was gazing down with a dull, vacant feeling at his heart.

"Are they not?" repeated the voice, in terrible excitement.

"They— Mr. De Jussac, they are loveliness itself. Plancine, I will not touch them. You must be the first."

He strode to the kneeling girl; lifted, almost roughly dragged her to her feet.

"Come!" he said; and, supporting her across the room, whispered madly in her ear: "Pretend! For God's sake, pretend!"

Plancine's swimming eyes looked down, looked upon a litter of perished rags of paper, and, lying in the midst of the rubbish, an ancient stained and cockled miniature of a powdered Louis *Seize* coquette.

This was all. This was the treasure the old crazed vanity had thought sufficient to build her nephew his fortune.

The diamonds! Probably these had long before been sacrificed to the armies ineffectively manoeuvring for the destruction of Monsieur "Veto's" enemies.

Plancine lifted her head. Thereafter George never ceased to recall with a glad pride the nobility that had shone in her eyes.

"My papa!" she cried softly, going swiftly to the bed; "they are beautiful as the stars that glittered over the old untroubled France!"

De Jussac sprang up on his pillow.

"The guillotine!" he cried. "The beams break into flowers! The axe is a shaft of light!"

And so the glowing blade descended.

Dinah's Mammoth

On a day early in the summer of the present year Miss Dinah Groom was found lying dead off a field-path of the little obscure Wiltshire village which she had named her "rest and be thankful." At the date of her decease she was not an old woman, though any one marking her white hair and much-furrowed features might have supposed her one. The hair, however, was ample in quantity, the wrinkles rather so many under-scores of energy than evidences of senility; and until the blinds were down over her soul, she had looked into and across the world with a pair of eyes that seemed to reflect the very blue and white of a June sky. No doubt she had thought to breast the hills and sail the seas again in some renaissance of vigour. No doubt her "retreat," like a Roman Catholic's, was designed to be merely temporary. She aped the hermit for the sake of a sojourn in the hermitage. She came to her island of Avalon to be restored of her weary limbs and her blistered feet, so to speak; and there her heart, too weak for her spirit, failed her, and she fell amongst the young budding poppies, and died.

I use the word "heart" literally, and in no sentimental sense. To talk of associations of sentiment in connection with this lady would be misleading. She herself would not have repudiated any responsibility for the term as applied to her; she would have simply failed to understand the term itself. There was no least affectation in this. Throughout her life of sixty years, as I gather, she acted never once upon principle. Impulse and inclination dominated her, and she would indulge many primitive instincts without a thought of conventions. Yet she was not selfish; or, at least, only in the self-contained and self-protective meaning of the word. She was a perfect animal, conscious of her supreme brute caste, shrewd, resourceful, and the plain embodiment of truth.

Miss Groom had, I think, a boundless feeling of fellowship with beauty of whatever description; but no least touch of that sorrow of affection which, in its very humanity, is divine. Her unswerving creed was that woman was the inheritrix of the earth, the reversion of which she had wilfully mortgaged to an alien race, and that she had bartered her material immortality for a sensation. For man she had no vulgar and jealous contempt; but she feared and shrank from him as something moved by scruples with which she had no sympathy. She understood the world of Nature, and could respond to its bloodless caresses and passions. She could *not* understand the moodiness that dwells upon a grievance, or that would sell its birthright of joy for a pitiful memory.

Yet (and here I must speak with discretion, for I have no sufficient data to go upon) there was that of contradictoriness in her character that, I have reason to believe, she had borne children, and had even been right and particular as to their temporal welfare until such time as, in the nature of things, they were of an age to make shift for themselves. This, virtually, I know to be the case; and that, once quit of the primitive maternal responsibility, she gave no more thought to them than a thrush gives to its fledglings when she has educated them to their first flights, and to the useful knack of cracking a snail on a stone.

My own feeling about Dinah Groom was that she had "thrown back" a long way over the heads of heredity, and that, in her fearlessness, in her undegenerate physique, in the animal regularity of her face and form, she presented to modern days a startling aboriginal type.

Beautiful—save in the sense of symmetry—she can never have been to the ordinary man; inasmuch as she would subscribe to no arbitrary standard of his dictating. She had a high, rich colour; but her complexion must always have been rough, and a pronounced little moustache crossed her upper lip, like an accent to the speech that was too distinct and uncompromising to be melodious. Her every limb and feature, however, was instinct with capability, and, in her presence, one must always be moved to marvel over that indescribable worship of disproportion that has grown to be the religion of a shapely race.

How I first became acquainted with Miss Groom it is unnecessary to explain. During the last three years of her life I was fortunate to be her guest in the Wiltshire retreat for an aggregate of many months. She took a fancy to me—to my solitariness and moroseness, perhaps—and she not only liked to have me with her, but, after a time, she fell into something of a habit of recalling for my benefit certain passages and experiences of her past life. In doing this, there was no suggestion of confidence; and I am breaking no faith in alluding to them. She was a fine talker—rugged, unpicturesque, but with an instinctive capacity of selection in words. If I quote her, as I wish to do, I cannot reproduce her style; and that, no doubt, would appear bald on paper. But, at least, the matter is all her own.

Now, I must premise that I arrogate to myself no exhibitory rights in this lady. She was familiar with and to many from the foremost ranks of those who "follow knowledge like a sinking star"; those great and restless spirits to whom inaction reads stagnation. To such, in all probability, I tell, in speaking of Dinah Groom, a twice-told tale; and, therefore—inasmuch as I make it my business only to print what is hitherto unrecorded—to them I give the assurance that I do not claim to have "discovered" their friend.

On a wall of the little embowered sitting-room hung a queer picture, by Ernest Griset, of the "Overwhelming of the Mammoths in the Ice." From the first this odd conception had engaged my curiosity,—purely for its fanciful side,—and one evening, in alluding to it, I made the not very profound remark that Imagination had no anatomy.

"They are true beasts," said Dinah.

"They are the mastodons of Cuvier, no doubt; but, then, Cuvier never saw a mastodon, you know."

"But I have; and I tell you Griset and Cuvier are very nearly right."

I expressed no surprise.

"In what were they astray?" I asked.

"The mammoth, as I saw it, had a huge hump—like the steam-chest of an enormous engine—over its shoulders."

"And where did you see it, and when?"

"You are curious to know?"

"Yes, I think I am; and there is a quiet of expectancy abroad. I hear the ghost of my dead brother walking in the corridor, Dinah; and we are all waiting for you to speak."

She smiled, and said, "Push me over the cigarettes."

She struck a match, kindled the little crackling tube, and threw the light out into the shrubbery. It traced a tiny arc of flame and vanished. The sky was full of the mewing of lost kittens, it seemed. The sound came from innumerable peewits, that fled and circled above the slopes of the darkening meadows below.

"What an uncomfortable seer you are!" she said, "to people this dear human night with your fancies. No doubt, now, you will read between the lines of that bird speech down there?" (She looked at me curiously, but with none of the mournful speculativeness of a soul struggling against the dimness of its own vision.) "To me it is articulate happiness—nothing more abstruse. Yes, I have seen a mastodon; and I was as glad to happen on the beast as a naturalist is glad to find a missing link in a chain of evidence. From the moment, I knew myself quite clearly to be the recovered heir to this abused planet."

She paused a moment, and contracted her brows, as if regretfully and in anger. "If I had only seen it sooner!" she cried, low; "before I had, in my pride of strength, tested the poison that has bewildered the brains of my sisters!"

Her general reserve was her self-armour against the bolts of the Philistines. What worldling would not have read mania in much that was spoken by this sane woman? Yet, indeed, if we were all to find the power to give expression to our inmost thoughts, madness and sanity would have to change places in the order of affairs.

"Once," said Dinah— "and it was when I was a young woman— a man in whom I was interested shipped as passenger on a whaling vessel. This friend was what is called a degenerate. Physically and morally he had yielded his claim to any share in that province of the sun, that his race had conquered and annexed only to find it antipathetic to its needs. Combative effort was grown impossible to him, as in time it will grow to you all. You drop from the world like dead flies from a wall. He could not physic his soul with woods, and groves, and waters. To his perceptions, life was become an abnormality—a disease of which he sickened, as you all must when the last of the fever of aggression has been diluted out of your veins. You die of your triumph, as the bee dies of his own weapon of offence; and you can find no antidote to the poison in the nature you have inoculated with your own virus.

"This man contemplated self-destruction as the only escape. He had sought distraction of his moral torments in travel long and varied. Many of the most beautiful, of the historically interesting places of the world, he had visited and sojourned in—without avail. His haunting feeling, he said, was that he did not belong to himself. Pursued by this Nemesis, he came home to end it all. He still proclaimed his spiritual independence; but it was immeshed, and he must tear the strands. This was wonderfully perplexing to me, and, out of my curiosity, I must persuade him to make one more attempt. His late efforts, I assured him, were nothing but an endeavour to cure nausea with sweet syrups. He would not get his change out of nature by such pitiful wooing. Let him, rather, emulate, if he could not feel, the spirit of his remote forbears, and rally his nerves to an expedition into the harsh and awful places of the earth. I would accompany him, and watch with and for him, and supply that of the fibre he lacked.

"He consented, and, after some difficulty (for there is an economy of room in whalers), we obtained passage in a vessel and sailed into the unknown. Our life and our food were simple and rugged; but the keen air, the relief from luxury, the novelty and the wonder, wrought upon my companion and renewed him, so that presently I was amused to note in him signs of a moral preening—some smug resumption of that arrogant air of superiority that is a tradition with your race."

Miss Groom here puckered her lips, and breathed a little destructive laugh upon her cigarette ash.

"It did not last long," she said. "We encountered very bad weather, and his nerves again went by the board. That was in the 60th longitude, I think (where whales were still to be found in those years), and seven hundred miles or so to the east of Spitzbergen. On the day—it was in August—that the storm first overtook us, the boats were out in pursuit of a 'right' whale, as, I believe, the men called it—a great bull creature, and piebald like a horse; and I saw the spouting of his breath as if a water main had burst in a London fog. The wind came in a sudden charge from the northwest, and the whale dived with a harpoon in its back; and in the confusion a reel fouled, and one of the boats was whipt under in a moment—half a mile down, perhaps—and its crew drawn with it, and their lungs, full of air, burst like bubbles. We had no time to think of them. We got the other boat-load on board, and then the gale sent us crashing down the slopes of the sea. I have no knowledge of how long we were curst of the tempest and the sport of its ravings. I only know that when it released us at last, we had been hurled a thousand miles eastwards. The long interval was all a hellish jangle in which time seemed obliterated. Sometimes we saw the sun—a furious red globe; and we seemed to stand still while it raced down the sky and ricocheted over the furthermost waves like a red-hot cannon ball. Sometimes in pitch darkness the wild sense of flight and expectation was an ecstasy. But through all my friend lay in a half-delirious stupor.

"At length a morning broke, full of icy scud, but the sea panting and exhausted of its rage. As a child catches its breath after a storm of tears, so it would heave up suddenly, and vibrate, and sink; and we rocked upon it, a ruined hulk. We were off a flat, vacant shore—if shore you could call it—whose margin, for miles inland, it seemed, undulated with the lifting of the swell. It was treeless desolation manifest; and on our sea side, as far as the eye could reach, the water bobbed and winked with countless spars of ice.

"I will tell you at once, my friend,—we were brought to opposite an inhuman swamp on the coast of Siberia, fifty miles or more to the west of North-east Cape; and there what remained of the crew made shift to cast anchor; and for a day and night the ragged ship curtsied to the land, like a blind beggar to an empty street, and we only dozed in our corners and wondered at the silence.

"By-and-by the men made a raft, and that took us all ashore. There was something like a definite coast-line, then; but for long before we touched it the undersides of the planks were scraping and hissing over vegetation. This was the winter fur of the land—thick, coarse tundra moss; and on that we pitched a camp, and on that we remained for long weeks while the ship was mending. It was a weird, lonely time. Once or twice strange, wandering creatures came our way—little, belted men, with hairless faces, who rode up on strong horses, and liked to exhibit their skilful management of them. They talked to us in their chirpy jargon (Toongus, I think it was called); but jargon it must needs remain to us.

"Well, we made a patch of the hulk, and we shipped in her again. We were fortunate to be able to do that, for, with every stiffish wind blowing inshore, we had feared she would drag her moorings and ground immovably on the swamps. The land, indeed, was so flat and low that, whenever the sea rose at all, it threshed the very plains and crackled in the moss; and we were glad, despite the risk, to leave so lifeless a place."

Dinah paused to light another cigarette, and to inhale the ecstasy of the first puff or so before she continued. Up through the still evening, from a curve of the main road that crooked an elbow to her front garden, came what sounded like the purring of a great cat—the wind in the telegraph wires.

"And I am now to tell you," she said, "about the mastodon?"

"As you please," I answered.

"I do please; for why should I keep it to myself? It makes no difference; only I warn you, if you quote me, you will be writ down a fool or a maniac. This relation lacks witnesses, for the whaler—that I subsequently quitted for another homing vessel—was never heard of in port any more."

She looked at me with some serious scrutiny before she went on.

"For these regions, it had been an extraordinarily hot summer—phenomenally hot, I understand; and to this—to the melting and breaking away of the ice from hitherto century-locked fastnesses, the captain attributed the wonderful experience that befell us. The sea was strewn with blocks and bergs, all hurrying onwards in the strong currents, as if in haste to escape the pursuing demon of frost that should re-fetter them; and their multitude kept the steersman's arms spinning till the man would fall half-fainting over the spoke-handles.

"Now, one morning early in September, a dense bright fog dropped suddenly upon the waters. We were making what sail we could—with our crippled spars and stunted trees of masts—and this it were useless to shorten, and so invite a rearward bombardment from the chasing hummocks. So we kept our course by the compass, and trailed on through a blind mist while fear drummed in our throats. The demoralization of my friend was by this time complete. For myself, I seldom had a thought but that Nature would sheathe her claws when she played with me.

"'This cannot last long!' said the captain.

"The words were on his lips when we struck with a noise like the splintering of glass. We were all thrown down, and my companion screamed like a mad thing. The captain rose and ran to the bows; and in a moment he came back and his beard was shaking.

"'God save us!' he cried, 'and fetch aft the rum!'

"There you have man in his invincible moods. They drank till they were in a condition to face death; and then they found that our situation was rather improved than otherwise by the collision. For—so it appeared—we had run full tilt for a perpendicular fissure in a huge block, and into that our bows were firmly wedged, the nature of the impact distributing the shock, and the berg itself carrying us along with it and protecting us.

"Now the dipping motion of the vessel was exchanged for a heavy regular wash along its stern quarters; for the bows were so much raised as that I felt a little strain on my knees as I went forward to satisfy my curiosity with a view of the icy mass into which we were penetrated. I waited, indeed, until the crew were come aft again from looking, and my friend crept timidly at my shoulder; but when we reached the stem, there was one of the hands, a little soberer than his fellows, sprawled over the bulwarks, and staring with all his eyes into the green lift of the wall against him.

"'Is it a mermaid you see, Killigrew?' I asked.

"The man shifted his gaze to me slowly and solemnly.

"'Nowt, nowt,' said he; 'but a turble monster, like a pram stuck in jelly.'

"I laughed, and went to his side. The fog, as I have said, was dense and bright, and one could see into it a little way, as into a milky white agate. But now and again a film of it would pull thin, and then sunlight came through and made a dim radiance of the ice.

"'I can make out nothing,' I said.

"He cocked an eye and leered up at me. 'Look steady and sober,' he said, 'and you'll make en owut like as in a glass darkly.'

"I gave a little gasp and my friend a cry before the words were issued from the man's mouth. Drawn by some current of air, the fog at the moment blew out of the cleft, like smoke from a chimney; and there, before our gaze, was a great curved tusk coming up through the ice and inside it.

"Now I clapped my hands in an agony, lest the fog should close in again, and the vision fade before my eyes; for, following the sweep of the tusk, I was aware of the phantom presentment of some monster creature lying imbedded within the ice, its mighty carcase prostrate as it had fallen; the conformation of its enormous forehead presented directly to our gaze. Its little toffee-ball eyes—little proportionately, that is to say—squinted at us, it seemed, through half-closed lids, and a huge, hairy trunk lay curled, like the proboscis of a dead moth, between its tree-like fore-legs. Away beyond, the great red-brown drum of its hide bellied upward on ribs as thick as a Dutch galliot's, and sprouting from its shoulders was the hump I have mentioned, but here, from its position, sprawled abroad and lying over in a shapeless mass.

"There was something else—horribly nauseating but for its strangeness. The brute had been partly disembowelled, as there was ample evidence to show, for the ice had preserved all.

"Suddenly my companion gave a high nervous shriek.

"'Look!' he cried— 'the hand! the hand sticking out of the side!'

"I saw in a moment; turned, and called excitedly to the captain. He—all the crew—came tumbling forward up the slippery deck. I seized him by the shoulder.

"'Do you see?' I screamed— 'the human hand beckoning to us from that great body!'

"He gazed stupidly, swaying where he stood.

"'One o' them bloomin' pre-hadymite cows!' he muttered; 'caught in the cold nip, by thunder! and some unfortnit crept into her for warmth.'

"I believed the creature's rude intuition had flown true.

"'Cannot you get at it?' I gasped.

"He stared at me. All in an instant a little paltry demon of avarice blinked out of his eye-holes.

"'Why,' he said slowly, 'who knows but it mayn't be a gal a-jingling from top to toe with gold curtain rings!'

"He was a furious dare-devil immediately, and quick, and savage, and peremptory. His spirit entered into his men. They went over the side with pikes and axes, and, scrambling for any foothold, set to work on the ice like maniacs. In the lust of cupidity they did not even think how they wrought against their own safety and that of the ship.

"The point of the uppermost tusk came to within a foot of the ice-surface. This they soon reached, and, prising frantically with crowbars, flaked off and rolled away half-ton blocks of the superincumbent mass. I need not detail the fierce process. In half an hour they had laid bare a great segment of that part of the trunk whence the hand protruded, and then they paused, and at a word flung down their tools.

"I was leaning over the bulwarks watching them. I could contain my excitement no longer.

"'Come,' I said to my friend, 'help me down, for I must go.'

"He climbed over, trembling, and assisted me to a standing on the ice. We scrambled along the track of *débris* left by the crew. At the moment half a dozen of the latter were rolling back a broad flap of the hide, in which they had found a long L-shaped rent revealed. Then a hoarse cry broke from them, and I stumbled forward and looked down, and saw.

"They lay beneath the mighty ribs as in a cage, of which the intercostal spaces were a foot in width, and the bars of a strength to maintain the enormous pressure of that which had surrounded and entombed them; they lay in one close group, their naked limbs smeared with the stain of their prison—a man, a woman, and a tiny child. From their faces, and their unfallen flesh, they might have been sleeping; but they were not; they were come down to us, a transfixture of death—prehistoric people in a prehistoric brute, and their eyes—their eyes!"

Dinah's voice trailed off into silence. Some expression that I could not interpret was on her face. There was regret in it, but nothing of pathos or mysticism. Suddenly she breathed out a great sigh and resumed her narrative.

"You will want to know how they looked, these lifeless survivors of a remote race from a remote time? I will try to tell you. The men hacked away the ribs with their axes, and laid bare the group lying in the hollow scooped out of the fallen beast. They were little people, and the man, according to your modern canons of taste, was by far the most beautiful of the three. He sat erect, with one uplifted arm projected through the ribs; as if, surprised by the frost-stroke, he had started to escape, and had been petrified in the act. His face, wondering and delicate as a baby's, was hairless; and his head only a pretty infantile down covered—a curling floss as radiant as spun glass. His wide-open eyes glinted yet with a hyacinth blue, and it was difficult to realize that they were dead and vacant.

"The woman was of coarser mould, ruddy, vigorous, brown-haired and eyed. She looked the very hamadryad of some blossoming tree, a sweet capricious daughter of the blameless earth. Everything luxuriated in her—colour, hair, and lusty flesh; and the child she held to her bosom with a manner that indescribably commingled contempt, and resentment, and a passion of proprietorship.

"This baby—joining the prominent characteristics of the two—was the oddest little mortal I have ever seen. What did its expression convey to me? 'I am fairly caught, and must brazen out the situation!' There! that was what it was; I cannot put it more lucidly. Only the thing's wee face was animal conscious for the first time of itself, and inclined to rejoice in that primitive energy of knowledge.

"Now, my friend, I must tell you how the sight operated upon me and upon my companion. For myself, I can only say that, looking upon that fine, independent fore-mother of my race, I felt the sun in my veins and the winy fragrance of antique woods and pastures. I laughed; I clapped my hands; I danced on the ice-rubbish, so that they thought me mad. But, for the other—the man—he was in a different plight. He was transfigured; his nervousness was gone in a flash. He cast himself down upon his knees, and gazed and gazed, his hands clasped, upon that sleek, mild progenitor of his, that pure image of gentle self-containment, whose very meekness suggested an indomitable will.

"Suddenly he, my friend, cried out: 'This is one caught in the process of materialization! It is not flesh; my God, no!'

"It seemed, indeed, as if it were as he said. I stopped in my capering and looked down. The tarry hinds standing by grinned and jeered.

"On the instant there came a splintering snap, and the floe rocked and curtsied.

"'Back!' yelled the captain. 'She's breaking through by the head!'

"He shrieked of the ship. She was clearing herself, had already shaken her prow free of the ice.

"There was a wild scamper for safety. I was carried with the throng. It was not until I was hauled on board once more that I thought of my friend. He still knelt where we had fled from him, a wrapt, strange expression on his face.

"'Come back!' I screamed. 'You will be lost!'

"Now at that he turned his head and looked at me; but he never moved, and his voice came to me quiet and exultant.

"'Lost!' he said, 'ay, for forty-three years: and here, here I find myself!'

"We dipped, and the wash of the water came about our bows. The block of ice swerved, made a sluggish half-pirouette and dropped astern.

"'Come!' I shrieked again faintly.

"With the echo of my cry he was a phantom, a blot, had vanished in the rearward fog; and thereout a little joyous laugh came to me.

"And that was a queer good-bye for ever, wasn't it?"

Jack and Jill

My friend, Monsieur —, absolutely declines to append his name
to these pages, of which he is the virtual author. Nevertheless, he
permits me to publish them anonymously, being, indeed, a little
curious to ascertain what would have been the public verdict as to
his sanity, had he given his personal imprimatur to a narrative on
the face of it so incredible.

"How!" he says. "Should I have believed it of another, when I
have such astonishing difficulty at this date in realizing that it was
I—yes, I, my friend—this same little callow *poupon*—that was an
actual hero of the adventure? Fidèle" (by which term we cover the
identity of his wife)— "Fidèle will laugh in my face sometimes, crying, 'Not thou, little cabbage, nor yet thy faithful, was it that dived
through half the world and came up breathless! No, no—I cannot
believe it. We folk, so matter-of-fact and so comical. It was of
Hansel and Gretel we had been reading hand-in-hand, till we fell
asleep in the twilight and fancied this thing.' And then she will
trill like a bird at the thought of how solemn Herr Grabenstock, of
the Hôtel du Mont Blanc, would have stared and edged apart, had
we truly recounted to him that which had befallen us between the
rising and the setting of a sun. We go forth; it rains—my faith! as
it will in the Chamounix valley—and we return in the evening
sopped. Very natural. But, for a first cause of our wetting. Ah! there
we must be fastidious of an explanation, or we shall find ourselves
in peril of restraint.

"Now, write this for me, and believe it if you can. We are not in a conspiracy of imagination—I and the dear courageous."

Therefore I *do* write it, speaking in the person of Monsieur —, and largely from his dictation; and my friend shall amuse himself over the nature of its reception.

"One morning (it was in late May)," says Monsieur —, "my Fidèle and I left the Hôtel du Mont Blanc for a ramble amongst the hills. We were a little adventurous, because we were innocent. We took no guide but our commonsense; and that served us very ill— or very well, according to the point of view. Ours was that of the birds, singing to the sky and careless of the snake in the grass so long as they can pipe their tune. Of a surety that is the only course. If one would make provision against every chance of accident, one must dematerialize. To die is the only way to secure oneself from fatality.

"Still, it is a wise precaution, I will admit, not to eat of all hedge fruit because blackberries are sweet. Some day, after the fiftieth stomach-ache, we shall learn wisdom, my Fidèle and I.

"'Fools rush in where angels fear to tread.' That, I know, comes into the English gospel.

"Well, I will tell you, I am content to be considered of the first; and my Fidèle is assuredly of the second. Yet did she fear, or I rush in? On the contrary, I have a little laughing thought that it was the angel inveighed against the dulness of caution when the fool would have hesitated.

"Now, it was before the season of the Alps; and the mountain aubergistes were, for the most part, not arrived at their desolate hill-taverns. Nor were guides at all in evidence, being yet engaged, the sturdy souls, over their winter occupations. One, no doubt, we could have procured, had we wished it; but we did not. We would explore under the aegis of no cicerone but our curiosity. That was native to us, if the district was strange.

"Following, at first, the instructions of Herr Baedeker, we travelled and climbed, chattering and singing as we went, in the direction of the Montenvert, whence we were to descend upon the Mer de Glace, and enjoy the spectacle of a stupendous glacier.

"'And that, I am convinced,' said Fidèle, 'is nothing more nor less than one of those many windows that give light to the monsters of the under-earth.'

"'Little imbecile! In some places this window is six hundred feet thick.'

"'So?' she said. 'That is because their dim eyes could not endure the full light of the sun.'

"We had brought a tin box of sandwiches with us; and this, with my large pewter flask full of wine, was slung upon my back. For we had been told the Hôtel du Montenvert was yet closed; and, sure enough when we reached it, the building stood black in a pool of snow, its shuttered windows forlorn, and long icicles hung from the eaves.

"The depression induced by this sight was momentary. We turned from it to the panorama of majestic loveliness that stretched below and around us. The glacier—that rolling sea of glass—descended from the enormous gates of the hills. Its source was the white furnace of the skies; its substance the crystal refuse of the stars; and from its margins the splintered peaks stood up in a thousand forms of beauty. Right and left, in the hollows of the mountains, the mist lay like ponds, opal and translucent; and the shafts of the pine trees standing in it looked like the reflections of themselves.

"It made the eyes ache—this silence of greatness; and it became a relief to shift one's gaze to the reality of one's near neighbourhood—the grass, and the rhododendron bushes, and even the dull walls of the deserted auberge.

"A narrow path dipped over the hill-side and fled into the very jaws of the moraine. Down the first of this path we raced, hand in hand; but soon, finding the impetus overmastering us, we pulled up with difficulty, and descended the rest of the way circumspectly.

"At the foot of the steep slope we came upon the little wooden hutch where, ordinarily, one may procure a guide (also rough socks to stretch over one's boots) for the passage of the glacier. Now, however, the shed was closed and tenantless; and we must e'en dispense with a conductor, should we adventure further.

"Herr Baedeker says, 'Guide unnecessary for the experienced.'

"'Fidèle, are we experienced?'

"'We shall be, *mon ami*, when we have crossed. A guide could not alter that.'

"'But it is true, *ma petite*. Come, then!'

"We clambered down amongst huge stones. Fidèle's little feet went in and out of the crannies like sand-martins. Suddenly, before we realized it, we were on the glacier.

"Fidèle exclaimed.

"'*Mon Dieu*! Is this ice—these blocks of dirty alabaster?'

"Alas! she was justified. This torrent of majestic crystal—seen from above so smooth and bountiful—a flood of the milk of Nature dispensed from the white bosom of the hills! Now, near at hand, what do we find it? A medley of opaque blocks, smeared with grit and rubbish; a vast ruin of avalanches hurled together and consolidated, and of the colour of rock salt.

"'*Peste!*' I cried. 'We must get to the opposite bank, for all that.

"*Mignonne, allons voir si la rose,*
Qui ce matin avoit desclose. . . .'"

"We clasped hands and set forth on our little *traversée*, our landmark an odd-shaped needle of spar on the further side. My faith! it was simple. The *paveurs* of Nature had left the road a trifle rough, that was all. Suddenly we came upon a wide fissure stretched obliquely like the mouth of a sole. Going glibly, we learnt a small lesson of caution therefrom. Six paces, and we should have tumbled in.

"We looked over fearfully. Here, in truth, was real ice at last—green as bottle-glass at the edges, and melting into unfathomable deeps of glowing blue.

"In a moment, with a shriek like that of escaping steam, a windy demon leapt at us from the underneath. It was all of winter in a breath. It seemed to shrivel the skin from our faces—the flesh from our bones. We staggered backwards.

"'*Mon ami! mon ami!*' cried Fidèle, 'my heart is a stone; my eyes are two blisters of water!'

"We danced as the blood returned unwilling to our veins. It was minutes before we could proceed.

"Afterwards I learned that these hellish eruptions of air betoken a change of temperature. It was coming then shortly in a dense rainfall.

"When we were recovered, we sought about for a way to circumambulate the crevasse. Then we remarked that up a huge boulder of ice that had seemed to block our path recent steps, or toeholes, had been cut. In a twinkling we were over. Fidèle—no, a woman never falls.

"'For all this,' she says, shaking her head, 'I maintain that a guide here is a sinecurist.'

"Well, we made the passage safely, and toiled up the steep, loose moraine beyond—to find the track over which was harder than crossing the glacier. But we did it, and struck the path along the hillside, which leads by the *Mauvais Pas* (the *mauvais quart d'heure*) to the little cabaret called the *Chapeau*. This tavern, too, was shut and dismal. It did not matter. We sat like sparrows on a railing, and munched our egg-sandwiches and drank our wine in a sort of glorious stupefaction. For right opposite us was the vast glacier-fall, whose crashing foam was towers and parapets of ice, that went over and rolled into the valley below, a ruin of thunder.

"Far beyond, where the mouth of the gorge spread out littered with monstrous destruction, we saw the hundred threads of the glacier streams collect into a single rope of silver, that went drawn between the hills, a highway of water. It was all a majestic panorama of grey and pearly white—the sky, the torrents, the mountains; but the blue and rusty green of the stone pines, flung abroad in hanging woods and coppices, broke up and distributed the infinite serenity of the snow fields.

"Presently, having drunk deep of rich content, we rose to retrace our steps. For, spurred by vanity, we must be returning the way we had come, to show our confident experience of glaciers.

"All went well. Actually we had passed over near two-thirds of the ice-bed, when a touch on my arm stayed me, and *ma mie* looked into my eyes, very comical and insolent.

"'Little cabbage,' she said; 'will you not put your new knowledge to account?'

"'But how, my soul?'

"She laughed and pressed my arm to her side. Her heart fluttered like a nestling after its first flight.

"'To rest on the little prowess of a small adventure! No, no! Shall he who has learnt to swim be always content to bathe in shallow water?'

"I was speechless as I gazed on her.

"'Behold, then!' she cried. 'We have opposed ourselves to this problem of the ice, and we have mastered it. See how it rears itself to the inaccessible peaks, the which to reach the poor innocents expend themselves over rocks and drifts. But why should one not climb the mountain by way of the glacier?'

"'Fidèle!' I gasped.

"'Ah!' she exclaimed, nodding her head; 'but poor men! They are mules. They spill their blood on the scaling ladders when the town gate is open.'

"Again I cried 'Fidèle!'

"'But, yes,' she said, 'it needs a woman to see. It is but two o'clock. Let us ascend the glacier, like a staircase; and presently we shall stand upon the summit of the mountain. Those last little peaks above the ice can be of no importance.'

"I was touched, astounded by the sublimity of her idea. Had no one, then, ever thought of this before?

"We began the ascent.

"I swear we must have toiled upwards half a mile, when the catastrophe took place.

"It was raining then—a dense small mist; and the ice was as if it had been greased. We were proceeding with infinite care, arm in arm, tucked close together. A little doubt, I think, was beginning to oppress us. We could move only with much caution and difficulty; and there were noises—sounds like the clapping of great hands in those rocky attics above us. Then there would come a slamming report, as if the window of the unknown had been burst open by demons; and the moans of the lost would issue, surging down upon the world.

"These thunders, as we were afterwards told, are caused by the splitting of the ice when there comes a fall in the barometer. Then the glacier will yawn like a sliced junket.

"My faith! what a simile! But again the point of view, my friend.

"All in a moment I heard a little cluck. I looked down. Alas! the fine spirit was obscured. Fidèle was weeping.

"'*Chut! chut!*' I exclaimed in consternation. 'We will go back at once.'

"She struggled to smile, the poor *mignonne*.

"'It is only that my knees are sick,' she said piteously.

"I took her in my strong arms tenderly.

"We had paused on a ridge of hard snow.

"There came a tearing clang—an enormous sucking sound, as of wet lips opening. The snow sank under our feet.

"'My God!' shrieked Fidèle.

"I held her convulsively. It happened in an instant, before one could leap aside. The bed of snow on which we were standing broke down into the crevasse it had bridged, and let us through to the depths.

"Will you believe what follows? Pinch your nose and open your mouth. You shall take the whole draught at a breath. *The ice at the point where we entered was five hundred feet thick; and we fell to the very bottom of it.*

"Ha! ha! Is it difficult to swallow? But it is true—it is quite true. Here I sit, sound and safe, and eminently sane, and that after a fall of five hundred feet.

"Now, listen.

"We went down, welded together, with a rush and a buzz like a cannon-ball. Thoughts? Ah! my friend, I had none. Who can think even in a high wind? And here the wind of our going would have brained an ox. Only one desperate instinct I had, one little forlorn remnant of humanity—to shield the love of my heart. So my arms never left her; and we fell together. I dreaded nothing, feared nothing, foresaw no terror in the inevitable mangling crash of the end. For time, that is necessary to emotion, was annihilated. We had outstripped it, and left sense and reason sluggishly following in our wake.

"Sense, yes; but not altogether sensation. Flashingly I was conscious here of incredibly swift transitions, from cold to deeper wells of frost; thence down through a stratum of death and negation, between mere blind walls of frigid inhumanity, to have been stayed a moment by which would have pointed all our limbs as stiff as icicles, as stiff as those of frogs plunged into boiling water. But we passed and fell, still crashing upon no obstruction; and thought pursued us, tailing further behind.

"It was the passage of the eternal night—frozen, self-contained; awful as any fancied darkness that is without one tradition of a star. Yet, struggling hereafter to, in some shadowy sense, renew my feelings of the moment, it seemed to me that I had not fallen through darkness at all; but rather that the friction of descent had kindled an inner radiance in me that was independent of the vision of the eyes, and full of promise of a sudden illumination of the soul.

"Now, after falling what depths God knows, I become numbly aware of a little griding sensation at my back, that communicated a whistling small vibration to my whole frame. This intensified, became more pronounced. Perceptibly, in that magnificent refinement of speed, our enormous pace I felt to decrease ever so little. Still we had so far outstripped intelligence as that I was incapable of considering the cause of the change.

"Suddenly, for the first time, pain made itself known; and immediately reason, plunging from above, overtook me, and I could think.

"Then it was I became conscious that, instead of falling, we were rising, rising with immense swiftness, but at a pace that momently slackened—rising, slipping over ice and in contact with it.

"The muscles of my arms, clasped still about Fidèle, involuntarily swelled to her. My God! there was a tiny answering pressure. I could have screamed with joy; but physical anguish overmastered me. My back seemed bursting into flame.

"The suffering was intolerable. When, at last, I thought I should go mad, in a moment we took a surging swoop, shot down an easy incline, and *stopped*.

"There had been noise in our descent, as only now I knew by its cessation—a hissing sound as of wire whirring from a drawplate. In the profound enormous silence that, at last, enwrapped us, the bliss of freedom from that metallic accompaniment fell on me like a balm. My eyelids closed. Possibly I fainted.

"All in a moment I came to myself, to an undefinable sense of the tremendous pressure of nothingness. Darkness! it was not that; yet it was as little light. It was as if we lay in a dim, luminous chaos, ourselves an integral part of its self-containment. I did not stir; but I spoke: and my strange voice broke the enchantment. Surely never before or since was speech exchanged under such conditions.

"'Fidèle!'

"'I can speak, but I cannot look. If I hide so for ever I can die bravely.'

"'*Ma petite!* oh, my little one! Are you hurt?'

"'I don't know. I think not.'

"Her voice, her dear voice was so odd; but, *Mon Dieu*! how wonderful in its courage! That, Heaven be praised! is no monopoly of intellect. Indeed, it is imagination that makes men cowards; and to the lack of this possibly we owed our salvation.

"Now, calm and freed of that haunting jar of descent, I became conscious that a sound, that I had at first taken for the rush of my own arteries, had an origin apart from us. It was like the wash and thunder of waters in a deep sewer.

"'Fidèle!' I said again.

"'I am listening.'

"'Hear, then! Canst thou free my right arm, that I may feel for the lucifers in my pocket?'

"She moved at once, never raising her face from my breast. I groped for the box, found it; and manipulating with one hand, succeeded in striking a match. It flamed up—a long wax vesta.

"A glory of sleek fires sprang on the instant into life. We lay imprisoned in a house of glass at the foot of a smooth incline rising behind us to unknown heights. A wall of porous and opaque ice-rubbish, into which our feet had plunged deep, had stayed our progress.

"I placed the box by my side ready for use. Our last moments should be lavish of splendour. Stooping for another match, to kindle from the flame of the near-expired one, a thought struck me. Why had we not been at once frozen to death? Yet we lay where we had brought up, as snug and glowing as if we were wrapped in bedclothes.

"The answer came to me in a flash. We had fallen sheer to the glacier bed, which, warmed by subterraneous heat, was ever in process of melting. Possibly, but a comparatively thin curtain of perforated ice separated us from the under torrent.

"The enforced conclusion was astounding; but as yet it inspired no hope. We were none the less doomed and buried.

"I lit a second match, turned about, and gave a start of terror. There, imbedded in the transparent wall at my very shoulder, was something—the body of a man.

"A horrible sight—a horrible, horrible sight—crushed, flattened—a caricature; the very gouts of blood that had burst from him held poised in the massed congelations of water.

"For how long ages had he been travelling to the valley, and from what heights? He was of a bygone generation, by his huge coat cuffs, his metal buttons, by his shoe buckles and the white stockings on his legs, which were pressed thin and sharp, as if cut out of paper. Had he been a climber, an explorer—a contemporary, perhaps, of Saussure and a rival? And what had been his unrecorded fate? To slip into a crevasse, and so for the parted ice to snap upon him again, like a hideous jaw? Its work done, it might at least have opened and dropped him through—not held him intact to jog us, out of all that world of despair, with his battered elbow!

"Perhaps to witness in others the fate he had himself suffered!

"I dropped the match I was holding. I tightened my clasp convulsively about Fidèle. Thank God she, at any rate, was blind to this horror within a horror!

"All at once—was it the start I had given, or the natural process of dissolution beneath our feet?—we were moving again. Swift—swifter! Fidèle uttered a little moaning cry. The rubbish of ice crashed below us, and we sank through.

"I knew nothing, then, but that we were in water—that we had fallen from a little height, and were being hurried along. The torrent, now deep, now so shallow that my feet scraped its bed, gushed in my ears and blinded my eyes.

"Still I hugged Fidèle, and I could feel by her returning grasp that she lived. The water was not unbearably cold as yet. The air that came through cracks and crevasses had not force to overcome the under warmth.

"I felt something slide against me—clutched and held on. It was a brave pine log. Could I recover it at this date I would convert it into a flagstaff for the tricolour. It was our raft, our refuge; and it carried us to safety.

"I cannot give the extravagant processes of that long journey. It was all a rushing, swirling dream—a mad race of mystery and sublimity, to which the only conscious periods were wild, flitting glimpses of wonderful ice arabesques, caught momentarily as we passed under fissures that let the light of day through dimly.

"Gradually a ghostly radiance grew to encompass us; and by a like gradation the water waxed intensely cold. Hope then was blazing in our hearts; but this new deathliness went nigh to quench it altogether. Yet, had we guessed the reason, we could have foregone the despair. For, in truth, we were approaching that shallower terrace of the glacier beyond the fall, through which the light could force some weak passage, and the air make itself felt, blowing upon the beds of ice.

"Well, we survived; and still we survive. My faith, what a couple! Sublimity would have none of us. The glacier rejected souls so commonplace as not to be properly impressed by its inexorability.

"This, then, was the end. We swept into a huge cavern of ice—through it—beyond it, into the green valley and the world that we love. And there, where the torrent splits up into a score of insignificant streams, we grounded and crawled to dry land and sat down and laughed.

"Yes, we could do it—we could laugh. Is that not bathos? But Fidèle and I have a theory that laughter is the chief earnest of immortality.

"To *dry* land I have said. *Mon Dieu!* the torrent was no wetter. It rains in the Chamounix valley. We looked to see whence we had fallen, and not even the *Chapeau* was visible through the mist.

"But, as I turned, Fidèle uttered a little cry.

"'The flask, and the sandwich-box, and your poor coat!'

"'*Comment?*' I said; and in a moment was in my shirt-sleeves.

"I stared, and I wondered, and I clucked in my throat.

"Holy saints! I was adorned with a breastplate on my back. The friction of descent, first welding together these, the good ministers to our appetite, had worn the metal down in the end to a mere skin or badge, the heat generated from which had scorched and frizzled the cloth beneath it.

"I needed not to seek further explanation of the pain I had suffered—was suffering then, indeed, as I had reason to know when ecstasy permitted a return of sensation. My back bears the scars at this moment.

"'It shall remain there for ever!' I cried, 'like the badge of a *cocher de fiacre*, who has made the fastest journey on record. 'Coachman! from the glacier to the valley.' '*Mais oui, monsieur.* Down this crevasse, if you please.'

"And that is the history of our adventure.

"Why we were not dashed to pieces? But that, as I accept it, is easy of elucidation. Imagine a vast crescent moon, with a downward nick from the end of the tail. This form the fissure took, in one enormous sweep and drop towards the mouth of the valley. Now, as we rushed headlong, the gentle curve received us from space to substance quite gradually, until we were whirring forward wholly on the latter, my luggage suffering the brunt of the friction. The upward sweep of the crescent diminished our progress—more and yet more—until we switched over the lower point and shot quietly down the incline beyond. And all this in ample room, and without meeting with a single unfriendly obstacle.

"'*Voilà, mes chers amis, ce qui me met en peine.*'

"Fidèle laughs, the rogue!

"'Ta, ta, ta!' she says. 'But they will not believe a word of it all.'"

Plots

"The limbs o' the plot—no more, I hope."—*Henry viii.*, Act i. sc. 1.

The literary virtuoso, putting his wits to gentle exercise in the fields of contemplative retrospection, must have often reviewed, in a sort of anaesthetic wonder, the self-condemnatory processes of the typical historical conspirator. By what insane rendering of principles he (this historical conspirator) thought to justify his machinations; by what motives, by what pressure of disordered ambitions, he was compelled to deeds foredoomed to failure; how he, an inconsiderable rebel, could ever have dreamed of penetrating deeper than through the remotest outworks of established authority, before he should rebound in fragments from the wall against which he had tilted—here are conundrums among which every browser in the records of the past has ineffectually nosed for a grain of reason. History is littered with the barren chaff. Cabals, schemes, intrigues—all short cuts into blind alleys—all, if not purposeless, at least ill-calculated—confuse the passage of events with an innumerable concourse of side-influences. There was never a hawk, it seemed, sailing stately on, but a cloud of chattering pipers teased its flight. Such are the conspirators who thought to confound the sure direction of history. The beams of the scaffolds of yesterday are grooved with the ropes that strangled them; the edges of the axes are notched from biting on their neckbones. Why they so wantonly conspired, absurdly staking their all upon a single ticket in a lottery of ten thousand tickets, could have no moral but that of the overproduction and consequent valuelessness of life. They speculated with the trash, one chance in many. Life to them, we must suppose, was no more than a red counter in a game of "Reversi." The turning up of a remote black disc might mean the quenching of a whole row of flaming pieces, among which might or might not figure their own particular one. It was the game, and they played it.

Well, they plotted—the Guy Fawkeses, the Marino Falieros, the Perkin Warbecks—they plotted solemnly, hopefully; and all the time it would seem impossible for any sane man to prognosticate other than sure disaster to their schemes. But what inclined each to his choice of plot—when the world hummed like a wood with viewless intrigue—would read stranger than fiction in the record, for it would be quoted from the history of the human heart.

From the Stars to the Supers! We have very few conspirators nowadays. Your author is almost your only plotter; but what inclineth him to the one scheme out of many that offer is as great a mystery as that other. He sits on saddle-bag instead of saddle; he wields the pen in place of the sword; he hath the freebooting alphabet at his command. The world lies at the point of his weapon; yet he seems often as wilful as Simon Fraser in his adoption of the purposeless intrigue.

What inclines him, indeed, to take or reject, unless it be that very thing that influences the *ordinary* person in his choice of a dish at a restaurant—the mood of the moment to which a hundred of little secret tributaries may have subscribed? There are gourmets among us (authors) who will sip and reject, or sip and approve, as daintily as bees in an April meadow; there are sybarites whose biliary humour is all for the sickly and oversatisfying; there are the simple appetites, of uniform unsensitive palate, to whose nets, it may be said, all that comes is fish—just appreciable changes on a single flavour. These should know their tastes, each selecting, appropriately to his own, from the bill of fare. In point of fact, they are quite wont to abuse them. Moved, no doubt, by the gastronomic enjoyment expressed in the face of his neighbour of the different temperament, any or either will select a dish antipathetic to his constitution, doing violence in the result to what he would indulge. The gourmet will toy with the plain joint of conservative fiction, thinking to express a new juice of astheticism from the commonplace; the sybarite will hope to stimulate a demoralised appetite with stinging *hors d'oeuvres* of epigram; the simple novelist (*Anglicè*, as one might say, the plain dealer or honest tradesman) will be moved to the discussion of a nauseating hash of "problems." They will all (to bring them together round a fount, so to speak, of inspiration) think that "Plot" is like a great Bodega cheese, for everyone that lists to cut from.

Heavens! what a salmis of figuratives! It were better to hark back to the leading comparison—to the unattached conspirators of history whose scheming came into the day's marketing, as it were. History keeps its sanity more or less over its detailing of the essayed plots of these. What a lunatic register it would be, did it try to enumerate the rejected ones!

What to leave in one's ink-pot! Does one let the liquid gall dry in it, there is to be seen a thick precipitate at the bottom. That is what fell from the pen when, in writing, one shook from it all but that which one desired to say. Here and there, if one looks closely, show up little prominences among the refuse. These are rejected plots, thrown away arbitrarily, or not, as the case may be. Possibly, if one now and again were reclaimed, liquefied into words and given pen-point, it might redeem itself in the eyes of its former contemner. The mood that cast them out may have relented. Let us, in our present one, at least have up two or three we wot of from the dregs, and reconsider their case.

The Plot of the Abhorred Cripple

He was an abhorred cripple, despised, an outcast—the scapegoat of Society. None, within his memory, had ever addressed him from an assumed common standpoint of equality. He hated his fellows. How to retaliate on them? How to command their fear, if not their respect? He joined a Secret Society—a modern

Vehmgericht. A man was to be slain. Lots were drawn for the deed; to the cripple fell its commission. He went forth—a lost soul wilfully obliterating its every footprint behind it as it walked, for that its pursuing Guardian Angel might hunt counter. He went forth into a desolate place, wandering blindly in his evil exultation, and came nigh to being engulfed in a quagmire. A stranger, riding afield at the critical moment, rescued him—nay, more, spoke to him fair, sympathetically, as in unaffected recognition of the gracious equality of all human souls. For the first time in his life he felt sane and self-respecting. And then, by way of a chance reference, he learnt that this stranger was he whom he was deputed to kill. He had wilfully eluded his Angel. The man he slew, and cast into the morass; and then at length his Angel overtook him, and looking into his face, shrouded its own, for evermore to be behind him a formless horror; and the marsh and the desolation of the waste enclosed his soul, as it were a tree age-long riveting itself about a toad that had once sought sanctuary in its hollowness.

Now—as if Heaven for his deed denied him the prerogative of unfulfilment—returning to the world, recognition, respect, prosperity, like full-ripe fruit, came away into his hand at a touch. Only, on the highest bough, heavy-bosomed love swelled without his reach. But, of its own weight, it drooped—drooped; until at last it came into his range of intimate vision—almost of touch—and he saw in it the fruit of his crime, the child of the man he had murdered. (What follows? Here the salvage gives out. We fancy that eventually the cripple, an apostate to his own religion of retaliation, is 'concluded' in his turn—and in the quagmire—by another member of the Vehmgericht. And what becomes of the lady? Doubtless she goes on "cutting bread and butter.")

THE PLOT OF THE FEARFUL HEAD
(*An Italic Story.*)

Some years ago a head (we think of an Earl of Suffolk, who was executed under order of Henry VIII.) was actually discovered, in an extraordinary state of preservation, in a box of sawdust. Very well: the head of our Earl (cut off for an extremely aggravated deed of wickedness) is also preserved in a box, and is an heirloom committed by the reprehensible creature himself to the custody of his descendants, each generation having to accept without question, and under the most fearful threat of anathema, the abominable trust. Now the head (never, by order of its original consigner, to be disturbed or revealed to mortal vision) remains in its box working havoc—like the prodigy of Glamis Castle—on all who, from scepticism or daredevilry, misdoubt its infernal influence upon the successive representatives of its race. None of these latter, however, so much as dreams of repudiating the malevolent trust—though it signifies to him, as to his predecessors, either a self-conscious process of dementation, or a gradual moral degeneracy—until, upon the succession of the —th Earl, love takes on its shoulders the burden of the accumulated terror. Armed only with her devotion and a mirror (perhaps she had been prettily reading of Perseus in the "Tanglewood Tales,") *She* "tackles" the curse in the gloaming, and, never withdrawing her eyes from its reflection in her glass, opens the baneful casket, sees a top-dressing of sawdust, and forces herself to lay bare with her fingers *that which lies beneath*. Then, in that awful moment, is revealed a severed human head—of indescribable inhuman expression—the wide blue eyes of which, protruding from the dusty flakes, *are looking at her*. Now comes the most ghastly crucial test—the battle between Love and Hate—between sin and purity. The eyes are drawing hers to turn from the negative, and address themselves to the positive, apparition. Does she succumb and obey, *she knows that she will shut down the unconquered curse into its coffer once more, and will then herself go raving mad*. The struggle sways her soul. Unnamable suggestions seem to circle round her head. The agony tears her. If she could only once sob, cry out! Suddenly she is conscious of a change taking place in the aspect of the horror. Its eyes seem to flicker—fade—fall in; an expression of terror grows out of and dominates the evil will. Seeming to gnash its teeth in rage and fear, the head collapses, sinks into dust—*and is gone*. Love, of course, seeks the floor in a swoon.

And, after all, it was only exposure to the air that the monstrosity had dreaded, manoeuvered to guard itself from, and eventually succumbed to. With the fading of its eyes, the curse is withdrawn. Indeed, Love can never very definitely recall the nature of the ordeal to which she was subjected; for the casket, upon examination, is found to contain nothing but dust and dusty fragments. The moral is, of course, of the self-damnatory processes of moral cowardice.

THREE PLOTS OF LOST AND RECOVERED TREASURES
I. OF THE TREASURE LOST IN THE CRATER

An old man (not of these islands) had, for all relations, two sons and a grandson. The sons he feared and hated, for he knew that, coveting his wealth, they desired his death; but the grandson he loved, and him he designed to make his heir. At length, foreseeing that the scarce governable cupidity of the two elder rogues would be like to end in violence to himself and the boy, he secretly realised on all his property, converted this into imperishable gems, secured the stones within a light belt of steel mail, and, fastening the treasure about his waist so that it was well concealed, took his grandson by the hand and led him in secrecy, at a fortunate moment, from the lonely house. He intended to go without sign—to sojourn, disguising his identity, in a distant place. The two—the old man and the boy—were inseparable companions. Now they went forth in love together, and their way led over a pass that skirted the crater of a usually dormant volcano. But the duet of rogues, though they knew nothing of the gems, had not been blind to the purposed flight; and they followed the runaways, and on the mountain came up with their father. But he, already scenting the pursuit, had hidden his grandchild in the hollow of a blasted rock, that hung nigh to the lip of the crater. Now the sons, blasphemously extolling Providence, realised upon the opportunity, and slew their father and cast his body into the crater, so that it disappeared within the nameless pit thereof. And they sought the boy, and, not finding him, reasoned of their own iniquity that the old man had, out of his irreclaimable venality, destroyed and hidden his companion by the way. Then home they went, "rejoicing in that tide," and, thinking to profit of their wickedness, were presently aware of the truth, and of how they were caught and mauled in the springe of their own setting.

Now the boy, witness of the parricide, emerged, when they were gone, from his hiding-place, and presently took service and became a shepherd on the mountain. And always he was wont to haunt the locality of the crime, driving his flock to the highest pastures. And this he did till the mountain began to throb and menace, moving in labour, and groaning like a thing that wearied of self-repression. Then one day there came to the crater edge two men—bestial lost souls, haggard and depraved. And they gazed over into the pit, and presently upon one another; and the boy from his eyrie in the riven stone saw them, and that they were his uncles. And the two spake, saying each to the other, "Go you down and seek to recover the belt, for else are we destitute, save we go to fatten ourselves for the gallows." Yet neither would descend, each dreading the terror of the place and the low-snoring gullet of the pit; and not less that, did he recover the treasure, the other should profit of his position to snatch the prize for himself, hurling back the adventurer to his death. So, quarrelling, in a little time they came to raging passion; and presently, in the blind grapple of fury, they stumbled on the brink, clutched, crashed over, and rolled screaming to their fate. New the deep-set mouth of the crater seemed to open, as a fish's mouth opens gasping at a worm, and into it the fated wretches were drawn. And immediately—as it were the casting forth of some gravel or foreign body taken with the other—a shower of scoria was discharged with a bellow from the orifice; and thereafter all fell still. But when at length the watcher dared to emerge and look over into the pit—there, shot upon a projecting sulphur-stone, within reach of his crook, was the belt of gems, oxidised and blackened, but whole. Thus it was, prosaically no doubt, that the two bodies in their foundering released some gases, long confined beneath that choked opening to the gullet of the crater, that was further plugged by the calcined remains of their former victim. But romance must give the old man's spirit some credit for the result.

II. OF THE DETECTIVE BALLOON

Peter Piper was in despair. For him, as he thought, the world held no further illusions. Money and credit, through the breaking of a bank, had failed him; his friends were paying back the capital of affection he had invested in them in instalments of cheap rebuke; his fiancée's papa had shown him the door. He thought all a curse of inheritance—the visitation of the sins of the father. For *his* had been a notorious miser; and when the miser's wealth chiefly crystallised into precious stones—had been all stolen one night, leaving behind it not so much as a single hop-o'-my-thumb pebble whereby to track the thief, the miser had died incontinently of a broken heart. Broken bank, broken credit, broken trust, broken heart—all "stony-broke"! Peter Piper sought about for an attractive means to a final break—that of the thread of his own existence. Wandering into a holiday enclosure, wherefrom was about to take place a balloon ascent, he saw, and jumped to, the method, scrambled into the empty car, and resisted all the aeronaut's attempts to dislodge him. In the racket and confusion that ensued, by some error the balloon was cut adrift, and Peter found himself committed alone to a course that was not altogether the one he had designed to take. For, alas! this course showed itself by far too irregular. He had intended only to be carried irresponsibly aloft, and so from an immeasurable altitude to drop over the basket-edge. He never could control his reason on or at heights. Now, no sooner was he soaring than his aspirations fell, but all desire to follow them had quitted him. He longed most ardently for the feel once more beneath his soles of the good flat earth, even were he consigned to nothing more profitable than a cinder heap. And in the meantime the balloon (a moderate one, say, of some twelve yards in diameter, and only partially filled with forty out of the fifty thousand cubic feet of gas that were its complement) swooped and tumbled along, within dangerous distance of those trees and spires that are their Casquets to aerial mariners. He was now tearing across "Crackskull" Common, midway on which stood up a gaunt and crumbling chimney-stock—the old-time flue to a ruined saw-mill. Crash!,—the enormous skin, palpitating like a huge irides-cent jelly-fish in a current, ripped through a clump of trees, spouted gas from half a dozen rents, dropped, reeled, rushed upwards on a dying wing, and came thud with its car midway upon the unstable chimney. That snapped like a carrot. In the midst of the downfall of wreckage, padded with the collapsed envelope Peter came to earth. When presently, in the midst of a clamorous concourse, he found his senses, it was to know their recovery incidental to one much more marvellous. For, from the disparted crest of the flue had been spilled, in its fall, the long-lost treasure of gems—the hoard of the defunct miser.

How had it come there? Why, to be sure, it was remembered that the mill had been owned in past years by an odd, eerie char-acter—a little grim, uncanny steeple-jack, who worked not, nei-ther span, save the web of secrecy that enwrapped him and his ruined eyrie on the common. And this gnome (long since passed) had nursed a grudge against the miser, and—

III. Of the Diver and the Devilfish

A diver, sent to raise a foundered chest of ingots, has just reeved his tackle to the load when he is approached by or monstrous squid. Two of the creature's tentacles embrace the man, three the locker, while three cling to rocks. The diver dares not signal to be hauled up, lest the gear snap under the enormous strain. Succeeding for a moment in fighting off the clutch of the two hideous arms, he sev-ers with his axe the three that are rock-fastened, and on the in-stant gives the signal for the chest to be raised. Through some sec-onds of agony he sees the tackle tighten, the load stir, hesitate, lift, with terrible leisureliness. Suddenly it shoots towards the surface, the squid flopping over, though still fastened to it. Wild swaying tentacles flog themselves towards him; the tip of one flips him and clings. It is torn away, writhing frantically at him. Reach-ing the surface with his treasure—like a self-stultifying miser—the insensate monster is destroyed by the diver's comrades.

TWO (SKELETON) PLOTS OF MYSTERIOUS DEATHS
I. OF THE POISONED FLIES

A certain spot on a forest road gains an evil notoriety from the fact that, during a short period, wayfaring bicyclists are frequently being thrown there and killed. Sometimes the injuries to the victims seem insufficient to have caused death. There is no extraordinary difficulty to be circumambulated, or peril to be considered at the place in question. That becomes uncanny, and travellers go roundabout to avoid it. At length some sapient illuminati resolve the mystery. They observe that the faces of the deceased (whatever the nature of the injuries) have a common *acrid* expression. They observe that the rocky banks through which the road is cut make, as it were, a ventilator, by way of which the draught of the whole valley passes. Anyone rushing through this gut must meet a very spindrift of wind and dust; and, latterly, he must have met worse—clouds of flies risen from settling, perhaps feeding, on some venom, most swiftly fatal to human life, that had been spilt on the further side of the gully. Now, if a fly or flies, reeking poison, were driven into the eye or eyes of a swiftly going traveller!—(Here are invited hypotheses,* agreeable to taste or reason. Only one of these, it may be suggested, is in question. The reader will, of course, know which.)

II. OF THE DEAD COOK UNDER THE COAL SHOOT

One morning is found, lying under the open circular shoot of a coal cellar beneath the pavement, the dead body of the general servant to a family living in a quiet street of a quiet suburb. She had evidently gone in the early morning to fetch coals, had mounted a heap of the stuff in order to the procuring of more light by removing the cap of the shoot, and had, while in this position, been struck and maltreated from above. Her scalp is abraded, her neck

---

* Sometimes a veterinary surgeon will, we believe, destroy a condemned dog or cat by dropping hydrocyanic acid into the corner of its eye.

dislocated. The pavement in the immediate neighbourhood of the orifice is slightly spattered with blood, while an indifferent track of blood-drops (fallen, it is presumed, from the instrument used) extends thence to the roadway. It would seem that the crown of the victim's head was, when assailed, actually projected, sprouting like a red tulip bud from the pavement. Now it is the very character of the injuries that baffles inquisition, for the damage to the scalp is superficial, and insufficient to account for the spilt blood, as in evidence. Moreover, even a red-haired cook will not allow her neck to be broken without a struggle, and here there was no sign of the occurrence of any.

So again we set our illuminati to work, and this is the solution of the mystery as they interpret it: A circus company is leaving the neighbourhood in the early morning. A young elephant—one of certain animals conducted through the empty streets—becoming either scared or skittish, breaks from the ranks and scuttles along the side-walk. Mary Jane, who has stationed herself immediately beneath the opened coal-shoot, hearing strange sounds, essays to project her inquisitive knowledge-box through the aperture, and has only got so far as to hung the latter, when the elephant shuffles up, and, unthinking, puts a foot upon the sprouting bulb, as upon a mere eccentricity of the pavement. Down goes Mary Jane, shutting upon herself, between the elephant and the coal, with a scratched scalp and a dislocated neck; and down also goes the animal's foot, wedging itself in the hole. And here it is, in the beast's frantic struggles to withdraw its limb, that the skin thereof is frayed and the blood scattered. (Note by illuminati: Diameter of blood corpuscle in man, 3,300th of an inch; of an elephant, 2,745th of an inch.)

THE PLOT OF THE PHENOMENAL CALCULATOR
AND THE QUANTITY SURVEYOR

Premiss: It has been related to us how a certain engineer, having the faculty of numerical calculation abnormally developed, would, while ciphering his astounding algorithms, wave his arms, crack his finger-joints, rush from chair to chair, and even leap from chair to table of the room in which he worked.

Plot: Miss Tottie Highclere, of the Theatre of Varieties, stands frequently—while attiring herself, in her lodgings, before her bed-room mirror—spellbound to witness the shadowy presentment of one who, in a room opposite her own across the street, appears to practise such fantastic and to her unaccountable evolutions as those referred to above. Her curiosity and her interest are greatly excited; her spirit of natural romance is stimulated by an occa-sional more intimate view of the subject of her secret regard, when, in the intervals of his apparently insane caprioles, he shows him-self, a melancholy young gentleman of preoccupied expression, at his window. Miss Tottie indulges a fancy, until it comes to tyrannise over her. The familiar tickle under the ribs of popular applause must dull of its allurement so long as a solution of this mystery is permitted to elude her. She sets herself to the unravelling task with as much affected impatience, and private enjoyment, as a woman expresses in the reeling out of a tangled skein of wool. Needless to say that, by means of her persistent and, so to speak, pachyderma-tous witchery, she is successful in picking up and following the clue. Details of the process it is idle to specify. A dozen of possible methods, serious or frolic, suggest themselves. Miss Tottie learns that her opposite neighbour—not the actual caperer—is a quantity surveyor (which we must conceive as a sort of practical mathema-tician, who works out his figures of bricks and timber for the builder); that he is himself a grossly ignorant man, having only that order of intelligence that enables its possessor to take full profit of the brains of his employes; and that he is making a rapid fortune by means of the caperer (a youthful phenomenal calcula-tor upon whom he has chanced, and whose natural genius for fig-ures he has been quick to turn to his own advantage, and for a consideration that spells starvation to the other). Miss Tottie fur-ther learns that the caperer (on the whole, a rather poor abnor-mality, and one quite unwitting of the material value of his gift) is never allowed to leave the house; and that therein he is bound to subjection by the triple cord of physical fear, moral cowardice, and the threat of prosecution for the recovery of a trifling loan advanced to him at one time by his employer. She learns it all—somehow; and she is indignant, and pitying, and sympathetic; and her coryphée blood boils while the fire burns; and she is quite an admirable Tottie.

Behold her, then—this little Fanfan of tricks and "turns"—delightedly conceiving and maturing her plans for a declaration of independence, for the triumph of innocence over a particularly despicable form of oppression. One day the quantity surveyor receives by post a stall ticket (available that night) for Miss Tottie Highclere's benefit performance at the Theatre of Varieties. The gross creature recalls, with a feculent laugh, how he has been made latterly the subject of certain suggestive oglings on the part of the actress who lives in the house opposite. He has all the arrogant faith of his kind in the power of reputable opulence to make the least desirable personality magnetic—an unjustified creed, of course. He knows, or thinks he knows, that the actual fruit of romance, like early strawberries, is for the high bidder. Shall he pay the price? He is something of a glutton, and he will. He goes to the theatre—makes even an occasion of it—and dines apoplectically at a restaurant before he takes a cab (and the full measure of it at a shilling) to the house. He does not guess that his inducement to this is a "plant"—*that his phenomenon is there before him.*

Presently, item, on the programme: Miss Tottie Highclere in the guise of show-woman to the *Lightning Calculator!* In a sort of gasping dream he sees his own abused phenomenon enter upon and take—in those very galvanic and fantastic plunges, with which he is so familiar—the stage; hears the shrill question; agonises through the expectant pause; shrinks beneath the resultant thunder of acclamation, and, foreseeing all that is implied in the glorious treachery, dies perhaps of apoplexy on the spot.

And as for Miss Tottie and her prodigy? Well, having set him on his legs, she remembers no doubt her own, and dances away on them to new fields of conquest, leaving the phenomenon in a mire of infatuation more stultifying than that of his ancient servitude.

PLOT OF THE MISUSED ABACUS

A scientific gentleman, who has undertaken to read at a conversazione a paper on some astronomical subject, that shall enable him practically to demonstrate the merits of a new arithmometer, or calculating machine, has the misfortune to fall indisposed on the very afternoon of his engagement. In despair, he will commission a lay friend to read his paper for him. "But how about the numerical demonstration?" says the friend. "Oh," says the scientific gentleman, "that is simple! Wherever illustrations are needed, I will write you exact directions on the margin of my MS. as to the management of the machine, the disposition of certain numbers, and the revolutions of the handle necessary to the working out of the desired sums." "Very well," says the confident friend; and off he goes presently to his appointment, with a box like a hurdy-gurdy under his arm. But the scientific gentleman's written directions prove, where not unintelligible, frequently illegible, and—(The potentialities for comic business are here so patent and so liberal, that it may be left to the fancy of any reader to supply a denouement.)

THE PLOT OF THE RIVAL SUITORS

Big Captain Bobadil and little Johnny Verulam are rivals for the hand of Sylvia. One afternoon, when they are facing one another green-eyed at her tea-table, Sylvia expresses her most imperious desire to see the coronation procession from the standpoint, or points, of the vagrom citizen. She would fill, however slenderly, no stationary chair; be anchored to no buoy of inglorious safety; flutter vain wings of yearning behind no plate-glass, nor dwell fixed to a stand like a stuffed specimen in a show-case. She would mingle with the people, taste of their liberal excitement, move with them, and get more fun out of a pennyworth of freedom than from all twelve inches of security at a guinea an inch.

"My dear," says her shocked Duenna, "think of the danger we should run in such a crowd!"

"We, Lavinia!" says Sylvia.

"We," says the Duenna very decidedly.

"Well," says Sylvia, conceding the plural, "we are both as thin as thin. There'd be nothing to squash, anyhow. Besides, we should have to engage an escort, of course."

Up jump the rivals, jibbing shoulder to shoulder for the honour, as if they are rudely fighting for place at the door of an omnibus.

"See, Mr. Verulam," says Sylvia, "your hair is ruffled and your collar burst from its stud. There is the moral, I am afraid. Captain Bobadil, who stands there quite strong and cool, must squire us—that is to say, if he cares to."

Behold, then, on Coronation Day, the Captain, large, elated, and plumed with arrogance, committed to his ecstatic charge, and piloting the two ladies through the press! He is full of a puffing condescension towards Fortune for her attention to him. When he thinks of little Verulam and his dandyprat assurance, "Poor little devil!" he says to himself. "I'm sorry, 'pin my"—puff— "soul, I am, to have to walk over him in this"—puff— "fashion; but, if he *will* presume upon that pitiful tale of inches"—puff.

Keep close to me, Miss Sylvia," he says aloud. It won't do for us to get separated, ya know."

The crush is, indeed, a little frightening; but the police will engineer the human mill, without hazard to its motion, so long as nothing jams. Perhaps the Duenna is a thought hysteric. Once or twice the Captain has to twitch his coat-tails from her fervid but bony clutch. She has a vague feeling that she is holding on to the rear rope of a bathing machine, and that if she slips it she will go under. Besides, if the truth must be told, the Bobadil is her golden goose. She would like to follow attached to him to the world's end, whereas she fears it is her fate but to be attached (professionally) to one who is attached to him.

All goes well till the party reaches St. Charles Street, a narrow court of communication between a park and a main thoroughfare. There has been no actual need for them to penetrate this crowded close. The moral of the digression lies in Captain Bobadil's knowledge that little Verulam is sulking in the Bow-window Club—whose front, standing flush with the pavement, faces to this St. Charles

Street—and in his, the Captain's, unworthy willingness to flaunt, *en passant*, his triumph in the eyes of his discomfited rival. And he has the reward of his venture. Verulam is actually there, standing in a ground-floor window, tragically conning the seething press of heads just beneath him—standing lowering, baleful, the ghost of a very Corsican brother.

With ineffable insolence, the Captain convoys his party, unconscious of the apparition, under the apparition's nose, and at that very moment the machine jams. The mob, by some unhappy coincidence of events, being driven or scared back from both points of exit, suddenly congests, and blocks the narrow artery of St. Charles Street. Immediately the machine shudders and screams through all its straining parts. Good-humour has at a thought become selfish panic; expectation, terror. Arms fight up to catch at straws of air; knee-joints feel as if turning to a numb jelly; the horrible fear-screech of women harrows and demoralises.

"Captain Bobadil," gasps poor Sylvia, "save me! I'm going to faint!"

Struggling, bullying, swaying, he yet—powerful man—forces a little breathing space of an inch or two, and turns in it, crouching as he can.

"Get on my back—my shoulders," he pants; "I'll carry you clear"; and he thunders at their maddened neighbours, "You fools! Help her up. It will make more room for you."

This prevails at least, for in an instant she is clinging on. But, before he can blunder a step forward, she is gone again—whether sucked back into the vortex, or pitched upon the heads of the mob, he is too frantic, too deafened by the din to gather.

"My God!" he yells; "don't give it up—for my sake, darling! Help her, you devils!"

He cannot look behind him. His lungs thud like a District engine's. And then, in an instant, she is there again; and he ejaculates one oath of rapture, and, jerking her as high towards his shoulders as is possible, makes a loop of his arms about her skirts, and sets himself furiously to the essay. His strong ribs bow inwards;

he can hardly breathe, but inch by inch he wins a way, until accident drifts him against an acquaintance.

"Help me," then he gasps, "Dicky—to save her—my own, my darling—has she fainted?"

Dicky has his troubles also; but he finds expression for a little amazement in the midst of them. However, he does his manful best—and at last, at last the pressure relaxes, the air lightens, the way is won. And it is at this very moment that Dicky turns confidential.

"I say," he asks, "your very own, eh—that up there?"

"Yes," says Captain Bobadil, daring everything on the throw.

"Oh!" says Dicky, "I didn't know—wish you joy, 'm sure—glad to have been of any use"; and he raises his hat and vanishes, at the instant that the Captain, reverently, ecstatically, hopefully, lowers to her feet—the Duenna.

The Duenna simpers, twitters, laughs a little shamefacedly.

"So very public," she says. But certainly—your declaration—sense of emergency—much may be excused."

He stares at her apoplectic.

"Sylvia!" he roars suddenly.

"Oh!" she says, "didn't you see? Such presence of mind—and strength—I shouldn't have thought him capable of it. Mr. Verulam, who was standing just above, pulled darling Sylvia off your shoulders through a window."

"Captain Bobadil," says Sylvia, "pray apologise no more. Any explanation of your conduct that once seemed called for is proved quite unnecessary. I was misled at first, I confess it very penitently, into thinking you guilty of the meanness, the wickedness of endangering our safety for no other object than that you might distress and humiliate a rival. I am so glad, so sorry, to know that I was wrong. A gentleman— 'Dicky,' they called him—was explaining things at the Bow-window Club, very shortly after—after— We were all very much surprised, I'm sure; but I congratulate you, with my whole heart, upon your engagement, as I hope you will me upon mine to Mr. Verulam. I hear Lavinia, I think, coming downstairs. Shall I—"

Curtain, as the Captain bolts, leaving his hat behind him on the hall table. It lifts again to reveal him on his way to South Africa in a false beard and a cricket cap.

THE PLOT OF THE STRANGE STONE

It is related (so the story says), in some hoary Chronicle, how that a certain wood acquired such an evil reputation that none but those, strangers, or who were under the press of extreme urgency, durst travel therein. Such as did, however, and came presently through, made a common tale of some influence, that had been constantly upon them from nigh their entrance into the thickets, persuading them from their path to a particular direction, and that must be combated and resisted, even with such a faintness and sweating as seize upon them that experience for the first time the masterful devil that may reveal itself in wind. Yet this was no wind; but rather the impulsion, so it appeared, of a dank and gloating stillness; and, yet again, not so much an impulsion as an allurement, that, making itself known by small degrees, waxed slowly, the deeper one penetrated, to a pitch near irresistible; and so, being withstood, waned by like gradations, as its point of seeming concentration was passed and left behind.

Now, it was noted that those who won, however hardly, through the haunted wood, were men of a mean condition—villains, churls, and so forth; and that in proportion as a traveller wore harness partial, or little, or none at all, so was the attraction strong, or feeble, or imperceptible to him. But, so surely as did knight—of whom, indeed, there came plenty, for Christ's or lady's sake, to dare the venture—enter cap-à-pie in quest to resolve the mystery, so certainly did he vanish from human ken, never more to issue or be heard of.

Once, now, there rode up a fair knight all clad in steel, and his esquire pillion behind him. And they dismounted at the edge of the thicket, because that it shut dense against the passage of a horse. Entering then on foot, they found a close woodland, most sweet and pranked with flowers of innocence, in all of which the donzel, being new-shriven, saw clearly the work of God. So that, coming shortly to a little pool, says he, "Master, fain were I to rest here, and doff and lave, for by're lady I am weary, and the wood as I see is withouten baile." To which the knight consenting, he doft his habergeon and hanger, and so was to strip off his acton of quilted leather, when he ware that his master, that had strolled yet forward, was drawn into the vortex of some influence and crying out to him to come and help him. At that the squire ran half-naked as he was; and he saw his master pulled, so it seemed, from his path, and disappearing, and coming again, and again vanishing, hauled into the brushwood. Now he followed, sweating, in the knight's track; and the other went before him, played, as he were a fish, by some devilish angler, and still, for all his plunging and withholding, reeled to his doom. Nor might it avail him to clutch at branch or thorn, or even to cast himself down, being for all his efforts drawn on, and at last with a swiftness that outstripped the pursuer. So for a furlong, it might be, when—lo! there, sleek from a ruin of trees, rose a great blue rock sullen and naked of vegetation. And the knight, caught swift at the end like a straw into a whirlpool, rushed, or was wrenched against this rock, whereto he was held in such manner as that he could move neither head nor limb. Then the fearful donzel, peering from covert, saw that the rock was all sown with armoured skeletons, clinging like limpets to a crag; and immediately there issued from some coign of concealment a body of men, near naked like himself, that robbed the knight of whatever that was precious in his possession, and so with their booty disappeared again, jeering and committing their captive of the rock to starvation. But the esquire coming up, when all was clear, tried to tear his master from that which held him, but could no more move him than he were the brand stuck in the four square stone of Arthur. Then, for that his lord was held from moving a finger in his own behoof, he unbuckled of his harness, piece by piece of it flying to the rock as it was released, till the knight, slipping forth, at the last, of his casque, stood on the ground a free man.

"Now," says he, "by God's grace I will rede you prestly this riddle. For hereby I see nothing less than a great mass of that quick-iron, the *ferrum vivum* of Pliny, that has the power to draw to itself both steel and iron, but metals none other; though it putteth my reason to St. Paul's sanctuary to trow that so mighty a piece, or of such far-reaching influence, could be deposited here by any than a supernatural agency. And that I am the more to believe, insomuch as the wretches that robbed me were, by mine oath, none other than fellows of the Count de Borne, whose castle tops the valley yonder, and who is suspected a robber and sorcerer. Yet, per-adventure," says he, "Providence hath taken its means through us that the accompt of his villainy be at length closed."

And even so it was proved. And the wicked Count, being pres-ently by threat of bell, book, and candle brought to confess, avowed that the mass of lodestone had, by his impious prayers, been pitched into the wood (as some say, in the form of a bolt or shoot-ing-star, that the devil, flying up, brake from the wall of heaven and cast down), that it might serve by its supernatural force of at-traction to gather for him a great harvest of spoil, and that spoil the richer because only those of a full equipment of arms might not resist it.

So runs the Chronicle; and, take that part of heaven's wall as ye will (yet what, indeed, in all conscience so draws men's hopes to it as heaven), within belief it is that the greater creation may contain materials like to our earth's, but more pronounced in their properties, and as such by the Divine Wisdom withheld from our too weak and partial control.

THE PLOT OF THE RUBBER-SOLED
BOOTS AND THE FOOT-WARMER

I am a diamond merchant. An unostentatious-looking bag I carry with me often contains some thousands of pounds' worth of

gems. Once, about to travel by the—night mail, I enter an empty
compartment at Liverpool Street terminus, sit down and place my
bag beside me. From the crowd and scurry on the platform a gentleman shortly emerges, enters my compartment, and bestows himself—drawing a voluminous rug over his hands and knees, and
yawning wearily—in a corner. An employé appears at the door with
foot-warmers. "If you please," say I. "No, thanks," says my fellow-
traveller. However, he stoops politely to help to shove the thing
past, and under, his own berugged legs, apparently fumbling with
it a minute while he gets a purchase. The next instant he slides it
over to me. "Boilin' hot, by Jove!" he says; and I thank him, and
put my feet on it. I always travel in rubber-soled boots. They are
warm, and discreetly unbetraying if one grows restive, when alone,
to pace up and down. Now, the moment I am secure of my warm
footstool, my friend rises, as if to readjust his rug, drops it instead—
and with it a little empty bottle—whisks about, collars my bag, and
in a flash is gone. The ruse, the act, has been so instant, that for
three seconds I sit paralysed. Then, conscious of an odd heaviness,
as it were, at my base, I spring erect, totter, double forward against
the opposite seat, struggle up again, again collapse backwards, and
begin to roar. My feet are glued to the foot-warmer as firmly as a
wooden soldier's to his stand!

Now a station constable is at the door. He hears, sees the bottle,
springs intelligent, and is suddenly down on his knees, with his
nose to the foot-warmer.

"Ah!" he says, rising, "acid and heat in combination, sir. He
spilt the stuff over when he stooped down. The soles of your boots
is all of a muck, and melted to the metal."

He pulls out a note-book.

"Nature of contents of bag?" says he officially.

"Oh!" I answer—as imperturbable for my part— "nothing—particular. Er—by a most unusual chance, I have my valuables in my
breast-pocket. I—er—wanted the bag for a couple of hedgehogs I'm
taking down to a friend. You're welcome to keep them, if you catch
the thief, which I should think, by appearances, you're extremely
likely to do."

AN ASTONISHING SENTENCE

"Gentlemen of the jury," said the clerk, are you agreed upon your verdict?"

"We are."

"Do you find the prisoner at the bar guilty or not guilty?"

"Guilty."

There was a little buzz of acquiescent relief in the court, as when a swarm of flies is disturbed by a passer-by and resettles on its carrion—in this instance represented by the gentleman in the dock, convicted of a very brazen and heartless species of fraud.

With the damnatory word, the prisoner, who had hitherto lounged carelessly back in his wooden pen, was observed to straighten himself and take a step forward, when he stood clutching the rail with his hands and staring fixedly at the judge.

"He's good for ten years," whispered a fat man amongst the spectators to his neighbour.

"Wait a bit," said the latter. "Old Coppergills has lunched up to the mercy point."

"There ain't a blessed doubt him there can get the benefit of."

"Wait a bit."

Mr. Justice Grimley, thus irreverently indicated, bore the reputation—because he liked well-cooked food—of holding himself in fief to his palate. As that was offended or gratified, it was said, so did he deal out the law of Rhadamanthus or the law of discretion. A hair in his soup might multiply itself to a cat-o'-nine-tails; a juicy fillet plead extenuating circumstances. So far, no doubt, justice was allowed something less than itself; but at least there was no denying, according to report, that Mr. Justice Grimley loved Burgundy, and that it had been known sometimes to make him nod to his fall.

Now, it was clear to the "how-many-beans-make-five" ones, at this point, that the judge had lunched to his liking. Therefore they awaited the sentence with some inclination to bet odds on lenity.

But those who had the honour—not to say the decency—of the bench at heart, showed at the same moment a tendency to dive amongst their papers with embarrassed faces, redly expectant of some unnamable fiasco.

The fact was, that Mr. Justice Grimley—returned from his private room, whither he had retired for refreshment during the absence of the jury—seemed (not to mince matters) to have lunched on the present occasion far too well. His face—looking puffed and grotesque as a mask through the dull January fog that lay dead in the court—was dyed of a clouded damask; his eyes shone vacuous and unspeculative, and those nearest him were vaguely aware that he was muttering incoherently to himself. This was shocking enough, but worse was to follow; and that came when Mr. Justice Grimley delivered sentence.

The voice was familiar, the matter astounding; for he told the prisoner, in so many words, that he might go. Legally phrased, the pronouncement was to the effect that he thought "the ends of justice would be met by binding over the prisoner, on his own recognisances, to come up for judgment if called upon."

There fell a flat silence. Then up jumped counsel for the prosecution, and expostulated so far as he dared. The fraud had been flagrant and proved up to the hilt; the prisoner—prisoner no longer—was an acknowledged impostor, a swindler (a prestidigitateur by profession) who had most basely traded upon the credulity of the poor and the ignorant.

There was some applause, repressed, and, following it, a stern, brief rebuke from the judge. During the whole scene the accused never shifted his position from the front of the dock; but those who had the curiosity to remark how he took his virtual acquittal, noticed that his teeth were set, and the apple of his throat was moving up and down, as if he combated some naturally strong emotion.

Now, at last (the judge being umpire, from whose decision there was no appeal), he bowed to the bench and hurriedly left the dock, the door of which was held open for him. Ten minutes later, acquitted of necessary formalities, he found himself free of the Law Courts, and with all the fog of London to blot him out of memory.

But Mr. Justice Grimley?

Full and astonished discussion buzzed about him. The junior Bar sniggered and whispered in groups; the senior nid-nodded in

juxtaposition of horse-hair, and with glances askance in his direction. After an interval, the next case was called. It was time the
judge noted the counsel engaged; but the judge sat silent at his
desk, an elbow resting upon it, his face dropped heavily in his hand.
Respectfully addressed, he made no response. There was a pause,
amid general amazement; then a senior member of the Bar, a personal friend of the judge, ascended the dais, and, bending, whispered in the high legal ear.

No response.

Mr. Justice Grimley was fast asleep.

Positively, it was necessary to shake him before so much as a
murmur could be won from his lips. Think of it! A first magistrate,
robed and bewigged, pounded into wakefulness like any sleepy
"tweenie"!

The gentleman on the daïs turned to the court, with a pallid,
awe-struck face.

"There is something wrong here," he said rather tremulously.
"He is as fast asleep as if counsel were in mid-argument."

"Pull his nose!" cried a voice from the gallery.

"Try the winding-up of a peroration," suggested a very young
barrister.

The senior member accepted the hint as an inspiration.

"That is my case, my lud," he said in a loud voice.

Mr. Justice Grimley immediately woke up.

He did more. He staggered to his feet and looked wildly about
him, swaying a little. Perhaps only the stiffness of his robes saved
him from falling. But the expression of his smile was so intensely
vacuous, that the senior member felt that, unless he could at once
be removed, the majesty of the law was a dead letter. Respectfully,
but firmly, he passed his arm under that of his superior.

"For Heaven's sake, let me conduct you without!" he whispered.
"You are indisposed."

The judge offered no resistance. He seemed entirely to acqui-
esce in the suggestion. As they made for the little door—like a the-
atrical R. C. entrance—that led from the daïs, the senior member
called over his shoulder, "His ludship is taken seriously ill. There
must be an adjournment *sine die*," and vanished with his charge,

the door snapping to behind them as if it had been pulled by a super.

Once in his private room, where on the table yet lay his near-untasted lunch—a congealed chop, and a small bottle of Pommard, less a single glass only—Mr. Justice Grimley sank into a chair, and into semi-stupor simultaneously.

Greatly agitated, the senior member set to pacing the room up and down, his brain a perfect yeast of ferment. At the thirty-fifth turn, he noticed that the judge's eyes were open and normal, and he stopped blank in front of him.

"Shapter," said the judge, "I have come to myself, you see. Oblige me by ringing the bell and sending for Jenkins, the restaurant-keeper, who provides my daily Burgundy."

The senior member, reserving his indignation, bowed stately, obeyed, and stood with mute lips of solemnity during the interval of waiting. The restaurateur was ushered in, bobbing, and kneading his hands.

"Jenkins," said Mr. Justice Grimley, "who brought over my wine this morning?"

"Let me see, m'lud. It was a new hand I tuk on yesterday, m'lud."

"Have you seen him since—since he brought it?"

"I have not, m'lud."

"Nor will you. Good afternoon."

Quit of the tradesman, Mr. Justice Grimley turned to the senior member.

"Shapter, the wine was hocussed."

"Hocussed? Impossible. By whom?"

"A confederate of that fellow—the prisoner."

"Impossible. But grant it was—that doesn't excuse your preposterous—"

"Stop a bit. I never sentenced the fellow at all." The other smiled, loftily incredulous.

"Ah, you'll come to believe. I never sentenced him at all, I say. I drank what you see has gone from the bottle, and was at once taken with a sort of walking stupor—capable of action, but speechless. When they summoned me, I went instinctively, gaping and imbecile. The court swam before me; it was like catalepsy. I could appreciate my surroundings, in a measure; but was no longer master of my voice or expression. The next thing I was conscious of was my own voice delivering a preposterous judgment, as you say."

"Your own voice, yes. Yet you assert—"

"I say I didn't speak. It was the prisoner pronouncing his own sentence."

"The prisoner?"

"You'll split your eyelids, my boy. Yes, the prisoner. I've seen and heard him more than once *ex curiâ*. He's one of the most expert ventriloquists in London."

Mr. Justice Grimley tumbled back, with a rolling bellow of laughter.

"It's rich, it's rich!" he whined, wiping his eyes. The rascal, oh, the rascal! To design and carry it out, and let himself off like that! He deserves a statue."

"You're dreaming, I say. The thing's impossible."

"Take a glass of that stuff, you stiff-necked Philistine."

"If it will please—and convince you."

Five minutes later the senior member was sitting hopelessly idiotic, while the judge writhed on his chair in helpless laughter.

THE FACE ON THE SHEET

This, you may take it, is the true version of a very extraordinary story, a garbled report of which at one time got into the papers. Its *bona fides*, as here written down, I can attest, for I was a native of Compton Martel, and present at the lecture ("Domestic Architecture," with dissolving views), at which the shocking scene took place.

I must premise that, some months before the date of the lecture, which was simply one of a series organised by a local "Literature, Science, and Art Society," Compton Martel had acquired an unenviable notoriety on account of an extremely brutal murder, that had for the once stained its rather boorish records with an ugly blot. The victim of the crime was one Martha Blumenthal, a middle-aged lady of eccentric habits and small popularity, who had lived by herself in an old Jacobean house at the extreme north end of the High Street.

This poor woman—a reputed miser, with, it must be confessed, a detestable misanthropic character had been found one morning murdered in her own hail. The fact that the man, who was in the habit of bringing her her daily milk from a neighbouring farm, had failed for some three or four mornings to procure an answer to his knockings, at length aroused suspicions, with the result that constables forced an entrance, and found the wretched creature lying dead, her skull starred and splintered, in a perfect pond of blood.

There were, of course, a frantic hue and cry, inflated rumour, extravagant speculation, and—a blank full-stop. The fox had run to earth, it seemed, and lay close.

That robbery had been the motive, was sufficiently evident; but only that had been removed from the house which was easy of carriage and concealment.

For long Compton Martel suffered a nightmare of insecurity. Then the vestry elections were to the fore, and interests shifted.

Still, in cottages on rainy days, or in the tap of the "Three Tuns," discussion wavered to the tragedy; and still, fitfully, local labourer and black-boding tramp were pitted one against another as candidates for a grisly distinction.

Now you shall hear how at that lecture the truth came to be known, and in a very awful fashion.

It was in the schoolroom (not "Board," for we hadn't come to that then), and the most of us who were respectable were present. Mr. Cornish, from the neighbouring town, peripatetic archaeologist and photographer, a stiff, dry talker, with a cold, insistent way about him that overawed clownish disrespect, was on the platform against the sheet, and his operator, with the lantern and slides, was posted at the back of the room. To the front, in the place of honour, was Barom Gramshaw of Leets, Lord of the Manor of Compton, President of the Society, and high patron of the interests it represented.

The lecturer had spoken of architecture technically and morally, of cornices, architraves, and columns, both from the structural point of view and from that of their expression of a national

character. He would trace the ethical evolution of any race through
the processes of its builders, and he would be, and was, most profoundly pedantic over it all, and most monstrously uninteresting.

Still we listened—thinking of the indemnifying pipe and glass
before the fire presently, no doubt. But we listened, nevertheless;
for I tell you there was something about the man that commanded
attention—an atmosphere, rather than a personality, the room being too dark to make out more of him than a black skimp figure
and a white blotch of face.

He was no stranger to us, however. Poking about in the neighbourhood with folding stand and camera, snapping at bits of wall,
cankered gravestones, half-tumbled byres, and such candle-ends
of "auld lichts," so to speak, as men of his kidney take their mental
sustenance of, his figure was most familiar to Compton Martel. To
secure a negative gave him a sense of possession in its subject, it
was said, that was as arrogant as ownership. And he, too, was suspected of being a miser.

Now the dissolving views were our milestones on a dreary road
of prolixity; and therefore a rustle of relief went round the room
when, after a fifteen-minutes preamble (or pre-maunder) on the
subject of the ethical significances of Jacobean architecture, he
came to the recurrent stop which was the prelude to something on
the sheet.

"You have in your own village," drawled the lecturer, "an elegant example of early Georgian work. I allude to a house that recently gained some unpleasant notoriety. That is nothing to the
point. What interests us is the extreme beauty of the porch, and of
the lines of the window above it. No earlier than this morning I
took a photograph of the subject, which I will now proceed to show
you in illustration. John!"

He signed to the man at the back to put in the slide. His speech
was commonplace enough, was it not ?—little in it to show how it
was to "thunder in the index."

On the disc of brilliant light a shadow fell—out of focus—click!
and it snapped into place.

There was a moment's dead silence. Then a stir went amongst
the audience, that suggested to me, I swear, the shudder of dying

limbs under bedclothes. A woman or two shrieked out in a stifled way, and I saw the man next to me lean forward, his eyeballs glinting like porcelain.

What was the matter? Why, this. On the sheet before us was depicted the upper part of the porch of Martha Blumenthal's house, with the window above it, *and through the window was looking a face hateful and ghastly beyond words!*

Remember that, by his own statement, Mr. Cornish had taken the photograph that very morning, and remember that the murder had been committed quite three months before, and that the house had remained ever since shunned and tenantless!

I heard the Hodge next to me fall back in his chair with a straining groan.

"Mawtha Bloomintail herself, by God!" he whispered.

There was menace of a general hysteric collapse, when old Gramshaw struggled to his feet and broke the spell on the nick of the moment.

"Mr. Cornish!" he cried, in a loud, wavering voice, "what does this mean—what does this mean, sir? It is not right nor decent, upon my word—it is in abominably bad taste, sir!"

There was no answer. Suddenly someone turned up the gas, and the horrible face went into a phantom of itself.

But an explanation of the silence was given in the figure of the lecturer, swaying, half-convulsed, his cheeks a sick white, his fingers picking at his collar.

Before a soul could help him, down he went his full length, with a dusty slap—and on the instant the face sunk out of the sheet, and there was only the porch and an empty window.

Then a dozen of us ran up, through the cries and babble of the women, and carried him into the little side room and stretched him on the table.

Now, this is an old story with those of us who received and retained the impression; and that I must say, because many, so it appeared, afterwards professed themselves unconscious of the vision, and as only affected by an unexplainable atmosphere while the photograph was exhibiting. Therefore it was that, in the result, we who both saw and remembered the hideous presentment, decided to lay no emphasis upon the circumstances that induced the murderer to his confession.

For it was Mr. Cornish who had committed the crime. So far, in its bald facts, you may read in certain past-dated newspapers. He was led to it, at once by his monomania for possession, and by the miserly reputation of the dark recluse in the old Jacobean house. In his hauntings of the ancient village he had learned of her habits, of her solitariness, of her conjectural hoards. It was miser cut miser. The lust of avarice came to a head in him, and, stimulated by the sense of security her isolation afforded him, he did the deed. One windy March morning, before the sleep was out of village eyes, he rapped at the door with the plaster shell over it. Martha Blumenthal came to the window above the porch, and looked down upon him. His aspect presented nothing fearful; the loaded stick in his hand might have been a light walking cane. Very possibly she knew him by sight, and had marked his innocuous pursuits. At any rate, she came to his summons and was murdered.

All this he gasped out on the table. What he might not explain was that abnormal development of the acquisitive in him, which could not only triumph over all traditions of culture, but could affect, and apparently feel, a callousness so astonishingly great as to enable him, without emotion, to illustrate an innocent phase of his character with material drawn from that character's most diseased propensities. But the pathology of crime bristles with such paradoxes.

As to the apparition—well, "Death and the sun are not to be looked at steadily," as M. Rochefoucauld says; and I prefer not to think of that face.

And Mr. Cornish died on the table. At the inquest they could find no more definite verdict than "Shock."

But that we had all had.

THE WIDOWS CLOCK

I was moved to pause outside the premises of Bull & Hacker, auctioneers. Unaccountable excitement exhaled from their very windows, grew intricate on their steps, congested at their doorway. Something out of the common, it was evident, was passing within.

I accosted a young man who was battling his way forth at the moment. The young man's face was a red mask of hilarity.

"What's up?" said he. "Oh, Lord! go and look. Old Bull's took mad, and he's knocking down the lots like skittles. There's some stuff goin' cheap there, there is."

He was borne past me, and I fought my way into the auction-room. I had a hard struggle to get within view of the rostrum; and then I saw a figure, with eyes like a Cheshire cat's, standing—or rather dancing—therein. It (the figure) was that, assuredly, of the urbane Mr. Bull; but he had put a copper saucepan-on his head, and tied up his side-whiskers with ribbons.

Two grinning, embarrassed-looking men in shirt sleeves had just placed upon the long table under the pulpit a very presentable plaster cast of the Capitoline Venus. The auctioneer addressed the company with quite exaggerated suavity.

"Look at that, gentlemen," said he: "pray don't look at me! My better half, gentlemen, and much better worth your consideration. A little stiff and cold, but a rare bargain if you keep her from putting rat poison in the soup.—How much for Mrs. Bull, now?—how much for the hard, unsympathetic lady? She's given me many a dressing, gentlemen, or she'd be better accommodated in that respect herself. A charitable soul indeed."

Here he cocked his saucepan over one eye, folded his arms, and ogling the company insinuatingly, suddenly bent down and bonneted with his hammer an old white-hatted broker who sat chuckling just underneath.

"The property of a gentleman going abroad!" he bellowed, recovering himself. "Must sell—must sell! Start your bids, and earn a reputation for gallantry in the Babylonian marriage market."

"A shillun," sniggered a sheepish-faced individual at the table. Mr. Bull snatched off his saucepan and beat it flat on the desk. "Gone for a shilling!" he roared, "and dear at the price." There had been a flank movement up the room. Blue-coated figures now rose from the crowd and seized the madman. A scene of wild uproar and confusion ensued. Presently I found myself in the street.

"How did it come about?" I said to a neighbour, as I endeavoured to coax the creases out of a crumpled tie.

"Drink," said he laconically. "Old Bull was always a soaker, he was."

"The sales won't hold, I suppose?" said I.

"They'll hold tight enough for them as cut their lucky with the stuff afore he was found out," answered my friend gruffly. "Why, he was a-selling things for songs at fust—rail good things, mind you," he said.

I departed, wondering; and certain inquiries I prosecuted set me wondering yet more.

The following day I made occasion to call upon my acquaintance Aubrey Standish. He is a curioso, and a young man of a most fastidious and delicate dilettanteism—of Catholic taste also, within the liberal limits of Art. At the same time he holds (or held) it his particular principle that, given such tact and knowledge as his own, an extreme virtuosity could be indulged on nothing larger than an ordinary household income, so to speak; in illustration of which his rooms (he had but three) were shrines containing treasures of heavenly *marqueterie* and *bijouterie*. Enamels, by Jean Petitot;

cinquecento intaglios in amethyst, and earlier cameos by Diosco-
rides; unique bits of gomroon porcelain ware from Chelsea; pot-
pourri in old Nankin vases; fragments of tapestry; exquisite painted
fans from the studios of M. Duvelleroy; swords in niello; a bronze
fish, presumptively by Benvenuto Cellini,—such and varied *bric-
à-brac*, sleeking from the chestnut glooms of Chippendale corner
cupboards, disposed with a crafty affectation of *insouciance* on
Louis XV. commodes, blinking soft slumberous eyes from green
plush-lined showcase tables, was the practical expression of
Aubrey's boasted principle. And he would assure you, with all the
enthusiasm of a nervous, lisping speech, that it needed but the
knowledge of how to sit effectively in the sunshine for the rarest
butterflies of Art to settle on one's hand. That was his rendering of
the *Tout vient à qui sait attendre*, which was a proverb too much
in the common way for one of his ultra-refinement; yet he was not
exalted above the exercise of some particularly mean qualities—
or, at least, so my Philistinism interpreted him.

Now he came skipping, in a Japanese silk dressing-gown, from
his bedroom, and put a thin, scented hand on each of my shoulders.

"What a sweet tie!" said he. "Permit me. It tones, with your
face, into the very aurelian tints of Giovanni Bellini."

"Oh, go to the devil!" said I crossly. "If I'm jaundiced, I'm jaundiced, that's all."

"My dear friend," said he, releasing me, "you're fretful. You take
life at too high a pressure. You exhale a humanity before which I
seem to shrink like a sensitive plant. I can never escape the feeling
when you visit me, that my little museum will fly into prismatic
splinters, like an opal too rudely unearthed."

I wanted, of course, to kick him; but bethought myself that this
was scarcely the way to enforce a certain mission on which I had
entered.

"Standish," said I.

"Now, now," said he, lifting his hands, palms to me, and closing
his eyes; "not the Charity Organisation again, my very sweet fellow!
Not some malodorous citizen with a compound fracture of his tail,

or a widow respectable in everything but the possession of twins. You wouldn't besmirch my preserves with such smut?"

"I'm to be bought out."

"Oh dear!" he said, with a little deprecating smile. "This is terrible. Do let me entreat your attention to that exquisite Bartolozzi. I picked it up last week for a mere song—literally, the merest swan-song of a dying consumptive."

"Standish, I want to put it to you"

He sank upon an Adams settee, sniffed at a tiny filagree vinaigrette, and fluttered a whisp of a handkerchief.

"I have learned to gather flowers of the wilderness. I have made a rose-crown of patience, till it blossoms about my head. Go on!" he murmured faintly.

"Standish, I will take no denial that you were at Bull & Hacker's sale yesterday."

"The subtlest penetration!" he whispered. "Were you there too?"

"Yes."

"Then," said he, "you were witness of a strange seizure."

"Not of yours," said I— "for it amounts to nothing else."

He only shrugged his eyebrows—a momentary spasm of astonishment.

"Was it not?" said I. "There is the very article, I see."

I had already "spotted," standing in the corner, what I sought— a lank "grandfather" clock in a Chippendale case. I nodded towards it significantly.

"It's by Smith of Crowland," said Standish, rallying, in the excitement of the collector. "His work was unique—the best of its kind. I assure you, I cannot recall a more vital illustration of my principles than is presented in that bargain."

"It is unique, you say?"

"I believe entirely. My one regret is, it doesn't go—or, at least, as yet I haven't been able to make it. And it was the durable quality of the Crowland clocks that gained them their reputation."

"Shall I examine it? I have a clever mechanical turn."

"By all means. I can trust you to handle it, I am sure."

He did not look as if he meant it; but I went and unbuttoned the door in the belly of the thing, and felt with my hand up along the pendulum.

"What would you say," said I, as I was thus engaged, "that this might have fetched under favourable conditions?"

"Eighty pounds," said Standish, with all the decision of a dealer.

"And you gave for it yesterday?"

"Eighteen pence."

His whole face creased with goblin merriment. His laugh was always a little hoarse, as if it were only the broken-out expression of what had been choking him for some time internally. Suddenly he came to his feet.

"You have set it going?" he cried.

"The pendulum was merely wired high up to the case. What time is it?"

He affected a fob, with dangling seals. He drew out what the Regency bucks called a warming-pan.

"Twenty minutes to twelve," he said.

Fortuitously, I had but to move the hands of the bargain a minute or two. "There's your clock going," said I, and shut the case.

"You are a genius!" he cried. "My happiness is complete. What an engaging possession is a practical head!"

"I'm glad you think so. It can always command its price, you mean; and so I may as well state it."

"Ha, ha! to be sure. The service of a friend is beyond price."

"Not in the least. I want eighty pounds for mine."

"Oh! of course. You're rating yourself higher than you do to the Income Tax assessors."

"I'm perfectly serious. I want eighty pounds—less eighteen-pence." He was beginning to laugh—checked himself, and stared at me in amazement, already with a touch of anger in it. "Are you daft?" he said.

"Not in the least. I'll explain myself. In taking advantage of that man's madness yesterday, Standish, I'm not at all sure you didn't give your economic principles an ugly look of felony."

His lip lifted, and he did not answer for a moment. Then said he, in a straitened voice—

"I see, I see. This is a blackmailing affair."

I kept my temper royally.

"No," I said. "And I shan't be at the trouble to refute such a charge. I appeal only to your sense of fair-play. You must have it, Standish, for all your virtuosity. Will you listen while I tell you the facts of the case?"

"Oh! I'll listen," he said.

"Very well. Now, I'll explain. That clock was the property of a wretched widow—a woman once in decent circumstances, but at last reduced to the hardest necessity. I've come across her in the way of my work on behalf of the Society; and a certain association of guess and inquiry has led me to the truth. Her husband was a Liverpool-Irish "patriot" of '81. I believe he was mixed up in the dynamite business. He died, however, years ago in prison. Piece by piece she has parted with every stick of their common property, till at last only the clock remained. That she could not find it in her heart to sell. *He* had always shown such an affection for it. No doubt even the worst of us have our little emotional associations. Perhaps it had once stood in his father's cottage. And so—though from the date of his arrest it had proved useless as a timepiece"— ("Ha!" murmured Standish, with a happy nod to me)— "she stuck to it. Then, at last, hunger and the devil broke her loyalty. Mr. Bull happened on the relic in a professional way, presumed its value, and being for all his sins something better than a collector, didn't offer to buy it for eighteenpence, but proposed, like an honest man, to include it, with a reserve, in one of his sales."

I came to an end, and looked at Standish.

"*Without* reserve, I think," said he.

"*With*," said I. "The man was as mad as a hatter. He had to be removed in the end."

"You greatly interest me," said Standish. "I assure you that— though, of course, I thought there was something a little exceptional about our friend's conduct—I had no inkling, at that early stage, that things would reach so disastrous a climax."

"I am quite ready to believe it. And, now you know, you will draw the widow a cheque for eighty pounds."

Standish shook his head, with quite a rippling little laugh.

"You are a sweet, droll fellow," he said: "the dearest utilitarian, by way of your friends' pockets. If I could materialise such a rare piece of Quixotism and put it in a case, I would give you the money on the spot—if I had it."

"At least send back the clock and let it be re-sold."

He looked at me, as if politeness alone restrained him from a positive guffaw.

"Unconscious humourist!" he murmured thickly. Then he explained very kindly. "The whole text of my capital is sunk in these things—these glorious trifles, every one of which represents an opportunity most patiently coveted. The margin only stands for my living expenses. Now, do you really imagine I will forego the little rewards, when they reach me, of such devotion?—and for the benefit of a dead savage's widow?" he added, with an irrepressible laugh.

"It was an accident, Standish."

"Such is our chance."

"Is it hopeless my trying to move you?"

"You have moved me already, my dear soul. Positively, a new value attaches in my eyes to this bargain in the knowledge that it is pronounced, in a certain sense, historical. Pray look at the matter impartially. Why should all the unselfishness be demanded of me who make no profession of dealing in these common virtues? Probably your bombazine widow is much better equipped with the article than I am. Comfort her with the Christian assurance that my expectations are realised, if hers are not. Now, pray don't say any more. It is painful and unprofitable to both of us. Let me show you an almost perfect example of a *gemma potaria*—a sardonyx drinking-cup that I picked"

I burst out, without more ado.

"Hang your drinking-cup!" I shouted; "you're just an inhuman swindler. Hang your drinking-cup, I say!"—and I made for the door.

Standish followed me, with imperturbable unconcern, down the stairs. At the moment, the liberated clock above began to strike midday.

"Hear it!" he cried triumphantly, pausing on a step. "It proclaims its emancipation! It speaks to its deliverer with a voice of silver! 'A bargain is a bargain,' it shrills. 'A—!!!'"

Where was I! My brain was stuffed with wool, it seemed, and my eyes were mere balls of smoked glass. In a moment I staggered to my feet. Another shape was poised tottering just above me. The stairway rolled with choking vapour, through which—as it slowly dissipated by way of an open skylight—a wreck of burst paper and broken banister rails was revealed.

As sight returned to me, I stared up at Standish. He looked like nothing so much as a torn Japanese doll. Then with one impulse we laboured up through the inferno, and stood at the doorway of the shattered museum.

I think there cannot have remained two consecutive inches of sound material anywhere in the room. The entire show was exploded into shivers. Porcelain, tapestry, enamels, with the cabinets that had enshrined them—all were committed in undistinguishable fragments to a common ruin. *Tout vient à qui sait attendre*: Everything comes to him that knows how to wait—even a very lively retribution for his sins.

"Standish," I said (I could only speak in croaks)— "the patriot's clock, Standish—it must have been set to midday! Standish—you have been a good angel to the bombazine widow!"

Lot 104

Mr. George George, house-surgeon at the Brantham-by-the-Sea Cottage Hospital, had acquitted himself with impunity of a traditionally fatal enterprise: he had drawn with his lips the poison from a clogged tube in a case of diphtheria, and had suffered no ill effects as a consequence. This was to stand remarkable, not for the act—which had infinite noble precedent—but for its sequel; yet, three days after the event, the young doctor would recall his deed with little else than a warmth of professional pride as over the successful conduct of a "case."

By then, it is true, he had some engrossing personal matters to occupy that much of the attention he could spare from his patients—matters that were to reach their curious culminating point, during the course of this third day, in a rencontre that would appear to have been designed of Providence for the express acknowledgment of merit. Introductorily, and essentially to the context, it may be premised that George George was young; that he was without money or substantial interest; that he had all the world to win.

His present post—his first—was just sufficiently remunerative to enable him to live unharassed of creditors. He had been fortunate in procuring it through the recommendation of a great-uncle, who was also an inhabitant of Brantham and a trustee to the estates of the hospital itself; and under the aegis of this worthy the house-surgeon had already passed the first half of his year of office, when suddenly his patron and relative died.

103

Now this, doubtless, was a matter for all decent regret; and it shall be said that the deceased's grandnephew was affecting no more than he felt (and that was honest measure, for he had had a liking for the old gentleman), when he was informed, to his utter astonishment, that his uncle had left him by will everything of which he had died possessed.

The shock was as genially stunning as is unexpected applause to an incipient orator; the reaction as depressing as might be the discovery, on the part of such orator, that he had been cried up ironically. For, so it appeared, George George had been bequeathed, in all inspiring phraseology, a heritage of emptiness.

How this was so became at once apparent. The departed trustee had been a Government pensioner. His income died with him. While he lived this had either sufficed simply for his wants, or else he had been—and such was his reputation—a deplorable skinflint. Results, however, would not appear to substantiate the latter charge. No securities, no dividend warrants, no personal estate or hoarded capital were disinterred from chest or bureau after the most uncommon investigation. His pension, it appeared, had rounded off at either end the testator's financial position; and the disappointed legatee had at last to face his disillusionment, and accept his inheritance for what it was worth. This was little enough in all conscience—a trifle of money at the bank, the almost moribund leasehold of a house in Bridge Street, and the furniture and personal effects (all of indifferent value) therein contained. The unhappy doctor's momentary dreams, of being able to realise his best ambition by purchasing a practice at the termination of his year of office, were dissolved into thin air.

Now, it was no good starting a grievance against Fate because his holiday mood had received a drenching, so to speak. It was not like him, moreover, to do so. He simply made the best of a disappointing job, and straightway put up to auction the whole of the household effects (which, in view of the near expiration of the lease, could be of no earthly use to him), with the object of converting them into at least an inconsiderable nucleus of capital.

Even here, however, disenchantment seemed to wait upon him. The day of the sale—conducted on the premises by Bull and Hacker—was chill and swampy; the attendance was poor, the bidding spiritless and inefficient.

The doctor—as before introduced, with the modest memory of his deed of heroism overclouded by present preoccupation—looked in during the course of the afternoon to see how matters were progressing. As to that he was seized at once with a discomfortable conviction. The lots were being knocked down with as cheap a jocularity as if they were skittles in an alley. Several, while he waited, were sold for an "old song," and it was the barb in the sting to him, as always to the uninitiated, to observe in each that incongruous association of objects, presumably much better offered apart, that it is the irreverent humour of auctioneers to exhibit in their tabulating of the household gods.

Item: a coal-scuttle, a scent-fountain, two clotheshorses, and sundries (the latter inclusive, apparently, of a charwoman's bonnet, and a framed photograph of somebody's aunt in a crinoline, standing by an Ionic pedestal)—six shillings. Item: a camp washstand, three dish covers, and a purdonium (which turned out to be nothing but the coal-scuttle over again)—two shillings. Item: plaque—the Wandering Jew (a fanciful description evolved of the fine genius of the auctioneer's clerk, inasmuch as the figure was obviously and even aggressively feminine—probably a Hecate painted in a flower-pot saucer by an amateur). But it fetched a good price—three-and-sixpence. Item: an ormolu and bronzed three-light gasalier.

At this point, something of a brisk rally occurred in the bidding. It was at the instance of a stranger, who, upon the calling of the lot (104 was its number), swiftly detached himself from the gloom of the outer ring of bystanders, and pushed his way to the front with an evident eye to business. He was a man of a certain professional cast, strongly built, loud in the style of those who are accustomed to appeal forcibly to audiences. His face was fleshy and colourless; his anointed curls, his eyebrows, and the blot of hair on his under lip were of a Brunswick black. His portly form was encased in a long threadbare overcoat with a sham Astrakhan collar, and on his head he wore at a rakish angle a scrupulously groomed silk hat with a preposterous curl of brim.

Mr. Hacker, the junior partner, who officiated at the rostrum in all second-class affairs, and who might even have pleaded guilty to some little weaknesses of collusion in sales technically known as "knockouts," noted the new-comer with the tail of his eye, and moistened his ferrety lips in foretaste of the blood his instinct told him he might expect to draw.

"For this excellent ormolu and bronze three-light gasalier," said he. "Now, gentlemen, name a price."

"Three bob," said a facetious broker.

"Four," snapped out the stranger.

"Five," "six," "seven," "eight," "nine," "ten" was run up rapidly in ineffective sequence. Then came a pause, the stranger having the last word.

"Ten shillin's!" said the auctioneer reproachfully; "this particularly elegant three-light ormolu gasalier going for ten shillin's! Come, gentlemen, isn't there one of you'll make an advance on the bid? Genuine ormolu and bronze, and fit for a ducal drawing-room."

He looked from face to face and poised his little mallet tentatively.

"Ten shillin's!" he repeated. His tone was that of a protesting incredulity. He might have been a convicted innocent hearing himself sentenced to ten years' penal servitude. One longed almost to assure this good man that he was only being made the victim of a hoax. Then he essayed humour—the humour of the rostrum that, like that of the Bench, sounds such a depressingly blank cartridge in the report.

"Why, the weights alone are worth the money! Take 'em off my mind, gentlemen. Come! say a suvereign. Won't anyone go an advance on ten shillin's? It's without reserve, gentlemen. There's no call for this extreme modesty."

He conned the blank faces once more, and shrugged his shoulders as if to repudiate all responsibility in so senseless a *fiasco*. The hammer in his hand rose slowly like that of a clock about to strike—lingered on the fall in a quick inspiration.

"Take him on, Charley," whispered a neighbour broker to the other. "He's fly."

"One pound."

"One pound ten," said the stranger.

"Two pounds."

"Two pounds one."

There was a murmur of protest. The auctioneer bent over his desk courteously.

"The conditions of sale," he said. "Above two pounds, no advance under two shillin's."

"Two pound ten, then," said the stranger.

The languid room woke to a sense of the humour of the situation.

"Three pounds," said the broker.

The stranger looked round defiantly.

"It's what I want," he said; "it'll soot my show, and I mean to have it."

There were cries of "Order, order!" and the room echoed with a ripple of laughter over this fatuous admission.

"Four pound," said the stranger immovably.

"It goes against my conscience," thought George George, "to profit by this victimising of a fool."

He waited, while they ran the fool up from six to ten pounds, and there, frighted perhaps by the magnitude of the issue, they let the joke lapse and chuckled themselves hoarse over the richness of the climax.

Ten pounds for a frame of indifferent old metal! It was an exhibition of tenacity all upon the insensate side.

The stranger seemed neither elated nor depressed by the result. He went and stood by his property until he could pay for and remove it, indifferently the cynosure of eyes that humoured their own derision of him a little covertly, in that they were conscious of a certain truculence in the expression of those under the unspeakable hat-brim.

The bidding, after this momentary effervescence of excitement, fell to a more dismal level of ineffectiveness than it had suffered hitherto. Very soon the person most interested in it tired of the reiteration of lame conclusions, and returned to his work more impressed than ever with the vanity of impulsive optimism. He busied himself over his cases and other matters for an hour or two, losing in occupation all but the shadowy memory of his disappointment; then went home for the cup of tea that is the solace to much heroic desperation. He had no living quarters at the hospital; but his dull lodgings were near at hand, and for them he made with a new distaste for their meanness that was half humour, half chagrin. His tiny sitting-room was lapped in darkness, for the fire was sunk to a mere belated spark, and the gas was turned down in the insufferable chandelier. With his fingers on the tap, George George dwelt a moment in retrospection on the queer little episode of the afternoon.

"Well," he thought, "it is ten pounds of eccentricity, at least, in my pocket."

His hand moved, the room leapt into light, and there before him on the hearthrug were standing—man and gasalier—the actual subjects of his meditations.

He jumped—he couldn't help it; then in an instant, with a violent effort, forced his nerves under control.

"What the—" he began, and stopped.

The stranger (placing his large hat on the table) bowed, with an expansive motion of his finger-tips from his mouth, as if he were caressing outwards the ends of a long moustache. Professionally, this manner of salutation may be interpreted to signify the "blowing a kiss" to applause. Then he put one hand a-kimbo, and waved the other grandiosely to the gasalier at his side.

"You're Doctor George?" said he.

"Certainly."

"Then, doctor, I've took the liberty of bringing you a little present."

"But, my good sir—"

"Hush!" said the stranger; and he went to the door on tiptoe and carefully shut and locked it.

"It's absolutely plain," thought the dismayed doctor. "I guessed it at the auction, and here's the confirmation. This person is an escaped lunatic."

The stranger had returned to the rug and his property. An odd smile was on his face. He thrust one hand, Napoleonic, into the breast of his coat.

"Sir," he began.

"There's nothing for it but to humour him," thought the young man.

He advanced and dragged forward his old elbow-chair—wintry as the evening, by token of its long-vanished spring—from its corner by the fire.

"Sit down," said he.

"No, sir," said the stranger promptly; "sooner in the presence of r'yalty than in yours!"

"Oh!" exclaimed the other, in a helpless voice.

"I were scurvy tempted," said the visitor; "I were scurvy tempted, I'll own it up fair. It's fortun' against the apple of my eye, says I; and, thank God, the man in me rose to the occasion, and the apple wins."

Mr. George recovered his decision and his professional manner. "That'll do," he said. "Now, my good fellow, come to the point and state your business."

Immediately his hands were seized in an emotional grasp. "I could kiss 'em!" cried the stranger; "s'elp me, I could kiss 'em and cry!"

The doctor wrenched himself free so roughly that the man staggered.

"Give me a moment, sir," pleaded the latter.

He passed the back of his hand across his eyes. To George's astonishment these swam with unmistakable tears.

"I'll come to the point," murmured the visitor. Then he gulped, produced a crimson bandana, blew his nose sonorously, and spoke up over a cushion of handkerchief.

"I'm own dad," said he, "to little Jemmy Montague as is down with the dipthiery."

With the words, the doctor's fog of indignant bewilderment began to dissipate. A little flush came to his cheek.

"Why didn't you say so before?" he protested. "Well, the boy's mending."

"Thanks to you, sir—thanks to the noblest act as ever merited a father's gratitood and the applause of a full house."

"Pooh!" said George George.

"Ah!" said the man, gasping and wiping his eyes. "Him as was good to do it, is good to say pooh to it, no doubt. I've been told the facts, sir. You saved my lad's life at the risk of your own. I say, God bless you for it; and I say He's blessed me, too, by showin' me how to rise and reward you out of the pit of my own temptation."

"I want no reward," said the doctor rather sharply. "But it will be something of one to me to hear your adequate explanation of why you have not hitherto, to my knowledge, been near the hospital since your boy was brought to it?"

"Could I help it, sir? I must move on and keep the pot a-b'ilin'. I swear I never guessed at Jemmy's danger. I come back here the moment I were free. S'elp me, you dunno what it is to tumble for a livin', and your heart burstin' with anxiety."

"To tumble? You are a mountebank, then?"

"I'm a hacrobat, sir—a street hacrobat; else I might never have been put in the way to reward jemmy's benefactor."

"I have told you I want no reward. You can't understand that, in a case like this, success is its own."

The acrobat shook his head.

"It's your own individual lawful property," he said. "I'm only the unworthy instrument under Providence, whose ways is past telling. To think that *you* should be the heir to that very identical house I've had my heye on a sixmonth. It were no chance, I'll swear, but a dispensation as learned me the truth at the last moment."

He turned to the gasalier.

"Here it is," he went on. "I brought it down in a cab the moment I could lay hands on it. Now look!"

The young doctor, still in two minds as to his visitor's sanity, advanced no further protest, but stood dumbly watching. From the ancient lumber the acrobat detached one of the three bulky ormolu weights, that lay upon the rug at the end of their chains. He raised it in his hands.

"Heavy, ain't it?" said he, and, placing it on the table, unhooked and deposited its two companions by its side.

"Now," said he, "if this don't answer to my expectations, I'm—"

Too suddenly flurried to finish the sentence, he seized a weight and held it between his knees, with the action of one drawing a recalcitrant cork from a bottle.

"Ah!" he cried triumphantly, and came erect, rapidly unscrewing a sort of stopper from the crown of the thing.

And then a "wonder came to light," for before George George's astonished eyes a clinking rain of gold pieces fell and scattered from a hollow vessel upon the table.

"Good!" chuckled the acrobat. "And now for the other two."

"Nine 'underd and seventy-five pound," said Mr. Montague, looking up breathless from a swift calculation. "All yours, sir, every penny of it, by will. Oh, I've learned the facts, and it's not a proportion of what you deserve."

"Tell me how you knew," said George George, speaking as if in a dream.

"That's explained in a sentence," answered the acrobat stoutly. "Top-balancing is part of my business. D'ye know what that means? No? Listen to this, then; my mate holds a pole perpendic'lar from a pocket in his belt, and up it I goes and balances. I sees a many things in course through fust-floor winders—things not always meant for me. That was the case in the present instance. We was comin' down Bridge Street last July in the dog-days, and stopped outside your uncle's house, The sash was up, for air. I see the old man shut into his room, gloatin' over his wealth, and I see the secret of his hiding-place. It were an instantaneous pictur', revealed to me in a flash; then the old screw made me out sudden, and rushed, with a hoath, and snatched down the blind. It struck a rare impression on me. I thought of it for months. When Jemmy was a-tumbling with all his little soul put into it, 'Ah, my lad!' I'd cogitate, 'if I could be present at the sale o' that old lickpenny's effects some day, I don't doubt I could leave ye a fortun'.' The fancy so dwelt with me, that somehow I've made out my season ever since in the neighbourhood of this here watering-place; and that's how my boy come to your horspital. It's a fact, sir; and now hear the end. This very mornin', hurryin' back from a week's tower on my way to visit Jemmy, I passed the house that had been so long in my thoughts, and see the sale of its effects advertised for one o'clock. It caught me by the throat like a spasm. 'By gum!' says I, 'now or never!' and I went in, took stock of the very article standin' there, sure enough, as innocent as emptiness—and felt myself a made man. Then I come on to the horspital and learned the truth of everything. It was common talk, this of your barren windfall. Jemmy himself knew all about it and told me, he did. 'Very well, Mr. Montague,' thinks I, 'you're either a devil or a human, and you've got to prove yourself.' Have I done so, sir? But, after all, it ain't much, puttin' you in the way of your own in exchange for Jemmy's life."

Upon minute investigation, there seemed to evolve itself from obscure documentary evidence a hint that George George's great-uncle had contemplated, amidst vain procrastination, the drawing up of a clue to the treasure's hiding-place for the ultimate benefit of his inheritor. Whether or no this were the case, two indisputable claims followed the discovery: the living young man's to the property; the dead miser's to a no longer disputed character for parsimony.

As for Mr. Montague, beyond a reluctant consent to receive back the ten pounds ventured by him in the service of Jemmy's benefactor, he steadfastly and persistently declined to accept for his probity any part, great or little, of the disinterred gold. And in this resolve we must hold him right.

THE LOST NOTES

The faculty of music is generally, I believe, inimical to the development of all the other faculties. Sufficient to itself is the composing gift. There was scarcely ever yet a born musician, I do declare, who, outside his birthright, was not a born ass. I say it with the less irreverence, because my uncle was patently one of the rare exceptions which prove the rule. He knew his Shakespeare as well as his musical-glasses—better than, in fact; for he was a staunch Baconian. This was all the odder because—as was both early and late impressed upon me—he had a strong sense of humour. Perhaps an eternal study of the hieroglyphics of the leger lines was responsible for his craze; for craze I still insist it was, in spite of the way he took to convince me of the value of cryptograms. I was an obstinate pupil, I confess, and withstood to the end the fire of all the big guns which he—together with my friend, Chaunt, who was in the same line—brought to bear upon me.

Well, I was honest, at least; for I was my uncle's sole provisional legatee, and heir presumptive to whatever small fortune he had amassed during his career. And day by day, as the breach between us widened, I saw my prospect of the succession attenuating, and would not budge from my position. No, Shakespeare was Shakespeare, I said and Bacon, Bacon; and not all the cyphers in the world should convince me that any profit was to be gained by either imagining or unravelling a single one of them.

"What, no profit!" roared my uncle. "But I will persuade you, young man, of your mistake before I'm done with you. Hum-ti-diddledidee! No profit, hey? H'm—well!"

Then I saw that the end was come. And, indeed, it was an open quarrel between us, and I was forbidden to call upon him again.

I was sorry for this, because, in his more frolicsome and uncontroversial moments, he was a genial companion, unless or until one inadvertently touched on *the* theme, when at once he exploded. Professionally, he *could* be quite a rollicking blade, and his settings of plantation songs were owned to be nothing less than lyric inspirations. Pantomime, too, in the light of his incidental music, had acquired something more than a classical complexion and, in the domain of knockabout extravaganza, not only did the score of "The Girl who Knew a Thing or Two" owe to him its most refined numbers, but also the libretto, it was whispered, its best Attic *bonnes-bouches*.

However, all that good company I must now forgo—though Chaunt tried vainly to heal the breach between us—and in the end the old man died, without any visible relenting towards me.

I felt his loss pretty keenly, though it is no callousness in me to admit that our long separation had somewhat dulled the edge of my attachment. I expected, of course, no testamentary consideration from him, and was only more surprised than uplifted to receive one morning a request from his lawyers to visit them at my convenience. So I went, soberly enough, and introduced myself.

"No," said the partner to whom I was admitted, in answer to a question of mine: "I am not in a position to inform you who is the principal beneficiary under our friend's will. I can only tell you—what a few days before his death he confided to us, and what, I think, under the circumstances, you are entitled to learn—that he had quite recently, feeling his end approaching, realized on the bulk of his capital, converted the net result into a certain number—five, I think he mentioned—of Bank of England notes, and . . . burned 'em, for all we know to the contrary."

"Burned them!" I murmured aghast.

"I don't say so," corrected the lawyer drily. "I only say, you know, that we are not instructed to the contrary. Your uncle" (he coughed slightly) "had his eccentricities. Perhaps he swallowed 'em; perhaps gave 'em away, at the gate. Our dealings are, beyond yourself, solely with the residuary legatee, who is, or was, his housekeeper. For her benefit, moreover, the furniture and effects of our late client are to be sold, always excepting a few more personal articles, which, together with a sealed enclosure, we are desired to hand over to you."

He signified, indeed, my bequest as he spoke. It lay on a table behind him: A bound volume of minutes of the Baconian Society; a volume of Ignatius Donnelly's *Great Cryptogram*; a Chippendale tea-caddy (which, I was softened to think, the old man had often known me to admire); a large piece of foolscap paper twisted into a cone, and a penny with which to furnish myself with a mourning ring out of a cracker.

I blushed to my ears, regarding the show; and then, to convince this person of my good-humoured sanity, giggled like an idiot. He did not even smile in reply, the self-important ass, but, with a manner of starchy condescension, as to a wastrel who was getting all his deserts, rose from his chair, unlocked a safe, took an ordinary sealed envelope from it, handed it to me, and informed me that, upon giving him a receipt, I was at liberty to remove the lot.

"Thanks," I said, grinding my astral teeth. "Am I to open this in your presence?"

"Quite inessential," he answered; and, upon ascertaining that I should like a cab called, sent for one.

"Good morning," he said, when at last it was announced (he had not spoken a word in the interval): "I wish you good morning," in the morally patronizing tone of a governor discharging a prisoner.

I responded coldly; tried, for no reason at all, to look threatening; failed utterly, and went out giggling again. Quite savagely I threw my goods upon the seat, snapped out my address, closed the apron upon my abasement, and sat slunk into the cavity behind, like a salted and malignant snail.

Presently I thumped the books malevolently. The dear old man was grotesque beyond reason. Really he needn't have left life cutting a somersault, as it were.

But, as I cooled outwardly, a warmer thought would intrude. It drew, somehow, from the heart of that little enclosure lying at the moment in my pocket. It was ridiculous, of course, to expect anything of it but some further development of a rather unkind jest. My uncle's professional connexion with burlesque had rather warped, it would appear, his sense of humour. Still, I could not but recall that story of the conversion of his capital into notes: and an envelope—!

Bah! (I wriggled savagely). It was idiotic beyond measure so to flatter myself. Our recent relations had precluded for ever any such possibility. The holocaust, rather! The gift to a chance passer-by, as suggested by that fool of a lawyer! I stared out of the window, humming viciously, and telling myself it was only what I ought to expect; that such a vagary was distinctly in accordance with the traditions of low comedy. It will be observed that I was very contemptuous of buffoonery as a profession. Paradoxically, a joke is never played so low as when it is played on our lofty selves.

Nevertheless, I was justified, it appeared. It may be asked, Why did I not at once settle the matter by opening the envelope in the cab? Well, I just temporized with my gluttony, till, like the greedy boy, I could examine my box in private—only to find that the rats had devoured all my cake. It was not till I was shut into my sitting-room that I dared at length to break the seal, and to withdraw—

Even as it came out, with no suggestion of a reassuring crackle, I realized my fate. And this was it: please to examine it carefully—

Now, what do you make of it? "*Ex nihilo nihil fit*," I think you will say with me. It was literally thus, carefully penned in the middle of a single sheet of music-paper—a phrase, or *motif*. I suppose it would be called—an undeveloped memorandum, in fact—nothing else whatever. I let the thing drop from my hand.

No doubt there was some capping jest here, some sneer, some vindictive sarcasm. I was not musician enough to tell, even had I had spirit for the endeavour. It was unworthy, at least, of the old man—much more, or less, than I deserved. I had been his favourite once. Strange how the *idée fixe* could corrode an otherwise tractable reason. In justice to myself I must insist that quite half my disappointment was in the realization that such dislike, due to such a trifle, could have come to usurp the old affection.

By and by I rose dismally, and carried the jest to the piano. (Half a crown a day my landlady exacted from me, if I so much as thumped on the old wreck with one finger, which was the extent of my talent.) Well, I was reckless, and the theme appeared ridiculously simple. But I could make nothing of it—not though Mrs. Dexter came up in the midst, and congratulated me on my performance.

When she was gone I took the thing to my chair again, and resumed its study despondently. And presently Chaunt came in.

"Hullo!" he said: "how's the blooming legatee?"

"Pretty blooming, thanks," I said. "Would you like to speculate in my reversion? Half a crown down to Mrs. Dexter, and the use of the tin kettle for the day."

"Done," he said, "so far as the piano's concerned. Let's see what you've got there."

He had known of my prospective visit to the lawyers, and had dropped in to congratulate me on that performance. I acquainted him with the result; showed him the books, and the tea-caddy, and the penny, and the remnants of foolscap—finally, handed him the crowning jest for inspection.

"Pretty thin joke, isn't it!" I growled dolefully. "Curse the money, anyhow! But I didn't think it of the old man. I suppose you can make no more of that than I can?"

He was squinting at the paper as he held it up, and rubbing his jaw, stuck out at an angle, grittily.

"H'm!" he said, quite suddenly, "I'd go out for a walk and revive myself, if I were you. I intend to hold you to that piano, for my part; and you wouldn't be edified."

"No," I said: "I've had enough of music for a lifetime or so! I fancy I'll go, if you won't think me rude."

"On the contrary," he murmured, in an absorbed way; and I left him.

I took a longish spin, and returned, on the whole refreshed, in a couple of hours. He was still there; but he had finished, it appeared, with the piano.

"Well," he said, rising and yawning, "you've been a deuce of a time gone; but here you are"—and he held out to me indifferently a little crackling bundle.

Without a word I took it from his hand—parted, stretched, and explored it.

"Good God!" I gasped: "five notes of a thousand apiece!"

He was rolling a cigarette.

"Yes," he drawled, "that's the figure, I believe."

"For me?"

"For you—from your uncle."

"But—how?"

He lighted, took a serene puff or two, drew the *jest* from his pocket, and, throwing it on a chair, "You'll have to allow some value to cryptograms at last," he said, and sat down to enjoy himself.

"Chaunt!"

"O," he said, "it was a bagatelle. An ass might have brayed it out at sight."

"Please, I am something less than an ass. Please will you interpret for me?" I said humbly.

He neighed out—I beg *his* pardon—a great laugh at last.

"O," he cried: "your uncle was true blue; he stuck to his guns; but I never really supposed he meant to disinherit you, Johnny. You always had the first place in his heart, for all your obstinacy. He took his own way to convince you, that was all. Pretty poor stuff it is, I'm bound to confess; but enough to run your capacities to extinction. Here, hand it over."

"Don't be hard on me," I protested, giving him the paper. "If I'm all that you say, it was as good as cutting me off with a penny."

"No," he answered: "because he knew very well that you'd apply to me to help you out of the difficulty."

"Well, help me," I said, "and, in the matter of Bacon, I'll promise to be a fool convinced against my will."

"No doubt," he answered drily, and came and sat beside me. "Look here," he said; and I looked:—

"You know your notes, anyhow," said he. "Well, you've only got to read off these into their alphabetical equivalents, and cut the result into perfectly obvious lengths. It's child's play so far; and, indeed, in everything, unless this rum-looking metronome beat, or whatever it may be, bothers you for a moment."

He put his finger on the crazy device perched up independently in the left-hand corner; and then came down to the lines again.

"Let that be for the moment," said he. "It don't much signify, after all. How do these notes go? that's the main question. Read 'em off."

I spelt them out, following his finger: "b a c e f e c a d e c."

"That's a good boy," he said. "And now, what are these things beyond, that have run off the lines, so to speak?"

"What are they? Why, I don't see what they can be but notes."

"Exactly. Five notes."

I stared at the bundle in my hand, and then up at Chaunt.

"O-o-o-o!" I exclaimed.

He uttered a loud ironic laugh. "Well," he said: "what does 'bacefdecadec' spell?"

I scratched my nose. "You tell me, please."

"O Jerusalem!" he cried, and took his pencil to the line, thus: bac | ef | de | cade | c—

"Well?"' he said again.

I shook my head.

He positively stamped. "Listen here," he cried: "bac ef de cad-e c'—*don't* you see?"

"No."

"O, you ineffable ass! 'Back of the caddy' (that's to say the teacaddy; there it is), 'see'—see what? What follows? Why, five notes, don't they? 'Back of the caddy see five notes'—and there they are."

I sank in a heap in my chair. Light had dawned on me. "And you found 'em there, I suppose?" I murmured "behind a false back or something?"

He nodded. "You're getting on."

"And, please, what's the thing at the top?" I continued faintly. "Let me get it all over at once."

"Ah!" he said: "there's a trifle more ingenuity in that, perhaps. What is it, to begin with? A demisemiquaver balanced on the top of an MY, eh?"

"So it appears to me."

"To any one. Don't be frightened. Try it every way round, and conclude with this: 'On the top of MY'—that is to say, '*on* MY,' which is my, 'a demisemiquaver': or, shorn of all superfluities (he pencilled it down), thus: 'on my demisemiquaver.' Now apply the same process."

I looked; pondered; felt myself instantly and brilliantly inspired; seized the pencil from him, and ticked off the measurements:—

"On my demise | mi | q | u | av | er."

"Exactly," said Chaunt, rising with the air of an at-length-released martyr, and proceeding to roll another cigarette: "'On my demise, my cue you have here.' 'Pon my word, without irreverence, it's worthier of the composer of 'Say, den, Julius, whar yo' walkin' roun'?' than of the author of 'Some Unnoticed Sides of Bacon.' But all one can say is that he adapted himself to the intellectual measure of his legatee. Have you got a match?"

I must end, I am really ashamed to say, with this. Anyhow, in one way my uncle was triumphant: I was convinced, at last and at least, of a value in cryptograms.

A Gallows-Bird

In February of the year 1809, when the French were sat down before Saragossa—then enduring its second and more terrific siege within a period of six months—it came to the knowledge of the Duc d'Abrantes, at that time the General commanding, that his army, though undoubtedly the salt of the earth, was yet so little sufficient to itself in the matter of seasoning, that it was reduced to the necessity of flavouring its soup with the saltpetre out of its own cartridges. In this emergency, d'Abrantes sent for a certain Ducos, captain on the staff of General Berthier, but at present attached to a siege train before the doomed town, and asked him if he knew whence, if anywhere in the vicinity, it might be possible to make good the deficiency.

Now this Eugène Ducos was a very progressive evolution of the times, hatched by the rising sun, emerged stinging and splendid from the exotic quagmires of the past. A facile linguist, by temperament and early training an artist, he had flown naturally to the field of battle as to that field most fertile of daring new effects, whose surprises called for record rather than analysis. It was for him to collect the impressions which, later, duller wits should classify. And, in the meantime, here he was at twenty a captain of renown, and always a creature of the most unflagging resourcefulness.

"You were with Lefebvre-Desnouettes in Aragon last year?" demanded Junot.

"I was, General; both before the siege and during it."

"You heard mention of salt mines in this neighbourhood?"

"There were rumours of them, sir—amongst the hills of Ulebo; but it was never our need to verify the rumours."

"Take a company, now, and run them to earth. I will give you a week."

"Pardon me, General; I need no company but my own, which is ever the safest colleague."

Junot glared demoniacally. He was already verging on the madness which was presently to destroy him.

"The devil!" he shouted. "You shall answer for that assurance! Go alone, sir, since you are so obliging, and find salt; and at your peril be killed before reporting the result to me. Bones of God! is every skipjack with a shoulder-knot to better my commands?"

Ducos saluted, and wheeled impassive. He knew that in a few days Marshal Lannes was to supplant this maniac.

Up and away amongst the intricate ridges of the mountains, where the half-unravelled knots of the Pyrenees flow down in threads, or clustered threads, which are combed by and by into the plains south of Saragossa, a dusky young goatherd loitered among the chestnut trees on a hot afternoon. This boy's beauty was of a supernal order. His elastic young cheeks glowed with colour; his eyebrows were resolute bows; his lips, like a pretty phrase of love, were set between dimples like inverted commas. And, as he stood, he coquetted like Dinorah to his own shadow, chasséd to it, spoke to it, upbraiding or caressing, as it answered to his movements on the ground before him—

"Ah, pretty one! ah, shameless! Art thou the shadow of the girl that Eugenio loved? Fie, fie! thou wouldst betray this poor Anita—mock the round limbs and little feet that will not look their part. Yet, betray her to her love returning, and Anita will fall and kiss thee on her knees—kiss the very shadow of Eugenio's love. Ah, little shadow! take wings and fly to him, who promised quickly to return. Say I am good but sad, awaiting him; say that Anita suffers, but is patient. He will remember then, and come. No shadow of disguise shall blind him to his love. Go, go, before I repent and hold thee, jealous that mine own shadow should run before to find his lips."

She stooped, and, with a fantastic gesture, threw her soul upon the winds; then rose, and leaned against a tree, and began to sing, and sigh and murmur softly:

> "'At the gate of heaven are sold brogues
> For the little bare-footed angel rogues'—

Ah, little dear mother! it is the seventh month, and the sign is still delayed. No baby, no lover. Alack! why should he return to me, who am a barren olive! The husbandman asks a guerdon for his care. Give me my little doll, Santissima, or I will be naughty and drink holy water: give me the shrill wee voice, which pierces to the father's heart, when even passion loiters. Ah, come to me, Eugenio, my Eugenio!"

She raised her head quickly on the word, and her heart leaped. It was to hear the sound of a footstep, on the stones far below, coming up the mountain side. She looked to her shirt and jacket. Ragged as they were, undeveloped as was the figure within them, she had been so jealous a housewife that there was not in all so much as an eyelet hole to attract a peeping Tom. Now, leaving her goats amongst the scattered boulders of the open, she backed into the groves, precautionally, but a little reluctant, because in her heart she was curious.

The footsteps came on toilfully, and presently the man who was responsible for them hove into sight. He wore the dress of an English officer, save for the shepherd's felt hat on his head; but his scarlet jacket was knotted loosely by the sleeves about his throat, in order to the disposition of a sling which held his left arm crookt in a bloody swathe. He levered himself up with a broken spear-shaft; but he was otherwise weaponless. A pistol, in Ducos's creed, was the argument of a fool. He carried *his* ammunition in his brains.

Having reached a little plateau, irregular with rocks shed from the cliffs above, he sat down within the shadow of a grove of chestnut and carob trees, and sighed, and wiped his brow, and nodded to all around and below him.

"Yes, and yes, and of a truth," thought he: "here is the country of my knowledge. And yonder, deep and far amongst its myrtles and mulberries, crawls the Ebro; and to my right, a browner clod amongst the furrows of the valleys, heaves up the ruined monastery of San Ildefonso, which Daguenet sacked, the radical; whilst I occupied (ah, the week of sweet malvoisie and sweeter passion!) the little inn at the junction of the Pampeluna and Saragossa roads. And what has become of Anita of the inn? Alack! if my little *fille de joie* were but here to serve me now!"

The goatherd slipped round the shoulder of a rock and stood before him, breathing hard. Her black curls were, for all the world, bandaged, as it might be, with a yellow napkin (though they were more in the way to give than take wounds), and crowned rakishly with a dusky sombrero. She wore a kind of gaskins on her legs, loose, so as to reveal the bare knees and a little over; and across her shoulders was slung a sun-burnt shawl, which depended in a bib against her chest.

Now the one stood looking down and the other up, their visions magnetically meeting and blending, till the eyes of the goatherd were delivered of very stars of rapture.

Was this a spirit, thought Ducos, summoned of his hot and necessitous desire? But the other had no such misgiving. All in a moment she had fallen on her brown knees before him, and was pitifully kissing his bandaged arm, while she strove to moan and murmur out the while her ecstasy of gratitude.

"Nariguita!" he murmured, rallying as if from a dream; "Nariguita!"

She laughed and sobbed.

"Ah, the dear little happy name from thy lips! A thousand times will I repeat it to myself, but never as thou wouldst say it. And now! Yes, Nariguita, Eugenio—thine own 'little nose'—thy child, thy baby, who never doubted that this day would come—O darling of

my soul, that it would come!"—(she clung to him, and hid her face)—
"Eugenio! though the blossom of our love delays its fruitage!"

He smiled, recovered from his first astonishment. Ministers of
coincidence! In all the fantastic convolutions of war, the merry,
the dance-macabre, should not love's reunions have a place? It was
nothing out of that context that here was he chanced again, and
timely, upon that same sweet instrument which he had once played
on, and done with, and thrown aside, careless of its direction. Now
he had but to stoop and reclaim it, and the discarded strings, it
seemed, were ready as heretofore to answer to his touch with any
melody he listed.

He caressed her with real delight. She was something more than
lovable. He made himself a very Judas to her lips.

"Anita, my little Anita!" he began glowingly; but she took him
up with a fevered eagerness, answering the question of his eyes.

"So long ago, ah Dios! And thou wert gone; and the birds were
silent; and under the heavy sky my father called me to him. He
held a last letter of thine, which had missed my hands for his. Love,
sick at our parting, had betrayed us. O, the letter! how I swooned
to be denied it! He was for killing me, a traitor. Well, I could not
help but be. But Tia Joachina had pity on me, and dressed me as
you see, and smuggled me to the hills, that I might at least have a
chance to live without suffering wrong. And, behold! the heavens
smiled upon me, knowing my love; and Señor Cangrejo took me to
herd his goats. For seven months—for seven long, faithful months;
until the sweetest of my heart's flock should return to pasture in
my bosom. And now he has come, my lamb, my prince, even as he
promised. He has come, drawing me to him over the hills, following the lark's song of his love as it dropped to earth far forward of
his steps. Eugenio! O, ecstasy! Thou hast dared this for my sake?"

"Child," answered the admirable Ducos, "I should have dared
only in breaking my word. *Un honnête homme n'a que sa parole.*
That is the single motto for a poor captain, Nariguita. And who is
this Señor Cangrejo?"

Some terror, offspring of his question, set her clinging to him
once more.

"What dost thou here?" she cried, with immediate inconsistency— "a lamb among the wolves! Eugenio!"

"Eh!"—he took her up, with an air of bewilderment. "I am Sir Zhones, the English capitaine, though it loose me your favour, mamselle. Wat! Damn eet, I say!"

She fell away, staring at him; then in a, moment gathered, and leapt to him again between tears and laughter.

"But this?" she asked, her eyes glistening; and she touched the bandage.

"Ah! that," he answered. "Why, I was wounded, and taken prisoner by the French, you understand? Also, I escaped from my captors. It comes, blood and splint and all, from the smashed arm of a sabreur, who, indeed, had no longer need of it."

"For the love of Christ!" she cried in a panic. "Come away into the trees, where none will observe us!"

"Bah! I have no fear, I," said Ducos. But he rose, nevertheless, with a smile, and, catching up the goatherd, bore her into the shadows. There, sitting by her side, he assured her, the rogue, of the impatience with which he had anticipated, of the eagerness with which he had run to realize this longed-for moment. The escapade had only been rendered possible, he said truthfully, by the opportune demand for salt. Doubtless she would help him, for love's sake, to justify the venture to his General?

But, at that, she stared at him, troubled, and her lip began to quiver.

"Ah, God!" she cried; "then it was not I in the first place! Go thy ways, love; but for pity's heart-sake let me weep a little. Yes, yes, there is salt in the mountains, that I know, and where the caves lie. But there are also Cangrejo—whom you French ruined and made a madman—and a hundred like him, wild-cats hidden amongst the leaves. And there, too, are the homeless friars of St. Ildefonso; and, dear body of Christ! the tribunal of terror, the junta of women, who are the worst of all—lynx-eyed demons."

He smiled indulgently. Her terror amused him.

"Well, well," he said; "well, well. And what, then, is this junta?"

"It is a scourge," she whispered, shivering, "for traitors and for spies. It gathers nightly, at sunset, in the dip yonder, and there waters with blood its cross of death. This very evening, Cangrejo tells me—"

She broke off, cuddled closer to her companion, and clasping her hands and shrugging up her shoulders to him, went on awfully—

"Eugenio, there was a wagon-load of piastres coming secretly for Saragossa by the Tolosa road. It was badly convoyed. One of your generals got scent of it. The guard had time to hide their treasure and disperse, but him whom they thought had betrayed them the tribunal of women claimed, and to-night—"

"Well, he will receive his wages. And where is the treasure concealed?"

"Ah! that I do not know."

Ducos got to his feet, and stretched and yawned.

"I have a fancy to see this meeting-place of the tribunal. Wilt thou lead me to it, Nariguita?"

"Mother of God, thou art mad!"

"Then I must go alone, like a madman."

"Eugenio, it is cursing and accurst. None will so much as look into it by day; and, at dusk, only when franked by the holy church."

"So greatly the better. Adios, Nariguita!"

It took them half an hour, descending cautiously, and availing themselves of every possible shelter of bush and rock, to reach a strangely formed amphitheatre set stark and shallow amongst the higher swales of the valley, but so overhung with scrub of myrtle and wild pomegranate as to be only distinguishable, and that scarcely, from above. A ragged track, mounting from the lower levels into this hollow, tailed off, and was attenuated into a point where it took a curve of the rocks at a distance below.

As Ducos, approaching the rim, pressed through the thicket, a toss of black crows went up from the mouth ahead of him, like cinders of paper spouted from a chimney. He looked over. The brushwood ceased at the edge of a considerable pit, roughly circular

in shape, whose sides, of bare sloping sand, met and flattened at
the bottom into an extended platform. Thence arose a triangular
gibbet, a very rack in a devil's larder, all about which a hoard of
little pitchy bird scullions were busy with the joints. Holy mother,
how they squabbled, and flapped at one another with their sleeves,
it seemed! The two carcasses which hung there appeared, for all
their heavy pendulosity, to reel and rock with laughter, nudging
one another in eyeless merriment.

Ducos mentally calculated the distance to the gallows below
from any available coign of concealment.

One could not hide close enough to hear anything," he murmured, shaking his head in aggravation; "and this junta of ladies—
it will probably talk. What if it were to discuss that very question
of the piastres? Nariguita, will you go and be my little reporter at
the ceremony?"

Anita, crouching in the brush behind him, whispered terrified:
"It is impossible. They admit none but priests and women."

"And are not you a woman, most beautiful?"

"God forbid!" she said. "I am the little goatherd Ambrosio."

He stood some moments, frowning. A scheme, daring and characteristic, was beginning to take shape in his brain.

"What is that clump of rags by the gallows?" he asked, without
looking round.

"It is not rags; it is rope, Eugenio."

He thought again.

"And when do they come to hang this rascal? " he said.

"It is always at dusk. O, dear mother!" she whimpered, for the
young man had suddenly slipped between the branches, and was
going swiftly and softly down the pit-side.

Already the basin of sand was filled with the shadows from the
hills. Ducos approached the gibbet. The last of the birds remaining arose and dispersed, quarrelling with nothing so much as the
sunlight which they encountered above.

"It is an abominable task," said the aide-de-camp, looking up
at the dangling bodies; "But—for the Emperor—always for the

Emperor! That fellow, now, in the domino—it would make us appear of one build. And as for complexion, why, he at least would have no eyes for the travesty. Mon Dieu! I believe it is a Providence."

There was a ladder leaned against the third and empty beam. He put it into position for the cloaked figure, and ran up it. The rope was hitched to a hook in the crosspiece. He must clasp and lever up his burden by main strength before he could slacken and detach the cord. Then, with an exclamation of relief, he let the body drop upon the sand beneath. He descended the ladder in excitement.

"Anita!" he called.

She had followed, and was at hand. She trembled, and was as pale as death.

"Help me," he panted— "with this—into the bush."

He had lifted *his* end by the shoulders.

"What devil possesses you? I cannot," she sobbed; "I shall die."

"Ah, Nariguita! for my sake! There is no danger if thou art brave and expeditious."

Between them they tugged and trailed their load into the dense undergrowth skirting the open track, and there let it plunge and sink. Ducos removed the domino from the body, rolling and hauling at that irreverently. Then he saw how the wretch had been pinioned, wrists and ankles, beneath.

Carrying the cloak, he hastened back to the gallows. There he cautiously selected from the surplus stock of cord a length of some twelve feet, at either end of which he formed a loop. So, mounting the ladder, over the hook he hitched this cord by one end, and then, swinging himself clear, slid down the rope until he could pass both his feet into the lower hank.

"*Voilà!*" said he. "Come up and tie me to the other with some little pieces round the waist and knees and neck."

She obeyed, weeping. Her love and her duty were to this wonder of manhood, however dreadful his counsel. Presently, trussed to his liking, he bade her fetch the brigand's cloak and button it over all.

"Now," said he, "one last sacramental kiss; and, so descending and placing the ladder and all as before, thou shalt take standing-room in the pit for this veritable dance of death."

A moment—and he was hanging there, to all appearance a corpse. The short rope at his neck had been so disposed and knotted—the collar of the domino serving—as to make him look, indeed, as if he strained at the tether's end. He had dragged his long hair over his eyes; his head lolled to one side; his tongue protruded. For the rest, the cloak hid all, even to his feet.

The goatherd snivelled.

"Ah, holy saints, he is dead!"

The head came erect, grinning.

"Eugenio!" she cried; "O, my God! Thou wilt be discovered—thou wilt slip and strangle! Ah, the crows—body of my body, the crows!"

"Imbecile! have I not my hands? See, I kiss one to thee. Now the sun sinks, and my ghostly vigil will be short. Pray heaven only they alight not on that in the bush. Nariguita, little heroine, this is my last word. Go hide thyself in the bushes above, and watch what a Frenchman, the most sensitive of mortals, will suffer to serve his Emperor."

It was an era, indeed, of sublime lusts and barbaric virtues, when men must mount upon stepping-stones, not of their dead selves, but of their slaughtered enemies, to higher things. Anita, like Ducos, was a child of her generation. To her mind the heroic purpose of this deed overpowered its pungency. She kissed her lover's feet; secured the safe disposition of the cloak about them; then turned and fled into hiding.

At dusk, with the sound of footsteps coming up the pass, the crows dispersed. Eugène, for all his self-sufficiency, had sweated over their persistence. A single more gluttonous swoop might at any moment, in blinding him, have laid him open to a general attack before help could reach him from the eyrie whence unwearying love watched his every movement. Now, common instance of the providence which waits on daring, the sudden lift and scatter of the swarm left his hearing sensible to the tinkling of a bridle, which came rhythmical from the track below. Immediately he fell, with all his soul, into the pose of death.

The cadence of the steely warning so little altered, the footsteps stole in so muffled and so deadly, that, peering presently through slit eyelids for the advent of the troop, it twitched his strung nerves to see a sinister congress already drawn soundless about the gibbet on which he hung. Perhaps for the first time in this stagnant atmosphere he realized the peril he had invited. But still the gambler's providence befriended him.

They were all women but two—the victim, a sullen, whiskered Yanguesian, strapped cuttingly to a mule, and a paunchy shovel-hatted Carmelite, who hugged a crucifix between his roomy sleeves.

Ducos had heard of these banded *vengeresses*. Now, he was Frenchman enough to appreciate in full the significance of their attitude, as they clustered beneath him in the dusk, a veiled and voiceless huddle of phantoms. "How," he thought, peeping through the dropped curtain of his hair, "will the adorables do it?" He had an hysterical inclination to laugh, and at that moment the monk, with a sudden decision to action, brushed against him and set him slowly twirling until his face was averted from the show.

Immediately thereon—as he interpreted sounds—the mule was led under the gallows. He heard the ladder placed in position, heard a strenuous shuffling as of concentrated movement. What he failed to hear (at present) was any cry or protest from the victim. The beam above creaked, a bridle tinkled, a lighter drop of hoofs receded. A pregnant pause ensued, broken only by a slight noise, like rustling or vibrating—and then, in an instant, by a voice, chuckling, hateful—the voice of the priest.

"What! to hang there without a word, Carlos? Wouldst thou go, and never ask what is become of that very treasure thou soldst thy soul to betray? The devil has rounded on thee, Carlos; for after all it is thou that art lost, and not the treasure. That is all put away—shout it in the ears of thy neighbours up there—it is all put away,

Carlos, safe in the salt mines of the Little Hump. Cry it to the whole
world now. Thou mayst if thou canst. In the salt mines of the Little
Hump. Dost hear? Ah, then, we must make thee answer."

With his words, the pit was all at once in shrill hubbub, noise
indescribable and dreadful, the shrieking of harpies bidden to their
prey. It rose demoniac—a very Walpurgis.

"No, no," thought Ducos, gulping under his collar. He was almost
unnerved for the moment. "It is unlawful—they have no right to!"

He was twisting again, for all his mad will to prevent it. He
would not look, and yet he looked. The monk, possessed, was
thrashing the torn and twitching rubbish with his crucifix. The
others, their fingers busy with the bodkins they had plucked from
their mantillas, had retreated for the moment to a little distance.

Suddenly the Carmelite, as if in an uncontrollable frenzy,
dropped his weapon, and scuttling to the mule, where it stood near
at hand, tore a great horse pistol from its holster among the trap-
pings, and pointed it at the in sensible body.

"Scum of all devils!" he bellowed. "In fire descend to fire that
lasts eternal!"

He pulled the trigger. There was a flash and shattering explosion. A blazing hornet stung Ducos in the leg. He may have started
and shrieked. Any cry or motion of his must have passed unnoticed in the screaming panic evoked of the crash. He clung on with
his hands and dared to raise his head. The mouth of the pass was
dusk with flying skirts. Upon the sands beneath him, the body of
the priest, a shapeless bulk, was slowly subsiding and settling, one
fat fist of it yet gripping the stock of a pistol which, overgorged,
had burst as it was discharged.

The reek of the little tragedy had hardly dissipated before Ducos
found himself. The sentiment of revolt, deriving from his helpless
position, had been indeed but momentary. To feel his own acces-
sibility to torture, painted torture to him as an inhuman lust. With
the means to resist, or escape, at will, he might have sat long in
ambush watching it; even condoning it as an extravagant posture
of art.

With a heart full of such exultation over the success of his trick that for the moment he forgot the pain of his wound, he hurriedly unpicked the knots of the shorter cords about him, and, jumping to the ground, waited until the shadow of a little depressed figure came slinking across the sand towards him.

"Eugenio!" it whispered; "what has happened? O, art thou hurt?"

She ran into his arms, sobbing.

"I am hurt," said Ducos. "Quick, child! unstrap this from my arm and bind it about my calf. Didst hear? But it was magnificent!. Two birds with a single stone. The piastres in pickle for us. Didst see, moreover? Holy Emperor! it was laughable. I would sacrifice a decoration to be witness of the meeting of those two overhead. It should be the Yanguesian for my money, for he has at least his teeth left. Look how he shows them, bursting with rage! Quick, quick, quick! we must be up and away, before any of those others think of returning."

"And if one should," she said, "and mark the empty beam?"

"What does it matter, nevertheless! I must be off tonight, after thou hast answered me one single question."

"Off? Eugenio! O! not without me?"

"God, little girl! In this race I must not be hampered by so much as a thought. But I will return for thee— never fear."

He still sat in his domino. She knelt at his feet, stanching the flow from the wound the pistol had made in his leg. At his words she looked up breathlessly into his face; then away, to hide her swimming eyes. In the act she slunk down, making herself small in the sand.

"Eugenio! My God! we are watched!"

He turned about quickly.

"Whence?"

"From the mouth of the pass," she whispered.

"I can see nothing," he said. "Hurry, nevertheless! What a time thou art! There, it is enough of thy bungling fingers. Help me to my feet and out of this place. Come!" he ended, angrily.

He had an ado to climb the easy slope. By the time they were entered amongst the rocks and bushes above, it was black dusk.

"Whither wouldst thou, dearest?" whispered the goatherd.

He had known well enough a moment ago—to some point, in fact, whence she could indicate to him the direction of the Little Hump, where the treasure lay; afterwards, to the very hill-top where some hours earlier they had forgathered. But he would not or could not explain this. Some monstrous blight of gloom had seized his brain at a swoop. He thought it must be one of the crows, and he stumbled along, raving in his heart. If she offered to help him now, he would tear his arm furiously from her touch. She wondered, poor stricken thing, haunting him with tragic eyes. Then at last her misery and desolation found voice—

"What have I done? I will not ask again to go with thee, if that is it. It was only one little foolish cry of terror, most dear—that they should suspect, and seize, and torture me. But, indeed, should they do it, thou canst trust me to be silent."

He stopped, swaying, and regarded her demoniacally. His face was a livid and malignant blot in the thickening dusk. To torture her? What torture could equal his at this moment? She sought merely to move him by an affectation of self-renunciation. That, of course, called at once for extreme punishment. He must bite and strangle her to death.

He moved noiselessly upon her. She stood spell-bound before him. All at once something seemed to strike him on the head, and, without uttering a sound, he fell forward into the bush.

Ducos opened his eyes to the vision of so preternaturally melancholy a face, that he was shaken with weak laughter over the whimsicality of his own imagination. But, in a very little, unwont to dreaming as he was, the realization that he was looking upon no apparition, but a grotesque of fact, silenced and absorbed him.

Presently he was moved to examine his circumstances. He was lying on a heap of grass mats in a tiny house built of boards. Above him was a square of leaf-embroidered sky cut out of a carte roof; to his left, his eyes, focusing with a queer stiffness, looked through an open doorway down precipices of swimming cloud. That was because he lay in an eyrie on the hillside. And then at once, into his white field of vision, floated the dismal long face, surmounted by an ancient cocked-hat, slouched and buttonless, and issuing like an august Aunt Sally's from the neck of a cloak as black and dropping as a pall.

The figure crossed the opening outside, and wheeled, with the wind in its wings. In the act, its eyes, staring and protuberant, fixed themselves on those of the Frenchman. Immediately, with a little stately gesture expressive of relief and welcome, it entered the hut.

"By the mercy of God!" exclaimed the stranger in his own tongue. Then he added in English: "The Inglese recovers to himself?"

Ducos smiled, nodding his head; then answered confidently, feeling his way: "A little, sir, I tank you. Thees along night. Ah! it appear all one pain."

The other nodded solemnly in his turn—

"A long night indeed, in which the sunksink tree very time."

"Comment!" broke out the aide-de-camp hoarsely, and instantly realized his mistake.

"Ah! devil take the French!" said he explanatorily. "I been in their camp so long that to catch their lingo. But I spik l'Espagnol, señor. It shall be good to us to converse there."

The other bowed impenetrably. His habit of a profound and melancholy aloofness might have served for mask to any temper of mind but that which, in real fact, it environed—a reason, that is to say, more lost than bedevilled under the long tyranny of oppression.

"I have been ill, I am to understand?" said Ducos, on his guard.

"For three days and nights, señor. My goatherd came to tell me how a wounded English officer was lying on the hills. Between us we conveyed you hither."

"Ah, Dios! I remember. I had endeavoured to carry muskets into Saragossa by the river. I was hit in the leg; I was captured; I escaped. For two days I wandered, señor, famished and desperate. At last in these mountains I fell as by a stroke from heaven."

"It was the foul blood clot, señor. It balked your circulation. There was the brazen splinter in the wound, which I removed, and

God restored you. What fangs are theirs, these reptiles! In a few days you will be well."

"Thanks to what ministering angel?"

"I am known as Don Manoel di Cangrejo, señor, the most shattered, as he was once the most prosperous of men. May God curse the French! May God" (his wild, mournful face twitched with strong emotion) "reward and bless these brave allies of a people more wronged than any the world has yet known!"

"Noble Englishman," said he by and by, "thou hast nothing at present but to lie here and accept the grateful devotion of a heart to which none but the inhuman denies humanity."

Ducos looked his thanks.

"If I might rest here a little," he said; "if I might be spared—"

The other bowed, with a grave understanding.

"None save ourselves, and the winds and trees, señor. I will nurse thee as if thou wert mine own child."

He was as good as his word. Ducos, pluming himself on his perspicacity, accepting the inevitable with philosophy, lent himself during the interval, while feigning a prolonged weakness, to recovery. That was his, to all practical purposes, within a couple of days, during which time he never set eyes on Anita, but only on Anita's master. Don Manoel would often come and sit by his bed of mats; would even sometimes retail to him, as to a trusted ally, scraps of local information. Thus was he posted, to his immense gratification, in the topical after-history of his own exploit at the gallows.

"It is said," whispered Cangrejo awfully, "that one of the dead, resenting so vile a neighbour, impressed a goatherd into his service, and, being assisted from the beam, walked away. Truly it is an age of portents."

On the third morning, coming early with his bowl of goat's milk and his offering of fruits, he must apologize, with a sweet and lofty courtesy, for the necessity he was under of absenting himself all day.

"There is trouble," he said— "as when is there not? I am called to secret council, señor. But the boy Ambrosio has my orders to be ever at hand shouldst thou need him."

Ducos's heart leapt. But he was careful to deprecate this generous attention, and to cry *Adios!* with the most perfect assumption of composure.

He was lying on his elbow by and by, eagerly listening, when the doorway was blocked by a shadow. The next instant Anita had sprung to and was kneeling beside him.

"Heart of my heart, have I done well? Thou art sound and whole? O, speak to me, speak to me, that I may hear thy voice and gather its forgiveness!"

For what? She was sobbing and fondling him in a very lust of entreaty.

"Thou hast done well," he said. "So, we were seen indeed, Anita?"

"Yes," she wept, holding his face to her bosom. "And, O! I agonize for thee to be up and away, Eugenio, for I fear."

"Hush! I am strong. Help me to my legs, child. So! Now, come with me outside, and point out, if thou canst, where lies the Little Hump."

She was his devoted crutch at once. They stood in the sunlight, looking down upon the hills which fell from beneath their feet—a world of tossed and petrified rapids. At their backs, on a shallow plateau under eaves of rock, Cangrejo's eyrie clung to the mountain-side.

"There," said the goatherd, indicating with her finger, that mound above the valley—that little hill, fat-necked like a great mushroom, which sprouts from its basin among the trees?"

"Wait! mine eyes are dazzled."

"Ah, poor sick eyes! Look, then! Dost thou not see the white worm of the Painpeluna road—below yonder, looping through the bushes?"

"I see it—yes, yes."

"Now, follow upwards from the big coil, where the pine tree leans to the south, seeming a ladder between road and mound."

"Stay—I have it."

"Behold the Little Hump, the salt mine of St. Ildefonso, and once, they say, an island in the midst of a lake, which burst its banks and, poured forth and was gone. And now thou knowest, Eugenio?"

He did not answer. He was intently fixing in his memory the position of the hill. She waited on his mood, not daring to risk his anger a second time, with a pathetic anxiety. Presently he heaved out a sigh, and turned on her, smiling.

"It is well," he said. "Now conduct me to the spot where we met three days ago."

It was surprisingly near at hand. A labyrinthine descent—by way of aloe-horned rocks, with sandy bents and tufts of harsh juniper between—of a hundred yards or so, and they were on the stony plateau which he remembered. There, to one side, was the coppice of chestnuts and locust trees. To the other, the road by which he had climbed went down with a run—such as he himself was on thorns to emulate—into the valleys trending to Saragossa. His eyes gleamed. He seated himself down on a boulder, controlling his impatience only by a violent effort.

"Anita," he said, drilling out his speech with slow emphasis, "thou must leave me here alone awhile. I would think—I would think and plan, my heart. Go, wait on thy goats above, and I will return to thee presently."

She sighed, and crept away obedient. O, forlorn, most forlorn soul of love, which, counting mistrust treason, knows itself a traitor! Yet Anita obeyed, and with no thought to eavesdrop, because she was in love with loyalty.

The moment he was well convinced of her retreat, Ducos got to his legs with an immense sigh of relief. Love, he thought, could be presuming, could be obtuse, could be positively a bore. It all turned upon the context of the moment; and the present was quick with desires other than for endearments. For it must be related that the young captain, having manoeuvred matters to this accommodating pass, was designing nothing less than an instant return, on the wings of transport, to the blockading camp, whence he proposed returning, with a suitable force and all possible dispatch, to seize and empty of its varied treasures the salt mine of St. Ildefonso.

"Pouf!" he muttered to himself in a sort of ecstatic aggravation; "this accursed delay! But the piastres are there still—I have
Cangrejo's word for it."

He turned once, before addressing himself to flight, to refocus
in his memory the position of the mound, which still from here
was plainly visible. In the act he pricked his ears, for there was a
sound of footsteps rising up the mountain path. He dodged behind a boulder. The footsteps came on—approached him—paused—
so long that he was induced at last to peep for the reason. At once
his eyes encountered other eyes awaiting him. He laughed, and left
his refuge. The new-comer was a typical Spanish Romany—slouch-
ing, filthy, with a bandage over one eye.

"God be with thee, Caballero!" said the Frenchman defiantly.

To his astonishment, the other broke into a little scream of
laughter, and flung himself towards him.

"Judge thou, now," said he, "which is the more wide-awake
adventurer and the better actor!"

"My God!" cried Ducos; "it is de la Platière!"

"Hush!" whispered the mendicant. "Are we private? Ah, bah!
Junot should have sent me in the first instance."

"I have been hurt, thou rogue. Our duel of wits is yet postponed.
In good time hast thou arrived. This simplifies matters. Thou shalt
return, and I remain. Hist! come away, and I will tell thee all."

Half an hour later, de la Platière—having already, for his part,
mentally absorbed the details of a certain position—swung rapidly,
with a topical song on his lips, down the path he had ascended
earlier. The sound of his footfalls receded and died out. The hill
regathered itself to silence. Ducos, on terms with destiny and at
peace with all the world, sat for hours in the shadow, of the trees.

Perhaps he was not yet Judas enough to return to Anita, awaiting him in Cangrejo's eyrie. But at length, towards evening, fear-
ing his long absence might arouse suspicion or uneasiness, he arose
and climbed the hill. When he reached the cabin, I he found it
empty and silent. He loitered about, wondering and watchful. Not
a soul came near him. He dozed; he awoke; he ate a few olives and

some bread; he dozed again. When he opened his eyes for the second time, the shadows of the peaks were slanting to the east. He got to his feet, shivering a little. This utter silence and desertion discomforted him. Where was the girl? God! was it possible after all that she had betrayed him? He might have questioned his own heart as to that; only, as luck would have it, it was such a tiresomely deaf organ. So, let him think. De la Platière, with his men (as calculated), would be posted in the Pampeluna road, round the spur of the hill below, an hour after sunset—that was to say, at fifteen minutes to six. No doubt by then the alarm would have gone abroad. But no great resistance to a strong force was to be apprehended. In the meantime—well, in the meantime, until the moment came for him to descend under cover of dark and assume the leadership, he must possess his soul in patience.

The sun went down. Night flowing into the valleys seemed to expel a moan of wind; then all dropped quiet again. Darkness fell swift and sudden like a curtain, but no Anita appeared, putting it aside, and Ducos was perplexed. He did not like this bodiless, shadowless subscription to his scheming. It troubled him to have no one to talk to—and deceive. He was depressed.

By and by he pulled off, turned inside-out and resumed his scarlet jacket, which he had taken the provisional precaution to have lined with a sombre material. As he slipped in his arms, he started and looked eagerly into the lower, vortices of dusk. In the very direction to which his thoughts were engaged, a little glow-worm light was burning steadily from the thickets. What did it signify—Spaniards or French, ambush or investment? Allowing—as between himself on the height and de la Platière on the road below—for the apparent, discrepancy in the time of sunset, it was yet appreciably before the appointed hour. Nevertheless, this that he saw made the risk of an immediate descent necessary.

Bringing all his wits, his resolution, his local knowledge to one instant focus, he started, going down at once swiftly and with caution. The hills rose above him like smoke as he dropped; the black ravines were lifted to his feet. Sometimes for scores of paces he would lose sight altogether of the eye of light; then, as he turned some shoulder of rock, it would strike him in the face with its nearer, radiance, so that he had to pause and readjust his vision to the new perspective. Still, over crabbed ridges and by dip of thorny gulches he descended steadily, until the mound of the Little Hump, like a gigantic thatched kraal, loomed oddly upon him through the dark.

And, lo! the beacon that had led him down unerring was a great lantern hung under the sagging branch of a chestnut tree at the foot of the mound—a lantern, the lurid nucleus of a little coil of tragedy.

A cluster of rocks neighboured the clearing about the tree. To these Ducos padded his last paces with a catlike stealth—crouching, hardly breathing; and now from that coign of peril he stared down.

A throng of armed guerrillas, one a little forward of the rest, was gathered about a couple more of their kidney, who, right under the lantern, held the goatherd Anita on her knees in a nailing grip. To one side, very phantoms of desolation, stood Cangrejo and another. The faces of all, densely shadowed in part by the rims of their sombreros, looked as if masked; their mouths, corpse-like, showed a splint of teeth; their ink-black whiskers hummocked on their shoulders.

So, in the moment of Ducos's alighting on it, was the group postured—silent, motionless, as if poised on the turn of some full tide of passion. And then, in an instant, a voice boomed up to him.

"Confess!" it cried, vibrating: "him thou wert seen with at the gallows; him whom thou foisted, O! unspeakable, thou devil's doxy! on the unsuspecting Cangrejo; him, thy Frankish gallant and spy" (the voice guttered, and then, rising, leapt to flame)— "what hast thou done with him? where hidden? Speak quickly and with truth, if, traitor though thou be, thou wouldst be spared the traitor's estrapade."

"Alguazil, I cannot say. Have mercy on me!"

Ducos could hardly recognize the child in those agonized tones.

The inquisitor, with an oath, half wheeled.

"Pignatelli, father of this accursed—if by her duty thou canst prevail?"

A figure—agitated, cadaverous, as sublimely dehumanized as Brutus—stepped from Cangrejo's side and tossed one gnarled arm aloft.

"No child of mine, alguazil!" it proclaimed in a shrill, strung cry. "Let her reap as she hath sown, alguazil!"

Cangrejo leapt, and flung himself upon his knees by the girl.

"Tell Don Manoel, chiquita. God! little boy, that being a girl (ah, naughty!) is half absolved. Tell him, tell him—ah, there—now, now, now! He, thy lover, was in the cabin. I left him prostrate, scarce able to move. When the council comes to seek him, he is gone. Away, sayst thou? Ah, child, but I must know better! It could not be far. Say where—give him up—let him show himself only, chiquita, and the good alguazil will spare thee. Such a traitor, ah, Dios! And yet I have loved, too."

He sobbed, and clawed her uncouthly. Ducos, in his eyrie, laughed to himself, and applauded softly, making little cymbals of his thumb-nails.

"But he will not move her," he thought—and, on the thought, started; for from his high perch his eye had suddenly caught, he was sure of it, the sleeking of a French bayonet in the road below.

"Master!" cried Anita, in a heart-breaking voice; "he is gone—they cannot take him. O, don't let them hurt me!"

The alguazil made a sign. Cangrejo, gobbling and resisting, was dragged away. There was a little ugly, silent scuffle about the girl; and, in a moment, the group fell apart to watch her being hauled up to the branch by her thumbs.

Ducos looked on greedily.

"How long before she sets to screaming?" he thought, "so that I may escape under cover of it."

So long, that he grew intolerably restless—wild, furious. He could have cursed her for her endurance.

But presently it came, moaning up all the scale of suffering. And, at that, slinking like a rat through its run, he went down swiftly towards the road—to meet de la Platière and his men already silently breaking cover from it.

And, on the same instant, the Spaniards saw them.

"Peste!" whispered de la Platière. "We could have them all at one volley but for that!"

Between the French force, ensconced behind the rocks whither Ducos had led them, and the Spaniards who, completely taken by surprise, had clustered foolishly in a body under the lantern, hung the body of Anita, its torture suspended for the moment because, its poor wits were out.

"How, my friend!" exclaimed, Ducos. "But for what?"

"The girl, that is all."

"She will feel nothing. No doubt she is half dead already. A moment, and it will be too late." "Nevertheless, I will not," said de la Platière.

Ducos stamped ragingly.

"Give the word to me. She must stand her chance. For the Emperor!" he choked—then shrieked out, "Fire!"

The explosion crashed among the hills, and echoed off.

A dark mass, which writhed and settled beyond the lantern shine, seemed to excite a little convulsion of merriment in the swinging body. That twitched and shook a moment; then relaxed, and hung motionless.

Jack the Skipper

"Will you favour me by looking at it, young gentleman?" said the petitioner.

It was a most curious little model, which the petitioner had taken reverently out of a handbag. He was a hungry, eager-looking man, in a battered bowler, shabby frockcoat, and a primordial "comforter" which might have been made for Job.

Mr. Edward Cantle, busy at his desk, paid no attention.

"It turns, sir, literally, on a question of fresh butter," said the petitioner. "Who gets it nowadays, or realizes how, between churn and table, every pat becomes a dumping-ground for bacilli? Here, you will observe, the whole difficulty is resolved. We lead the cow into the cart itself, milk her into a separator, turn her out, drive off, and the revolution of the wheels completes the process. See? No chance for any freebooting germ! The result is simplicity itself—the customer's butter made actually on the way to his door."

Mr. Cantle put his pen in his mouth, blotted what he had been at work on, examined it cursorily but surely, rose, walked to the counter, and presented a form to the petitioner, all something with the air of a passionless police-inspector. He was a tall young man, loose-limbed, and with all his hardness, like a melancholy Punch's show character, in his head. Much converse with cranks had engendered in him an air of perpetual unspoken protest, of exasperated resignation. For he was a trusted clerk in the office of the Commissioners of Patents for Inventions.

"Exactly," he mumbled over the goose-quill. "That's a matter for your provisional specification. Good morning."

"It's the most wonderful—"

"Of course—they all are. Good morning."

"It will revolutionize—"

"Naturally. You will make your petition and declaration in the proper forms. Good morning."

The inventor essayed another effort or two, met with no response, quavered out a sigh, packed up his treasure and vanished. The sound of his exit neither relaxed nor deepened a wrinkle on the brow of the neatly groomed Government official. He simply went on with his work.

At half-past one o'clock, it being Saturday, he—we were going to say "knocked off," but the expression would be a libel on his methodical refinement. He took a hansom—selecting a personably horsed one—to his chambers in Adelphi Terrace; lunched off four *pâté de foie gras* sandwiches, already awaiting him under a silver cover, and a glass of chablis; changed his dress for a river suit of sober-tinted flannel and a Panama hat; charged himself with a morocco handbag, also ready prepared; drove to Waterloo, and took a first-class ticket, and the train—he favoured the South-Western because it was the quieter line of two in this connexion—to Windsor. Arrived there, he was hailed and joined by a friend on the platform.

"Glad you're come, Ned. I'm off colour a bit. You never are."

It was hardly an attractive reception. Mr. Cantle glanced interrogatively at his companion, the Honourable Ivo Monk, son of Lord Prior.

"No?" he said. "What's disturbing you, Monk?"

"O, the devil, I think!" said the young man peevishly. "Come along, do, out of this."

Together they walked down to the river in almost absolute silence. Mr. Cantle had agreed to join his friend for an agreeable week-end on the water. It looked promising. He thought a little, and came to a characteristically uncompromising decision.

"Is it anything to do with Miss Varley?"

"Yes, it is."

"She—they have a houseboat here, haven't they?"

"Yes."

"Close by?"

"More or less. Just above Datchet."

"Then, I think, perhaps I'd better—"

"Then, I think, perhaps, you'd not. You don't know anything about it. It's not what you suppose."

"O!"

A punt, in luxurious keeping with the tastes of its owner, awaited them at the steps. It was equipped with a number of little lockers for wine and food, a wealth of the downiest cushions, and an adjustable tilt with brass hoops for "roughing it" at nights on the water. For the Honourable Ivo was at the moment an aquatic gipsy, wandering at large and at whim, and scorning the effeminate pillow.

They loitered through Romney lock, talking commonplaces, and below relinquished their poles and sat and drifted until the reeds held them up. It was a fair, sweet afternoon, full of life and merriment, and, in view of the crowding craft, the remotest from ghostliness.

"Would you like to see her?" said Mr. Monk suddenly and unexpectedly.

Cantle was never to be taken off his guard.

"If it will please you, it will please me," he said.

They resumed the poles and made forward. To their left a little sludgy creek went up among the osiers; and, anchored at its mouth, rocked the vulgarest little apology for a houseboat. It seemed just one cuddy, mounted on a craft like a bomb-ketch, which it filled from stem to stern; and what with its implied restrictedness, and dingy appearance, and stump of a chimney, one could not have imagined a less inviting prison in which to make out a holiday. Yet there was a lord to this squalid baby galliot, and to all appearance a very contented one, as he sat smoking a pipe, with his legs dan-

gling over the side. Monk nodded to him, and the man nodded back
with a grin.

"Who's that?" asked Mr. Cantle, when out of earshot.

"O, a crank! You should recognize the breed better than I do."

Mr. Cantle, thoughtfully nursing his jaw, with a frown on his
face, had left off punting.

"Don't you know him?" he said suddenly.

"We exchange civilities," answered the other; "the freemasonry
of the river, you understand. *There's* the Varleys' boat."

Forging under the Victoria Bridge, they had come in view of a
long line of houseboats moored under the left bank against a withy
bed, opposite the Home Park. At one of these, hight the "Mermaid,"
very large and handsome, they came to, and fastening on, stepped
aboard. A sound of murmuring ceased with their arrival, and Cantle
had hardly become aware of two figures seated in the saloon, before he was being introduced to one of them.

Miss Varley was certainly "interesting"—tall and "English," but
with an exhausted air, and her eyes superhumanly large. She
greeted the stranger sweetly, and her fiancé with a rather full, pathetic look.

"Mamma's resting a little," she said, in a bodiless voice, "and
Nanna's been reading to me. Papa comes down by the seven o'clock
train."

"And what's Nanna been reading?" asked the young man.

The old nurse held up the volume. It was the Holy Book. Monk
ground his teeth.

"Hush, Master Ivo!" whispered the woman. "You only distress her."

"I'd rather see her reading a yellow-back on a July day on the
river."

The girl put a hand on his arm. "When the call has come? When
my days are numbered, Ivo?" she said. He almost burst out in an
oath.

"I'd rather, if I were you, be recognized and called by my own
name and nature," he said bitterly. "But it's all nonsense, Netta.
Do, for God's sake, believe it!"

He was so obviously overwrought, the situation was so painful, that his friend persuaded him, on personal grounds, to leave.
They punted across, dropped down a distance, and brought up
under the bank in a quiet spot.

"Very well," said Cantle. "You'll tell me, perhaps, what's the
matter?"

"Can't you see? She's dying."

He dropped his face into his hands, with a groan of impotent
suffering.

"There's some mystery here," said his friend quietly.

Monk looked up, and burst out in a sudden lost fury—

"There is, by God! Jack the Skipper!"

Cantle was rolling a cigarette imperturbably.

"Who's—Jack the Skipper?" he drawled.

"I wish you could tell me," cried the other. "I wish you could
show these the way to his throat!" He held out his hands. "They'd
fasten!" he whispered.

He came all of a sudden, quite quietly, and sat by his friend.
"It's been going on for three weeks now," he said rapidly. "They
call him that about here—a sort of skit on the other—the other
beast, you know. He appears at night—a sort of ghoulish, indescribable monster, black and huge and dripping, and utters one beastly
sound and disappears. Nobody's been able to trace him, or see
where he comes from or goes to. He just appears in the night, in all
sorts of unexpected places—houseboats, and bungalows, and shan-
ties by the water—and terrifies some lonely child or woman, and is
gone. The devil!—O, the devil! We've made parties and hunted him,
to no good. It's a regular reign of terror hereabouts. People don't
dare being left alone after dark. He frightened the little Cunning-
ham child into a fit, and it's not expected to recover. Mrs. Bancock
died of an apoplexy after seeing it. And the worst of it is, a deadly
superstition's seized the place. Its visit's got to be supposed to
presage death, and—" He seized Cantle's hand convulsively.

"Damn it! It's unnatural, Ned! The river's haunted—here, in
Cockney Datchet—in the twentieth century! You don't believe in
such things—tell me you don't! But Netta—"

His head sank on his breast. Cantle blew out a placid whiff of smoke.

"But—Miss Varley?" he said.

"You know—you've heard, at least," said the other, "what she was. The *thing* suddenly stood before her, when she was alone, one night. Well—you see what she is now."

"I don't see, nevertheless, why she don't—"

"Pack and run? No more do I. Put it to her if you like. I've said *my* say. But she's in the grip—thinks she's had her call—and there's no moving her. Cantle, she's just dying where she stands."

Cantle's cigarette made a tiny arc of light, and hissed in the river. He had heard of epidemic hysteria. The world was full of cranks.

"Now," he said, "drop the subject, please. Shall I tell you of some fools I've come across in my time?"

He related some of his experiences in the Patent Office. The most impudent invention ever proposed, he said, was a burglar's tool for snipping out and holding by suction in one movement a disk of window glass. His dry self-confidence had a curiously reassuring effect on the other. While they ate and drank and smoked and talked, the life of the river had become gradually attenuated and delivered to silence; a mist rose and hung above the water; sounds died down and ceased, concentrating themselves into the persistent dismal yelp of a dog somewhere on the bank above; the lights in the houseboats thinned to isolated sparks—twelve o'clock clanged from a distant. tower.

Then, all at once, he was alert and quietly active. "Monk, listen to me: I'm going to cure Miss Varley."

"Ned!"

"Take the paddle and work up—up the river, do you hear? I'll sit forward."

The ghost of a red moon was rising in the east. They slipped on with scarce a sound. A sort of lurid glaze enamelled the water. All of a sudden a sleek bulk rose ahead right in their path, wallowed a moment like a porpoise, and disappeared.

"Good God!" cried Monk, in a choking voice, half rising from his seat.

"Keep down!" whispered his friend.

"Cantle! Did you see it? Cantle! It was he!"

"Keep, down!"

They paddled on, past the last of the boats, through the bridge, on as far as the squat little bomb-ketch bulking black and menacing at the mouth of the creek.

"Hold on!" whispered Cantle. "Run her out of sight into the reeds. We must wade on board there."

"There? That fellow Spindler's boat?"

"Of course, now. That was his name."

"What do you mean?"

"You'll soon know."

They accomplished the feat, though near mud-foundered by the way, and scrambled, dripping, on board. The door of the cuddy yielded to their touch. Monk was beginning to gather dim light.

"Don't let me," he whispered, almost sobbing. "Keep my hands off him."

"Leave him to me," said Cantle gravely.

Not a sound of life greeted them. They stole into the cabin and closed the door, almost, upon themselves.

"We must yield him to-night for the sake of to-morrow," murmured Cantle.

"Ned! If he goes again—"

"Hush! It's not probable he'd risk a second visit, knowing her watched."

The crack brightened as the moon rose: glowed into a ribbon of light. Suddenly Cantle gripped the other's wrist.

A stealthy puddling, sucking sound close by reached, their ears. Over the side came swarming a great shapeless fishy creature, which settled with a sludgy wallop on the little triangle of foredeck almost at their feet. Monk gave a soft, awful gasp, and, with the sound, Cantle had dashed open the door and flung himself upon the monster.

"Quick!" he cried; "you've got matches! Light a candle—lamp— anything! Lie still, Mr. Spindler. It's all up. I know you and your Marine Secret Service suit! A knife now, Monk! Out he comes."

He was merciless with the blade when he got it, slashing and cutting at the oilskin suit, splitting it from top to toe. Mr. Spindler's red beard and extravagant face came out of it like a death's-head out of its chrysalis.

"There goes the proud monument of a lifetime," said the madman. He had made no effort to resist. The first blow at this darling of his invention had seemed to hamstring him, morally and materially.

For he was just one of Mr. Cantle's cranks—had once invented a submarine travelling suit, with which he had hoped to inaugurate a new system of Secret Service for the Admiralty. It was an ingenious enough device, with some scheme of floating valves through which to breathe; but the authorities, after holding him on and off, would have none of it. Then the fate of many inventors had befallen him. Between practical ruin and a moral sense of wrong, he had gone crazy, and vowed warfare on the mankind which had discarded him. It should comprehend, too late, the uses of instant appearance and disappearance to which his invention could be put. He went mad, and ended his days in an asylum.

On the Monday morning Mr. Cantle posted back to the Patent Office; on the Tuesday Miss Varley was reading De Maupassant's "Mademoiselle Fifi" under the awning of the "Mermaid's" roof; and on the Wednesday Mr. Ivo Monk got her to name the day.

THE FIVE INSIDES

I'll example you with thievery.— "Timon of Athens."

The dear old lady was ninety, and it was always Christmas in the sweet winter of her face. With the pink in her cheeks and the white of her hair, she came straight from the eighteenth century in which she was born. They were not more at odds with nature than are the hips and the traveller's joy in a withered hedge; and if at one time they paid to art, why it was a charitable gift to a poor dependent—nothing more, I'll swear.

People are fond of testing links with the past. This sound old chatelaine had played trick-track, and dined at four o'clock. She had eaten battalia pie with "Lear" sauce, and had drunk orgeat in Bond Street. She had seen Blücher, the tough old "Vorwarts," brought to bay in Hyde Park by a flying column of Amazons, and surrendering himself to an onslaught of kisses. She had seen Mr. Consul Brummell arrested by bailiffs in the streets of Caen, on a debt of so many hundreds of francs for so many bottles of *vernis de Guiton*, which was nothing less than an adorable boot-polish. She had heard the demon horns of newspaper boys shrill out the Little Corporal's escape from Elba. She had sipped Roman punch, maybe;—I trust she had never taken snuff. She had—but why multiply instances? Born in 1790, she had taken just her little share in, and drawn her full interest of, the history, social and political, of all those years, fourscore and ten, which filled the interval between then and now.

152

Once upon a time she had entered a hackney-coach; and, lo! before her journey was done, it was a railway coach, moving ever swifter and swifter, and its passengers succeeding one another with an ever more furious energy of hurry-scurry. Among the rest I got in, and straight fell into talk, and in love, with this traveller who had come from so far and from scenes so foreign to my knowledge. She was as sweet and instructive as an old diary brought from a bureau, smelling of rose-leaves and cedar-wood. She was merry, too, and wont to laugh at my wholly illusory attachment to an age which was already as dead as the moon when I was born. But she humoured me; though she complained that her feminine reminiscences were sweetmeats to a man.

"You should talk with William keeper," she said. "*He* holds on to the past by a very practical link indeed."

It was snowy weather up at the Hall—the very moral of another winter (so I was told) when His Majesty's frigate "Caledonia" came into Portsmouth to be paid off, and Commander Playfair sent express to his young wife up in the Hampshire hills that she might expect him early on the following morning. He did not come in the morning, nor in the afternoon, nor, indeed, until late in the evening, when—as Fortune was generous—he arrived just at the turn of the supper, when the snow outside the kitchen windows below was thawing itself, in delirious emulation of the melting processes going on within, into a rusty gravy.

"You see," said Madam, "it was not the etiquette, when a ship was paid off, for any officer to quit the port until the pennant was struck, which the cook, as the last officer, had to see done. And the cook had gone ashore and got tipsy; and there the poor souls must bide till he could be found. Poor Henry—and poor little me! But it came right. *Tout vient à qui sait attendre.* We had woodcocks for supper. It was just such a winter as this—the snow, the sky, the very day. Will you take your gun, and get me a woodcock, sir? and we will keep the anniversary, and you shall toast, in a bottle of the Madeira, the old French rhyme."

I had this rhyme in my ears as I went off for my woodcock—

Le bécasseau est de fort bon manger,
  Duquel la chair resueille l'appetit.
Il est oyseau passager et petit:
  Est par son goust fait des vins bien juger.

I had it in my ears, and more and more despairingly, as I sought the coverts and dead, ferns and icy reed-wrecked pools, and flushed not the little *oyseau passager* of my gallantry's desires. But at last, in a silent coomb, when my feet were frozen, and my fingers like bundles of newly-pulled red radishes, William keeper came upon me, and I confided my abortive wishes and sorrows to his velveteen bosom.

He smiled, warm soul, like a grate.

"Will'ee go up to feyther's yonder, sir," said he; "and sit by the fire, and leave the woodcock to me? The old man'll be proud to entertain ye."

"I will go," I said meanly. "But tell me first, William, what is your very practical link with the past?"

He thought the frost had got into my blood; but when I had explained, he grinned again knowingly.

"'Tain't me my lady meant, sir," he said. "Tis old feyther, and his story of how the mail coach was robbed."

The cottage hung up on the side of the coomb, leaning its back to an ash wood, and digging its toes well into the slope to keep itself from pitching into the brook below. There were kennels under the faggot stacks, a horse-shoe on the door, red light behind the windows. It looked a very cosy corner after the white austerity of the woods. William led me to it, and introducing me and my errand to his father, left the two of us together by the fire.

It was a strange old shell of a man, russet and smooth yet in the face; but his breath would sometimes rattle in him to show how dried was the kernel within. Still his brown eye was glossy, and his voice full and shrewd; and in that voice, speaking straight and clear out of the past, and in an accent yet more of the roads than of the woods, he told me presently the story of the great mail robbery.

"It ruined and it made me, sir," said he; "for the Captain, hearing as how the company had sacked me for neglect of duty, and knowing something of my character, swore I'd been used damnably, and that he'd back his opinion by making me his gamekeeper. And he did that; and here I be, waiting confident for him to check my accounts when I jine him across the river."

He pointed to a dusky corner. There hung on the wall an ancient key-bugle, and an old, old napless beaver hat, with a faded gold band about it.

"I was twenty-five when I put *they* up there, and that was in the year '14; and not me nor no one else has fingered them since. Because why? Because it was like as if my past laid in a tomb underneath, and they was the sign that I held by it without shame or desire of concealment.

"In those days I was guard to the 'Globe' coach, that run between London and Brighton. We made the journey in eight hours, from the 'Bull and Mouth' in Aldersgate to the 'New Inn' in North Street—or t'other way about; and we never stopped but for changes, or to put down and take up. Sich was our orders, and nothing in reason to find fault with 'em, until they come to hold us responsible to something besides time. Then the trouble began.

"Now, sir, as you may know, the coachman's seat was over the fore-boot, and, being holler underneath, was often used as a box for special parcels. So it happened that this box was hired of the owners by Messrs. Black, South, and Co., the big Brighthelmstone bankers, in order to ship their notes and cash, whenever they'd the mind to, between London and the seaside, and so escape the risks and expense of a private mail. The valiables would be slid and locked in—coachman being in his place—with a private key; and George he'd nothing to do but keep his fat calves snug to the door, till someun at the other end came with a duplicate key to unlock it and claim the property. Very well—and very well it worked till the fifteenth of December in the year eighteen hundred and thirteen, on which day our responsibility touched the handsome figure—so I was to learn—of £4000 in Brighton Union bank notes, besides cash and securities.

"It was rare cold weather, much as it is now, save that the snow was shallower by a matter of two inches, and no more bind in it than dry sand. We was advertised to start from the 'Bull' at nine; and there was booked six insides and five out. At ten minutes to the hour up walks a couple of Messrs. Pinnick and Waghorn's clerks from the borough, with the cash box in whity-brown paper, looking as innocent as a babby in a Holland pinifore. George he comes out of the shades, like a jolly Corsican ghost, a viping of his mouth; the box is slung up and fastened in; coachman climbs to his perch, and the five outsides follow-my-leader arter him to theirs, where they swaddle 'emselves into their wraps strait-veskit-vise, and settin' as miserable as if they was waitin' to have a tooth drawed. Not much harm there, you'll say—one box-seat, two behind, two with me in the dickey—all packed tight, and none too close for observation. Well, sir, we'll hear about it.

"Out of the six insides, all taken, there was three already in place: a gentleman, very short and fierce, and snarling at everything; gentleman's lady, pretty as paint, but a white timidious body; gentleman's young-gentleman, in ducks and spencer and a cap like a concertina with the spring gone. So far so good, you'll say again, and no connexion with any other party, and leastways of all with the insides as was yet wanting, and which the fierce gentleman was blowin' the lights out of for bein' late.

"'Guard,' says he, goin' on outrageous, while the lady and the young gentleman cuddled together scared-like in a corner, 'who are these people who stop the whole service while they look in the shop-vinders? If you're for starting a minute after the stroke,' says he, 'dash my buttons,' he says, 'but I'll raise all hell to have you cashiered!'

"All right, sir,' I says. 'I knows my business better'n you can tell it me—' and just as I spoke, a hackney kerridge come rumbling into the yard, and drew up anigh us.

"'Globe?' says a jolly, fat-faced man, sticking his head out of it. All right, Cato—' and down jumps a black servant, in livery, that was on the box, and opens the door.

"The fat man he tumbled out—for all the world like a sheetful of washing a wallopin' downstairs—Cato he got in, and between them they helped from the hackney and across to the coach as rickety a old figure as ever I see. He were all shawls and wraprascal. He'd blue spectacles to his eyes, a travellin' cap pulled down on 'em, his mouth covered in; and the only evidence of flesh to be seen in the whole of his carcass, was a nose the colour of a hyster. He shuffled painful, too, as they held him up under the arms, and he groaned and muttered to himself all the time he were changing.

"Now, sir, you may suppose the snarling gentleman didn't make the best of what he see; and he broke out just as they was a-hauling the invalid in, wanting to know very sarcastic if they hadn't mistook the 'Globe' for a hearse. But the fat man he accepted him as good humoured as could be.

"'It's nothing affectionate, sir,' says he. 'Only paralysis, which ain't catching. The gentleman won't trouble you.'

"'Not for my place,' says the fierce gentleman, bristling up like a dog. 'Damme, sir, not for my place. O, I can see very well what his nose is a-pinting to, and dam-me if it isn't as monstrous a piece of coolness as ever I expeerunced. *These* seats, sir, are the nat'ral perkisite of a considerate punctiality, and if your friend objects to travelling with his back to the 'orses—'

"'Now, now,' says the fat man— 'nothing of the sort. You don't mind sitting with your back to the 'orses, do you, nunky?'

"'Eh,' says the old man, 'usky-like, and starting a bit forward— 'No, no, no no, no, no, no—' and he sunk into the front cushions, while Cato and the fat 'un dispodged him to his comfort.

"Time, gentlemen!' says I.

"'Wait a bit,' says snarler. 'It can't never be—why, surely, it can't never be that the sixth inside is took for a blackamoor?'

"'Alfred,' says the lady, half veeping: 'pray let things be. It's only as far as Cuckfield we're goin', arter all.'

"'A poor argiment, my dear,' says he, 'in favour of suffering forty miles of a sulphurious devil.'

"'Pray control yourself, sir,' says the fat man, still very ekable. 'We've booked three places, for two, just to be comfortable. Our servant rides outside.'

"Well, that settled it; and in another minute we was off. I laughed a bit to myself as I swung up; but I hadn't a thought of suspicion. What do *you* say, sir? Would you have? Why, no, of course not—no more than if you was a Lyons Mail. There was the five o' them packed in there, and one on the roof behind the coach-man—three divisions of a party as couldn't have seemed more un-connected with one another, or more cat and dog at that. Yet, would you believe it, every one of them six had his place in the robbery that follered as carefully set for him as a figure in a sum.

"As for me, sir, I done my duty; and what more could be ex-pected of me? At every stage I tuk a general look round, to see as things were snug and nat'ral; and at Croydon, fust out, I observed as how the invalid were a'ready nodding in a corner, and the other two gents settled to their 'Mornin' Postses.'

"Beyond Croydon the cold begun to take the outsides bitter; and the nigger got into a vay of drummin' with his feet so aggera-wacious, that at last George he lost his temper with him and told him to shut up. Well, he shut up that, and started scrapin' instead; and he went on scrapin' till the fierce gentleman exploded out of the vinder below fit to bust the springs.

"'Who's that?' roars he— 'the blackamoor? Damme!' he roars, 'if you aren't wus nor a badger in more ways than one,' he roars.

"'All right, boss,' says the nigger, grinning and lookin' down. 'Feet warm at last, boss,' and he stopped his shufflin' and begun to sing.

"Now, sir, a sudden thought—I won't go so far as to call it a suspicion—sent me, next stop, to examine unostentatious-like the neighbourhood of them great boots. But all were sound there, and the man sittin' well tucked into his wraps. It wasn't like, of course, that he could a' kicked the panels of the box in without George knowin' somethin' about it. And he didn't want to neither; *for he'd finished his part of the business a'ready*. So he just sat and smiled at me as amiable as Billy Vaters.

"Well, we went on without a hitch; and at Cuckfield the three back insides turned out into the snow, and went for a bespoke po'-chaise that was waitin' for 'em there. But, afore he got in, the fierce gentleman swung round and come blazin' back to the vinder.

"'My compliments, sir,' says he, 'at parting; and, if it should come to the vorst,' he says, 'I'd advise you to lay your friend pretty far under to his last sleep,' he says, 'or his snores'll wake the dead.'

"'Hush,' says the fat 'un. 'It's the drowndin' spirit in him comin' up to blow like a vale.'

"'Is it?' says the fierce gentleman. 'Then it's my opinion that the outsides ought to be warned afore he gives his last heave—' and he went off snortin' like a tornader.

"The fat man shook his head when he were gone. His mildness, having sich a figger, was amazing. He sat with his arm and shoulder for a bolster to old paralysis, who was certainly going on in style.

"'Now, sir,' says I, 'the whole blessed inside is yourn till the end of the journey.'

"'Thank you, guard,' says he; 'but I won't disturb my friend, and we'll stay as we are, thank you.'

"I got up then, and on we went—last stage, sir, through Clayton, over the downs, whipping through Pyecombe and Patcham, swish through Preston turnpike, and so into East Street, where we'd scarce entered, when there come sich a hullabaloo from underneath as if the devil, riding on the springs, had got his tail jammed in the brake. Up I jumps, and up jumps the blackamoor, screeching and clawing at George, so as he a'most dropped the ribbins.

"'Eh, boss!' he yelled. 'De old man—down dere!—damn bad!'

"George he pulled up; and I thought he'd a bust, till I climbed over and loosened his neckercher, and let it all out. Then down we got—nigger and I, and one or two of the passengers—and looked in. 'What the thunder's up?' says I. The fat man were goin' on awful, sobbin', and hiccup-in', and holding on to old paralysis, as were sunk back in the corner.

"'I'm afraid he's dyin',' he said. 'I'm afraid he's dyin'! O, why did I ever give way to him, and let him come!'

"Well, we all stood pretty foolish, not knowing what to say or do, when his great tricklin' face come round like a leg o' mutton on a spit, and, seein' the nigger, bust into hystrikes.

"O, Cato!' he roars; 'O Cato, O Cato! Sich a loss if he goes!' he roars. 'Run on by a short cut, Cato,' he says, 'and see if you can find a doctor agen our drawin' up at the "New Inn."'

"That seemed to us all a good idea, though, to be sure, there was no cut shorter than the straight road we was in. But anyhow, before we could re'lise it, the nigger was off like a arrer; and one of the gentlemen offered to keep the fat man company. But that he wouldn't listen to.

"'If he *should* come round,' he said, 'the shock of a stranger might send him off agen. No, no,' he said: 'leave me alone with my dying friend, and drive on as quick as ever you can.'

"It were only a matter of minutes; but afore we'd been drawed up half of one afore the inn, a crowd was gathered round the coach door.

"'Is he back?' says the fat man— 'Is Cato come back with a doctor? No, I won't have him touched or moved till a doctor's seen him.'

"Then all at once he was up and out, rampageous.

"'Where is he?' he shrieks. 'I can't vait no longer—I'm goin' mad—I'll find one myself'—and, afore you could say Jack Robinson, he was off. I never see sich a figger run so. He fair melted away. But the crowd was too interested in the corpse to follow him.

"Well, sir, he didn't come back with a doctor, and no more did Cato. And the corpse may have sat there ten minutes, and none daring to go into it, when a sawbones, a-comin' down the street on his own account, was appealed to by the landlord for a verdict, seein' as how by this time the whole traffic was blocked. He got in, and so did I; and he bent over the body spread back with its wraps agen the corner.

"'My God!' I whispers— 'there's no breath comin' from him. Is he dead, sir?'

The sawbones he rose up very dry and cool.

"'No,' he says, 'there ain't no breath comin' from him, nor there never will. It ain't in natur' to expect it from a waxworks.'

"Sir, I tell you I looked at him and just felt my heart as it might be a snail that someun had dropped a pinch of salt on.

"'Waxworks!' I says, gaspin'. 'Why, the man spoke and groaned!'

"'Or was it the gentleman you was tellin' me of as did it for him?' says the sawbones, still as dry as cracknels.

"Then I took one jump and pounced on the thing, and caught it up;—and I no sooner 'ad it in my 'ands, than I knew it were a dummy—nothing more nor less. But what I felt at that was nothin' to the shock my pullin' it away give me—for there, behind where it had set, was a 'ole, big enough for a boy to pass, cut right through the cushions and panels into the fore boot; and the instant I see it, 'O,' I says, 'the mail's been robbed!'"

The old man, who had worked himself up to a state of practised excitement, paused a dramatic moment at this point, until I put the question he expected.

"And it had been?"

"And it had been," he said, pursing his lips, and nodding darkly. "In the vinter of '13, sir—the cleverest thing ever planned. It made a rare stir; but the 'ole truth was never known till years arterwards, when one o' the gang (it was the boy as had been, now growed up) were took on another charge, and confessed to this one. The fat man were a ventriloquist, you see. That, and to secure the 'ole six insides to themselves while seemin' strangers was the cream of the job. They cut into the boot soon arter we was clear of London, and passed the boy through with a saw and centre-bit t'other side o' Croydon. He set to—the young limb, with his pretty innocent ducks!—tuk a piece clean out of the roof just under the driver's seat, and brought down the cash-box; while Mr. Blackamoor Cato kep' up his dance overhead to drown the noise of the saw. The box was opened and emptied, and put back in the boot where it was found; and the swag, for fear of accidents, was all tuk away at Cuckfield."

He came to an end. I was aware of William gamekeeper, the younger, standing silent at the door, with a couple of speckled auburn trophies in his hand. The fire leapt and fluttered. I rose with a sigh—then with a smile.

"Thank you, William," I said gratefully, as I took the woodcock. "How plump they are; and how I love these links with the past."

The Strength of the Rope

Si finis bonus est, totum bonum erit.

There were notices, of varying dates, posted in prominent places about the cliffs to warn the public not to go near them.— unless, indeed, it were to read the notices themselves, which were printed in a very unobtrusive type. Of late, however, this Dog-berrian *caveat* had been supplemented by a statement in the local gazette that the cliffs, owing to the recent rains succeeding prolonged frost, were in so ill a constitution that to approach them at all, even to decipher the warnings not to, was—well, to take your life out of the municipal into your own hands.

Now, had the Regius Professor a bee in his bonnet? Absurd. He knew the risks of foolhardiness as well as any pickpocket could have told him. Yet, neither general nor particular caution availed to abate his determination to examine, as soon as we had lunched, the interior formation of a cave or two, out of those black and in-numerable, with which the undercliff was punctured like a warren.

I did not remonstrate, after having once discovered, folded down under his nose on the table, the printed admonition, and heard the little dry, professorial click of tongue on palate which was wont to dismiss, declining discussion of it, any idle or super-fluous proposition. I knew, my man—or automaton. He inclined to the Providence of the unimaginative; his only fetish was science. He was one of those who if unfortunately buried alive, would turn

162

what opportunity remained to them to a study of geological deposits. My "nerves," when we were on a jaunt (fond word!) together, were always a subject of sardonic amusement with him.

Now, utterly unmoved by the prospect before him, he ate an enormous lunch (confiding it, incidentally, to an unerring digestion), rose, brushed some crumbs out of his beard, and said, "Well, shall we be off?"

In twenty minutes we had reached the caves. They lay in a very secluded little bay—just a crescent of sombre sand, littered along all its inner edge with débris from the towering cliffs which contained it.

"Are you coming with me?" said the Regius Professor.

Judged by his anxious eyes, the question might have been an invitation, almost a shamefaced entreaty. But the anxiety, never more than apparent, was delusive product of the preposterous magnifying-glasses which he wore. Did he ever remove those glasses, one was startled to discover, in the seemingly aghast orbs which they misinterpreted, quite mean little attic windows to an unemotional soul.

"Not by any means," I said. "I will sit here, and think out your epitaph."

He stared at me a moment with a puzzled expression, grinned slightly, turned, strode off towards the cliffs, and disappeared, without a moment's hesitation, into the first accessible burrow. I was moved on the instant to observe that it was the most sinister-looking of them all. The tilted stratification, under which it yawned oblique, seemed on the very poise to close down upon it.

Now I set to pacing to and fro, essaying a sort of mechanical preoccupation in default of the philosophy I lacked. I was really in a state of clammy anxiety about the Professor. I poked in stony pools for little crabs, as if his life depended on my success. I made it a point of honour with myself not to leave off until I had found one. I tried, like a very amateur pickpocket, to abstract my mind from the atmosphere which contained it, only to find that I had brought mind and atmosphere away together. I bent down, with my back to the sea, and looking between my legs sought to regard life from a new point of view. Yet, even in that position, my eyes and ears were conscious, only in less degree, of the spectres which were always moving and rustling in the melancholy little bay.

Tekel upharsin. The hand never left off writing upon the rocks, nor the dust of its scoring to fall and whisper. That came away in flakes, or slid down in tiny avalanches—here, there, in so many places at once, that the whole face of the cliffs seemed to crawl like a maggoty cheese. The sound was like a vast conspiracy of voices—busy, ominous—aloft on the seats of an amphitheatre. They were talking of the Regius Professor, and his consideration in making them a Roman holiday.

Here, on no warrant but that of my senses, I knew the gazette's warning to be something more than justified. It made no difference that my nerves were at the stretch. One could not hear a silence thus sown with grain of horror, and believe it barren of significance. Then, all in a moment, as it seemed to me, the resolution was taken, the voices hushed, and the whole bay poised on tiptoe of a suspense which preluded something terrific.

I stood staring at the black mouth which had engulfed the Regius Professor. I felt that a disaster was imminent; but to rush to warn him would be to embarrass the issues of his Providence—that only. For the instant a fierce resentment of his foolhardiness fired me—and was as immediately gone. I turned sick and half blind. I thought I saw the rock-face shrug and wrinkle; a blot of gall was expelled from it—and the blot was the Professor himself issued forth, and coming composedly towards me.

As he advanced, I turned my back on him. By the time he reached me I had made some small success of a struggle for self-mastery.

"Well," he said. "I left myself none too much of a margin, did I?"

With an effort I faced about again. The base of the cliff was yet scarred with holes, many and irregular; but now some of those which had stared at me like dilated eyes were, I could have sworn it, over-lidded—the eyes of drowsing reptiles. *And the Professor's particular cave was gone.*

I gave quite an absurd little giggle. This man was soulless—a monstrosity.

"Look here," he said, conning my face with a certain concern, "it's no good tormenting yourself with what might have happened. Here I am, you know. Supposing we go and sit down yonder, against that drift, till you're better."

He led the way, and, dropping upon the sand, lolled easily, talking to himself, by way of me, for some minutes. It was the kindest thing he could have done. His confident voice made scorn of the never-ceasing rustling and falling sounds to our rear. The gulls skated before my eyes, drawing wide arcs and figures of freedom in the air. Presently I topped the crisis, and drew a deep breaths

"Tell me," I said— "have you ever in all your life known fear?"

The Regius Professor sat to consider.

"Well," he answered presently, rubbing his chin, "I was certainly once near losing hold of my will, if that's what you mean. Of course, if I had let go—"

"But you didn't."

"No," he said thoughtfully. "No—luckily."

"You're not taking credit for it?"

"Credit!" he exclaimed, surprised. "Why should I take credit for my freedom from a constitutional infirmity? In one way, indeed, I am only regretful that I am debarred that side of self-analysis."

I could laugh lovelily, for the first time.

"Well," I said, "will you tell me the story?"

"I never considered it in the light of a story," answered the Regius Professor. "But, if it will amuse and distract you, I will make it one with pleasure. My memory of it, as an only experience in that direction, is quite vivid, I think I may say—" and he settled his spectacles, and began:

"It was during the period of my first appointment as Science Demonstrator to the Park Lane Polytechnic, a post which my little pamphlet on the Reef-building Serpulae was instrumental in procuring me. I was a young man at the time, with a wide field of interests, but with few friends to help me in exploring it. My holidays I generally devoted to long, lonely tramps, knapsack on back, about the country.

"It was on one of these occasions that you must picture me entered into a solitary valley among the Shropshire hills. The season was winter; it was bitterly cold, and the prospect was of the dreariest. The interesting conformations of the land—the bone-structure, as I might say—were blunted under a thick pelt of snow, which made walking a labour. One never recognizes under such conditions the extent of one's efforts, as inequalities of ground are without the contrast of surroundings to emphasize them, and one may be conscious of the strain of a gradient, and not know if it is of one foot in fifty or in five hundred.

"The scene was desolate to a degree; houseless, almost tree-less—just white wastes and leaden sky, and the eternal fusing of the two in an indefinite horizon. I was wondering, without feeling actually dispirited, how long it was to last, when, turning the shoulder of a hill which had seemed to hump itself in my path, I came straight upon a tiny hamlet scattered over a widish area. There were some cottages, and a slated school building; and, showing above a lower hump a quarter of a mile beyond, the roofs and tall chimney of a factory.

"It was a stark little oasis, sure enough—the most grudging of moral respites from depression. Only from one place, it seemed, broke a green shoot. Not a moving figure was abroad; not a face looked from a window. Deathlily exclusive, the little stony build-ings stood apart from one another, incurious, sullen, and self-contained.

"There was, however, the green shoot; and the stock from which it proceeded was the school building. That in itself was unlovely enough—a bleak little stone box in an arid enclosure. It looked hunched and grey with cold; and the sooty line of thaw at the foot of its wall only underscored its frostiness. But as if that one green shoot were the earnest of life lingering within, there suddenly broke through its walls the voices of young children singing; and, in the sound, the atmosphere of petrifaction lifted somewhat.

"Yes? What is it? Does anything amuse you? I am glad you are so far recovered, at least. Well—

"I like, I must confess, neither children nor music. At the same time, I am free to admit that those young voices, though they dismissed me promptly on my way, dismissed me pleased, and to a certain degree, as it were, reinvigorated. I passed through that little frigid camp of outer silence, and swung down the road towards the factory. As I advanced towards what I should have thought to be the one busy nucleus of an isolated colony, the aspect of desolation intensified, to my surprise, rather than diminished. But I soon saw the reason for this. The great forge in the hills was nothing but a wrecked and abandoned ruin, its fires long quenched, its ribs long laid bare. Seeing which, it only appeared to me a strange thing that any of the human part of its affairs should yet cling to its neighbourhood; and stranger still I thought it when I came to learn, as I did by and by, that its devastation was at that date an ancient story.

"What a squalid carcass it did look, to be sure; gaunt, and unclean, and ravaged by fire from crown to basement. The great flue of it stood up alone, a blackened monument to its black memory.

"Approaching and I entering, I saw some writhed and tortured guts of machinery, relics of its old vital organs, fallen, withered, from its ribs. The floor, clammy to the tread, was littered with tumbled masonry; the sheet iron of the roof was shattered in a hundred places under the merciless bombardment of the weather; and, here and there, a scale of this was corroded so thin that it fluttered and buzzed in the draught like a ventilator. Bats of grimy cobweb hung from the beams; and the dead breath of all the dead place was acrid with cold soot.

"It was all ugly and sordid enough, in truth, and I had no reason to be exacting in my inspection of it. Turning, in a vaulting silence, I was about to make my way out, when my attention was drawn to the black opening of what looked like a shed or annex to the main factory. Something, some shaft or plant, revealing itself from the dim obscurity of this place, attracted my curiosity. I

walked thither, and, with all due precaution because of the littered
ground, entered. I was some moments in adapting my vision to
the gloom, and then I discovered that I was in the mill well-house.
It was a little dead-locked chamber, its details only partly deci-
pherable in the reflected light which came in by the doorway. The
well itself was sunk in the very middle of the floor, and the projecting wall of it rose scarce higher than my knees. The windlass,
pivoted in a massive yoke, crossed the twilight at a height a little
above my own; and I could easily understand, by the apparent
diameter of its barrel, that the well was of a considerable depth.

"Now, as my eyes grew a little accustomed to the obscurity, I
could see how a tooth of fire had cut even into this fastness. For
the rope, which was fully reeled up upon the windlass, was scorched
to one side, as though some exploded fragment of wood or brick-
work had alighted there. It was an insignificant fact in itself, but
my chance observation of it has its importance in the context; as
has also the fact that the bight of the rope (from which the bucket
had been removed) hung down a yard or so below the big drum.

"You have always considered me a sapient, or at least a ratio-
nal creature, have you not? Well, listen to this. Bending over to
plumb with my eyes the depth of the pit (an absurdity, to begin
with, in that vortex of gloom), I caught with my left hand (wisdom
number two) at the hanging end of rope in order to steady myself.
On the instant, the barrel made one swift revolution, and stuck.
The movement, however, had thrown me forward and down, so that
my head and shoulders, hanging over, and actually into, the well,
pulled me, without possibility of recovery, from my centre of grav-
ity. With a convulsive wrench of my body, I succeeded in bringing
my right hand to the support of my left. I was then secure of the
rope; but the violence of the act dragged my feet and knees from
their last desperate hold, and my legs came whipping helpless over
the well-rim. The weight of them in falling near jerked me from
my clutch—a bad shock, to begin with. But a worse was in store for
me. For I perceived, in the next instant, that the rusty, long-dis-
used windlass was beginning slowly to revolve, *and was letting
me down into the abyss.*

"I broke out in a sweat, I confess—a mere diaphoresis of nature; a sort of lubricant to the jammed mechanism of the nerves. I don't think we are justified in attributing my first sensations to fear. I was exalted, rather—promoted to the analysis of a very exquisite, scarce mortal, problem. My will, as I hung by a hair over the abysm, was called upon to vindicate itself under an utmost stress of apprehension. I felt, ridiculous as it may appear, as if the surrounding dark were peopled with an invisible auditory, waiting, curious, to test the value of my philosophy.

"Here, then, were the practical problems I had to combat. The windlass, as I have said, revolved slowly, but it revolved persistently. If I would remain with my head above the well-rim—which, I freely admit, I had an unphilosophic desire to do—I must swarm as persistently up the rope. That was an eerie and airy sort of treadmill. To climb, and climb, and always climb, paying out the cord beneath me, that I might remain in one place! It was to repudiate gravitation, which I spurned from beneath my feet into the depths. But when, momentarily exhausted, I ventured to pause, some nightmare revolt against the sense of sinking which seized me, would always send me struggling and wriggling, like a drowning body, up to the surface again. Fortunately, I was slightly built and active; yet I knew that wind and muscle were bound sometime to give out in this swarming competition against death. I measured their chances against the length of the rope. There was a desperate coil yet unwound. Moreover, in proportion as I grew the feebler, grew the need for my greater activity. For there were already signs that the great groaning windlass was casting its rust of ages, and was beginning to turn quicker in its sockets. If it had only stuck, paused one minute in its eternal round, I might have set myself oscillating, gradually and cautiously, until I was able to seize with one hand, then another, upon the brick rim, which was otherwise beyond my reach. But now, did I cease climbing for an instant and attempt a frantic clutch at it, down I sank like a clock weight, my fingers trailed a yard in cold slime, and there I was at my mad swarming once more— the madder that I must now make up for lost ground.

At last, faint with fatigue, I was driven to face an alternative resource, very disagreeable from the first in prospect. This was no less than to resign temporarily my possession of the upper, and sink to the under world; in other words, to let myself go with the rope, and, when it was all reeled out, to climb it again. To this course there were two objections: one, that I knew nothing of the depth of the water beneath me, or of how soon I should come to it; the other, that I was grown physically incapable of any further great effort in the way of climbing. My reluctance to forgo the useless solace of the upper twilight I dismiss as sentimental. But to drop into that sooty pit, and then, perhaps, to find myself unable to reascend it! to feel a gradual paralysis of heart and muscle committing me to a lingering and quite unspeakable death—that was an unnerving thought indeed!

"Nevertheless, I had actually resolved upon the venture, and was on the point of ceasing all effort, and permitting myself to sink, when—I thought of the burnt place in the rope.

"Do you grasp what that sudden thought meant to me? Death, sir, in any case; death, if, with benumbed and aching hands and blistered knees, I continued to work my air-mill; death, no earlier and no later, no less and no more certainly, if I ceased of the useless struggle and went down into the depths. So soon as the strain of my hanging should tell direct upon that scorched strand, that strand must part.

"Then, I think, I knew fear—fear as demoralizing, perhaps, as it may be, short of the will-surrender. And, indeed, I'm not sure but that the will which survives fear may not be a worse last condition than fear itself, which, when exquisite, becomes oblivion. Consciousness *in extremis* has never seemed to me the desirable thing which some hold it.

"Still, if I suffered for retaining my will power, there is no doubt that its loss, on the flash of that deadly reflection, would have meant an immediate syncope of nerve and an instant downfall; whereas—well, anyhow, here I am.

"I was fast draining of all capacity for further effort. I climbed painfully, spasmodically; but still I climbed, half hoping I should die of the toil of it before I fell. Ever and again I would glance faintly up at the snarling, slowly-revolving barrel above me, and mark how death, as figured in that scorched strand, was approaching me nearer at every turn. It was only a few coils away, when suddenly I set to doing what, goodness knows, I should have done earlier. I screamed—screamed until the dead marrow must have crawled in the very bones of the place.

"Nothing human answered—not a voice, not the sound of a foot-fall. Only the echoes laughed and chattered like monkeys up in the broken roof of the factory. For the rest, my too-late outburst had but served to sap what little energy yet remained to me.

"The end was come. Looking up, I saw the burnt strand reeling round, a couple of turns away, to the test; and, with a final gulp of horror, I threw up the sponge, and sank.

"I had not descended a yard or two, when my feet touched something."

The Regius Professor paused dramatically.

"O, go on!" I snapped.

"That something," he said, "yielded a little—settled—and there all at once was I, standing as firmly as if I were in a pulpit.

"For the moment, I assure you, I was so benumbed, physically and mentally, that I was conscious of nothing in myself but a small weak impatience at finding the awful ecstasy of my descent checked. Then reason returned, like blood to the veins of a person half drowned; and I had never before realized that reason could make a man ache so.

"With the cessation of my strain upon it, the windlass had ceased to revolve. Now, with a sudden desperation, I was tugging at the rope once more—pulling it down hand over hand. At the fifth haul there came a little quick report, and I staggered and near fell. The rope had snapped; and the upper slack of it came whipping down upon my shoulders.

"I rose, dimly aware of what had happened. I was standing on the piled-up fathoms of rope which I had paid out beneath me. Above, though still beyond my effective winning, glimmered the moon-like disk of light which was the well mouth. I dared not, uncertain of the nature of my tenure, risk a spring for it. But, very cautiously, I found the end of the rope that had come away, made a bend in it well clear of the injured part, and, after many vain attempts, slung it clean over the yoke above, coaxed down the slack, spliced it to the other, and so made myself a fixed ladder to climb by. Up this, after a short interval for rest, I swarmed, set myself swinging, grasped the brick rim, first with one hand, then with both, and in another instant had flung myself upon the ground prostrate, and for the moment quite prostrated. Then presently I got up, struck some matches, and investigated."

The Regius Professor stopped, laughing a little over the memory.

"*Do* go on!" I said.

"Why," he responded, chuckling, "generations of school children had been pitching litter into that well, until it was filled up to within a couple yards of the top—just that. The rope, heaping up under me, did the rest. It was a testimony to the limited resources of the valley. What the little natives of to-day do with their odd time, goodness knows. But it was comical, wasn't it?"

"O, most!" said I. "And particularly from the point of view of the children's return to you for your dislike of them."

"Well, as to that," said the Regius Professor, rather shame-facedly, "I wasn't beyond acknowledging a certain indebtedness."

"Acknowledging? How?"

"Why, I happened to have in my knapsack one of my pamphlets on the Reef-building Serpulae; so I went back to the school, and gave it to the mistress to include in her curriculum."

Bullet-Proof

So far as I know, the true story of the Bugsley Vacuum Jacket has never yet been made public. Now the death of the distinguished officer, who was associated with the patentee in the production of what has virtually revolutionised modern warfare, has removed what polite embargo lay upon the tongues of the informed, and there can be no indiscretion or ill-taste in admitting the "general" to the humours of an anecdote, which the "particular" was wont often to relate in private, with a keen sense of the nature of the laugh which it raised against himself.

The circumstances which, many years ago, led to the resignation, by Major Cheverel Manton, of his official position in Pall Mall will be still within the recollection of many. The gallant officer had pledged himself and his credit to the impenetrability of a certain bullet-proof coat designed by a Mr. Bugsley, and his strength of faith in the invention had lacked only the force to convince the superior impenetrability of his department. His demand for a trial being persistently ignored, he took, finally, the extreme step of resigning his commission, as the most practical form of protest possible against, as he considered it, the ruinous supineness of the War Office. That the result came to justify this step served the enlightened public, of course, for a delirious scandal by and by; yet, no doubt, the War Office had had its excuse, and one even—as Major Manton himself was moved presently to admit—of a more than commonly reasonable complexion. For the fact had been that, while Mr. Bugsley was a notorious patenter of chimeras, his

backer—always a "cranky," hot-tempered man—had only recently
at the time recovered from a severe influenza, and was supposed
still subject to hallucinations.

Whatever the official rendering of the case, however, the evolution of the famous service jacket, from its first practical test in
the Borstall explorative expedition to its ultimate adoption by the
Government authorities, is a certain matter of history; and assuredly the late Major Manton never had reason to regret his firm
confidence in the virtues of an invention, which compensated him
with a fortune for the position he sacrificed to uphold it.

The story, as related by the Major, ran as follows: "I was one of
the officials of the Ordnance. It was part of my duties to interview
cranks. Do you realise what that means—the ineffable weariness
of flesh and waste of time? I dare say you have no conception of
the number of people in the world who are busily engaged in trying to extract sunbeams out of cucumbers. A single day spent at
the War Office would enlighten you, perhaps. I suppose that, as
human nature swings at the eternal balance between offence and
defence, it is natural that a disproportion of inventive genius should
flow Pall-Mallwards. There is no such fruitful inspiration, of the
right sort, as that which points to the most economic method of
destroying one's enemies. Of all creative cranks, the man who invented or adapted the guillotine stands, in my opinion, at the head
of the poll. Bugsley, for all his versatility, couldn't touch him.

"That man had haunted me for years—a suave apparition. You
never saw him? He couldn't survive his only success, and was found
sitting at his desk dead and smiling over the post which had brought
him Borstall's testimonial to the efficacy of the jacket.

"The first time I saw him was on an afternoon in the late nine-
ties. I had been pestered out of reason that day, I remember, and
was in a bad mood for considering any further Colney Hatch patents—sights that would enable a man to kill with his eyes shut,
powders that would explode automatically on the least little inter-
national friction, plugs for compressed rations to be carried in a
rifle-barrel, and buttons each a receptacle for a condensed meat
lozenge. I had been harassed, I say, and my temper was no doubt a

bit short when Bugsley was shown in to me. There was nothing repugnant about the man; but I developed an instinctive antagonism to him on the spot. He was very short and thick and ungainly, with an enormous smiling face and knock knees. As he stood rattling the pence in his trouser-pockets, with his feet finned out, his little fat thighs pressed together, and his great beaked nose tilted up at an angle, he reminded me of nothing so much as the aldermanic turtle. I saw a calm and unctuous assurance in his smile, and snapped out at him instanter:

"'State your business, if you please. I've no time to spare. A word will do.'

"He answered at once, looking sideways at the ceiling, 'I have a little fancy—Vacuums. There's a fortune in it.'

"That was his obsession—and he never looked away from the ceiling, but casually, in expressing it. Vacuums, vacancy, vacuity—the man's mind was gone on the craze. I don't know how to put it fairly. There is the jacket to speak for him; but, before that, there were certainly other things. His single idea was that where nothing was, nothing could happen—that all strategy in warfare should be directed to enticing the enemy to waste his energies and his ammunition upon emptiness.

"In this first case it was a design for a gun he brought. The weapon was to fire smokeless powder; but there was an arrangement in the breech for ejecting laterally, and simultaneously with the discharge, a miniature blank shell, filled with black powder, which, bursting at a point some two or three hundred yards distant, should mislead the enemy as to the position of your piece, and draw their fire upon nothing.

"I explained, briefly, some technical difficulties, and got rid of the man—as I thought. But not a bit of it. A month later he turned up again, smiling at the ceiling, and offered me a plan for a refracting instrument, which was to project the apparition of bodies of men moving upon the enemy from as many points as you liked, while the living troops which produced them were to be all confounded in the most diabolical and confusing way with the illusions. If I had hesitated over the first suggestion, as sincere in its way, I saw at once now the true character of the eccentric, and dismissed him without ceremony. A month later he called again, and took the ceiling into his confidence, with that eternal and imperturbable catch-phrase of his, 'I have a little fancy. There's a fortune in it.' This time it was a sort of compound heliograph, for dazzling the eyes of a whole troop of the enemy's horse when either making or resisting a cavalry-charge. I told him to go, and he went. I gave orders that he was not to be admitted again, and he was not admitted. Did that save me? Nothing of the sort. A few weeks later I was leaving the office, when a shadow emerged from a doorway, and an oily voice whispered in my ear, 'I have a little fancy, Major. There's a fortune in it.' It was for a sort of captive balloon, it appeared, to be floated, a tempting mark, over the enemy's lines, with two dummy aeronauts in the car stuffed with high explosives, and designed to spread destruction around the moment the thing should be brought down. I faced the creature decisive.

"'Mr. Bugsley,' I said; 'I have heard many of your inventions now, and this is really the last I wish to be told about, You mustn't approach me again, and I must tell you that your genius is wasted in these directions. Your province, if you will believe me, is in the large domain of pantomime, and I should recommend you to apply at Drury Lane.'

"He smiled, murmured 'Vacuums,' and fell back. But I was mistaken in supposing I had laid the apparition of him. He took to haunting me by post, in typewritten copy; his large placid face mooned at me round street corners, or was pressed against the glass of shop-fronts while I trafficked within; he put advertisements in the papers, addressed to Major C. M., and relating, in a sort of loose cypher, the details of new lunacies. I found myself studying these against my will; I developed a sickening subconsciousness of his presence in my neighbourhood; I thought about him constantly. Bit by bit he seemed to weave his insane personality into the very fibre of my being, and I grew to loathe the imposition, as it were, of a dual personality thrust upon me—only my Mr. Hyde was horribly benevolent, and the murderous moiety was myself. My dreams grew disturbed because of him, and my temperature constantly stood at a perilous figure. This state of things may have continued, in varying moods, for a year or two, when I got my big dose of influenza which pretty well laid me flat. I had to chuck everything, and rusticate. The demon of the complaint must be my apology for what followed.

"You know how it takes some people, even the sanest? That is the devil of what they call its convalescence. One can endure the fever and the pain and the nausea; but the suicidal depression during recovery! One looks out on the world through warped spectacles. Everything seems to have gone irredeemably crooked, ugly; everything presents a baffling front, and nothing, it appears, can by any hope shake itself straight again. I was in a foul bad way; and one day I sat, muffled in my dressing-gown, brooding my ruin, moral and material, and eyeing a revolver, army-service pattern, which lay on a table beside me. It was loaded in all its seven chambers, and I waited only the word of the demon to take it up.

"'I have a little fancy,' said a voice; and there he stood before me. Bugsley, and no other! That was in my bungalow down in Buckinghamshire, and how he had tracked me there the Lord only knows. But it didn't matter. The vision had had to materialise for me, and here was its most appropriate form. I took up the revolver and arose, grinning like a lynx. There were seven chambers—four for him and three for me.

"He had not altered by a crease, save that he looked even stouter and stumpier than his wont. His short frock-coat was buttoned almost to bursting across his chest; his gills were swollen and his eyes projecting. He gave his bow-window a resounding thwack.

"'Don't do that,' I said, 'or you'll break the glass.'

"He smiled like one in a beatitude.

"'No fear, Major,' he said. 'This time, I have done it.'

"'You have,' I said sternly. 'On your head be it!'

"It was his stomach I fired at, however. I couldn't help it; the mark was so sure and obtrusive.

"I waited a panic moment for the smoke to clear—and then I saw him. He was standing with his little legs straddled, his hands behind his back, and that ineffable smile on his face.

"'Don't mind me,' he said. 'Try again.'

"A sort of dementia seized me. One after the other I emptied the remaining six chambers at the impervious figure, and then threw down the weapon and reeled to a chair, at the moment that my servant, rushing from a distance, broke into the room. The man stood appalled before the apparition of the chuckling stranger, the reeking room, and my own livid face; and in that instant the intruder had thrown open his coat, and revealed underneath—what you all know now.

"'Behold,' said he, 'the Bugsley Vacuum jacket—bullet-proof, Major, as you must have convinced yourself. There's a fortune in it.'

"That was the way he excused me. It all passed for an experiment. He was a good soul, and he hadn't left me a cartridge for my own affairs.

"There's the story."

PRISCILLA PIPKIN

"And the long carpet rose along the gusty floor."

Priscilla Pipkin came on a windy evening and left on a windy morning. All night I heard the gale flapping in my blind, and dreamed of flying skirts, and at breakfast Priscilla was gone. There was no lamp alight, as usual, under an empty kettle; no stove-brush on my chair; no toast-rack at all (Priscilla would occasionally put my letters in it and post the toast under my bedroom door). Priscilla Pipkin, in short, had disappeared, like the baseless fabric of a vision, and left not a rack behind her.

Mrs. Hoskins, my landlady, when I rang her up to explain, explained. She had always mistrusted the girl, she said; she wore such small boots. There was an artful hussy hid somewhere behind that print apron. Priscilla, it appeared, had come straight down from her attic that morning and give her notice—not a month's, or a week's, or a day's, if you please; but had just up'd with her nose like a silk pairasole, and walked out of the house as grand as my lady. It was possible, Mrs. Hoskins thought, that a letter she had received by the early post had inspired her to this astonishing decision. But, whatever the case, Priscilla Pipkin, forgoing a month's wages and the possibility of a tip from the lodger, was gone on the wings of the wind.

"She'd neither stop nor explain," said Mrs. Hoskins bitterly; "but carried off her things, as she'd brought 'em, in a newspaper

179

parcel as big as a target, and pinned down at the corners; and what I may come to think of it all, the Lord deny me."

I begged that for the moment she would think of it in connection with my breakfast, and asked if there were any letters for me.

"No, sir," said Mrs. Hoskins; "though the postman come; I hear him. But I suppose Priscilla's was the only one."

Here was an additional aggravation. I had looked—with a confidence justified by nothing but inexperience—for a letter that morning from a certain "trustee," whose duty it should have been to pay me the first fourth of a yearly allowance of five hundred pounds on this, the first day of May. He had not done so—I supposed to impress me with the insignificance of my claim on his attention. He was a beast, and beastly rich—a great sweltering Croesus, with thin yellow hair streaking his head like soap, swollen eyes, and an ill-tempered mouth, with a purse of chin hanging from it as if he kept his gold there. In his view, I knew, I was a young ass, lately estated, whom it was his grudging responsibility to supply with the means to fresh wasteful imbecilities; and that, while I was as certain of my own young old-worldliness, of my inherent precaution and moderation, as I was of his detestable cynicism. "But I will convince him of my business capacities," I fumed, "if I have to do it by quoting to his face his own lack of 'em. Just a day or two's grace first!"

The day or two ran into a week; and then, desperate, I took cab to the City. To my astonishment Croesus received me with affability.

"You should have acknowledged that cheque, my boy," he said. "You aren't come, I suppose, to ask for an advance on the next? No, no; that would never do. I can't possibly entertain such a proposal."

"I haven't made it, sir," I said coldly. "I haven't received any cheque from you, that's all."

"Not?"

He sat back in his chair, one arm out on the desk, fiddling with a pen, and squinted at me, with his left eye closed, intolerably.

"O! that's it, is it?" he said quietly. "Well, you're beginning early."

"Don't you believe me?"

"Of course I do. But the cheque was sent."

"I never received it, I say."

He touched a bell; sent a clerk for the book; showed me the counterfoil—thirtieth of April, a hundred and twenty-five pounds, pay to the order of, etc.—and threw the book, with an air of insolent finality, on the desk.

"There it is," he said.

"It did not reach me."

"Well, I can't help that."

"Can't help it, sir? Am I to go without my money, because—because it was lost in the post?"

"You can sue me, if you like. The thing's been done before; and ended, I believe, in favour of the drawer. But it's an open question. The cheque was posted—there'll be my letter-book to prove it—and with that I wash my hands of the matter. I dare say one of your—one of your friends will be opening an account with it by and by. Good morning!"

What was the beast implying? That I was manoeuvring to obtain a further advance on the strength of an understanding with an accomplice? My blood boiled.

"You'll be sorry for this," I said, rising.

"All right," he said. "I'll be prepared with the sackcloth when my time comes."

I left him without another word. Outside, a paper-boy was announcing in a shrill voice: "Romance in 'igh life. Lady of quality steals a letter addressed to her 'ostess."

Like a smack, the words smote the blood to my cheek. Priscilla Pipkin!

It was she, of course. The letter, the circumstances, the informal "bolt." How could I have doubted it for a moment! Priscilla was the culprit.

I did not pause to consider in what way it would be possible for the girl to avail herself of that unnegotiable plunder. The thought of the sight, of the temptation, was enough. The draft was a potential treasure, at least. Priscilla had got it—perhaps in her pocket;

perhaps enclosed in the newspaper parcel which was like a target. *En avant* for Priscilla Pipkin.

I consulted a friend of mine, Charlie Glossop. He was dead against my approaching Scotland Yard.

"Police go for the criminal; swag's a secondary consideration with 'em," he said. "You take my advice, and employ a private enquiry agent. Find out what's become of the cheque, and settle the girl after. I know a chap who's the very moral of what you want—Hawkesby's his name, Long Acre."

Mr. Hawkesby, on Glossop's initiative, came to visit me. I told him that it would be as well to keep the affair very private.

"Else why apply to Hawkesby, sir?" he said. "A fair field and no favour's all that he asks."

He was elaborately designed to fit the part of the stage detective—an astute, quiet person, with side-whiskers (removable); a respectable top-hat, rather narrow in the brim; a frock-coat, somewhat short, and buttoned tightly about an upright, fairly portly figure; very black brows and blue eyes underneath, impenetrable but observant. His mind was obviously scored with information about all those things which a population of four millions particularly desires shall not be known about itself. Add to this a superhuman capacity for detecting motives, a condemning guile, a power of fascinating like the serpent's, and you have Mr. Hawkesby—at least according to the portrait of himself which he sketched for me. He gave me a feeling of fearful confidence at once.

He asked me for the outlines of the case. They appeared simple to absurdity to my unsophisticated mind; but Hawkesby thought otherwise.

"Here's what I like," he said, "a provocation to the best in me."

"It don't seem very difficult," I protested.

"Ah!" he answered. "That's the amateur mind. You wouldn't say it if you'd had my experience. Beware most when all seems plain sailing." (Sherlock Holmes.) "I've built my reputation and made my little pile on that understanding, sir. What about Mrs. Hoskins, now, and her point of view?"

"Why, I questioned her—very cautiously, of course," I answered deprecatingly; "and she told me that she knew nothing whatever about the girl—had taken her on at a moment's notice and without a character."

"Of course she'd say that," said Hawkesby triumphantly. He rubbed his chin, conning me shrewdly.

"What would you think, now," he pondered, "of the two being all this time in collusion?"

The suggestion struck me dumb. Mrs. Hoskins, the garrulous, the fussy, but the immaculate! No; I could not, I would not believe it. Yet, from that moment, the horrible insinuation began to poison my very fount of trustfulness in human nature. Henceforth all appearances were to be estimated by their speciousness. Hawkesby had emancipated me.

"Well," he said, "you leave her to me. I'll turn her inside out in no time." And he left me.

The next day an old lady called upon Mrs. Hoskins (I saw her come and go from my sitting-room window)—a tottery, whining old body, in a respirator and blue spectacles. Later, Mrs. Hoskins enlightened me, voluntarily, as to the old lady's mission. She had come about "that Pipkin," it appeared. The girl had applied to her for "tweenie's" place, and had referred her to Mrs. Hoskins for a character. "And I give her a rare one, my eye," said the landlady.

"Didn't you ask her what was the girl's present address?" I demanded in great excitement.

"No, to be sure," she answered. "What should I want with it?"

"Nor her own?"

"No, sir. It didn't matter to me."

Was this a criminal admission? I tried to think it out.

That evening Hawkesby paid me a visit.

"I've got some news for you," I began at once. He winked. Some subtle quality in the act confounded and silenced me.

"I dare say," he said. "Mrs. H. hasn't been letting on to you about her visitor to-day, I suppose?"

"Yes, she has."

"And didn't you twig?"

"Twig what?"

"The old lady."

"What about her?"

"She was me, that's all."

I began to comprehend his methods.

"Well," I said; "did you find out anything?"

"Something," he answered; "but this Rome isn't going to be built in a day. We're getting on; that's enough."

I saw him constantly after this—was always either entertaining or running up against him, in fact. I acquired an infernal shrewdness in identifying him under his innumerable disguises. Sometimes it would be a bricklayer, shouldering a hod to nowhere; sometimes an evangelical person, after the Stiggins type, distributing tracts; sometimes an itinerant and snuffling tradesman hawking boot laces along the kerb. Once, I am sure, I recognised him under the helmet of a policeman; and he was certainly the traveller who endeavoured to persuade Mrs. Hoskins to put her name down for a sewing machine on the hire system. The provincial and rather over-fatuous looking curate, too, whom I saw looking in upon me one day, his nose pressed against the glass of my window, was Hawkesby without a doubt, yearning to convince me of his fertility of invention.

He generally, after each of these essays, paid me a visit, bringing the comforting assurance that we were "beginning to move now." Then he would sound me, cunningly, on the subject of my penetration of his latest disguise, and appear pleased with my confession of recognition, though, one might have thought, it could be held rather to discount the cleverness of his "make-up." But he took a childish delight in the parts he played, and—so it seemed to me—was quite satisfied with their utter irrelevance and inanity, so long as I was an appreciative observer.

"You see, you're in the know, sir," he would confess jocundly; "but the public isn't, and takes me at my own valuation. Bless you! I can wind 'em round my little finger. I made seventy-five per cent profit on those bootlaces."

I began to see deeper than ever into his methods—and his "pile." Detectiveness, if I may use the word, embraces a multitude of "pickings."

And then, suddenly convinced, perhaps, of my thorough mastery of his *modus operandi*, he disappeared—or, at least, I saw him no more for quite a long time.

The respite, I admit, was a complete relief to me. I had come to think any atmosphere would be better than that atmosphere of exotic and luxuriant suspicion in which my scepticism of all human motives had been forced of late into a preposterous growth. I wanted to be my young credulous self again; I was ready even to waive the question of the cheque, if only Hawkesby would leave me alone to skimp and deny myself, and recover lost ground thereby. And when I thought of the bill he might be running up against me, I shivered.

But the respite was only a respite—by no means a reprieve. All too soon I was in his thrall again.

His manner had taken on a new seriousness; the weight of fresh problems and responsibilities had scored his brow with thunder. The range of his enquiries, he told me, was widening and ever widening. He left me almost in tears.

At length the end came. One day he suddenly appeared before me, his face suffused with a light of sombre triumph. The eccentric course of his enquiries, he said, had whirled him inevitably at last to the seashore. He had certain information that Priscilla Pipkin had gone to America.

And then Mrs. Hoskins came in.

She apologised; didn't know I was engaged, and so on. But the fact was that she had done a body wrong by her insinuations, and, being an honest woman, couldn't abide to rest till she had made the truth known. She thought, in brief, the explanation due to me that Priscilla Pipkin had had her reasons for departing suddenly as she had that morning, having received by the post an invitation, or an order, rather, from her young man (recently promoted) to come and marry him at once on that first of May, parsons obliging, or for ever hold her peace. To which peremptory citation

Priscilla Pipkin had incontinently succumbed, and was now in Mrs. Hoskins's kitchen, on a visit to her former mistress, the proud possessor of the surname and affections of Mr. Bertie Birdekin.

"And very modest she bears it, that I will say," said Mrs. Hoskins.

I looked at Hawkesby. He was equal to the occasion.

"A double," he whispered. "I shouldn't have thought her up to it." Then he addressed Mrs. Hoskins affably.

"And where's this Mrs. Birdekin been living since her marriage?" he said.

"Why, that's the queer part of it," answered my landlady. "No farther away than the next street, sir, if you'll believe me."

"I believe you, of course, ma'am," he said, with a knowing emphasis on the pronoun, and a wink to me to imply: "We haven't travelled where we have to be made Mrs. Birdekin's gulls!" Then he continued aloud: "And now, ma'am, with your permission, we will wait upon this young woman."

Mrs. Hoskins looked surprised; but preceded us to the kitchen. There, sure enough, was Priscilla, in a hat with a whole cherry-orchard in it. She blushed and giggled as she rose to greet me.

"A moment," said Hawkesby, as I stuck undecided. "We—my friend here and me—have been wanting to see you, Mrs. Birdekin; very much we have."

Priscilla gaped, dumbfoundered.

"Quite a romance," said Hawkesby, "upon my word—your being hooked like that, I mean, by a letter—and the only one, too, that came by that post, I understand."

"No," said Priscilla; "there were another."

"O, indeed!" said Hawkesby. "For whom?"

"For the lodger, sir."

"Dear, dear! how very strange. Would you be surprised to hear, now, that he never received it?"

"I put it under his door, sir," said Priscilla, breathing a little hard.

"Would you mind showing us, now, exactly where?"

Somehow, then, we were all trooping upstairs. I felt horribly mean and treacherous—shaken, moreover, with a premonition of scenes unthinkable to follow. It was Priscilla who threw open the door, and who scanned the room with a lost air, as if baffled in the hope that the letter, unaccountably overlooked by us, might be lying there on the threshold all the time.

"I shot it in for certain," she said, half weeping.

"It were a windy morning; perhaps it went under the carpet."

Hawkesby, with a smile of ineffable toleration, lifted the hem of the thing—and there was the letter.

A dead silence ensued. Then I looked for Hawkesby. He was nowhere to be seen. He had folded his tent like the Arab, and as silently stolen away. I began giggling like a maniac; and then checked myself with a gasp.

"O! that's all right," I said. "I couldn't make it out, and wanted you to tell me, that was all; but—but you were gone. It was unwise of you to leave us in that way, Priscilla; but, never mind—my wedding present shall carry interest with it, now I know where to send it."

"You're very good, sir," she said, drying her eyes. "Bert's badly in need of an accordion."

The Man Who Had Dined Too Well

"Sit down, Mr. Archibald Dalrymple," said the tea-broker, with a sarcastic emphasis on the name, as if its distinction were a mere aristocratic pretence. "Sit down, sir."

He noticed with disfavour how the young man, despite his agitation, slightly pulled up the knees of his irreproachable trousers as he obeyed. The act brought into prominence a couple of long thin feet in varnished boots, at the vision of which Mr. Huggins sniffed audibly. He was too extreme a Tory not to be sensible of his own shortcomings, literally, in the leg and foot department. A bluff insistence on the proverbial inadequacy of clothes to prove the gentleman was his solitary refuge from a self-consciousness of his own thick inelegance, and the general incompetency of tailors to better it. It was certainly hard that this whipper-snapper, on a hundred and nothing a year, should possess, on no warrant but that of his birth, what he with all his thousands was denied—the personality of a gentleman. Therefore he was sarcastic at the expense of his visitor's name and boots, and insulting in his use of the only counter-check at his command to all which they implied. Impecuniosity, the young man must learn, was not the less subject, because patrician, to the dictatorialness of wealth.

"It's a dirty day," he said; "and I suppose you never thought of doing anything but walk?"

The interview, by the way, was in his own drawing-room; the hour, midday on a Sabbath.

"I hope, sir," said Mr. Dalrymple, with an ingratiatory smile, "that you've no fault to find with that sort of providence?"

He was tall and slender, with a pale not very wise face; but, like many aristocratic unintelligences, he seemed capable of a certain fixity of purpose.

"That depends," said the tea-broker, "on what's behind it. The more you're justified in cabs and such-like ostentations, the better you'll be advised to chuck 'em."

"Honestly, I'm not justified in any ostentation," said the young man.

"Exactly," said the tea-broker; "and you've come, I understand, to ask me for the hand of my daughter, who is. Now, how you're going to reconcile me, as a plain man of business, to that, is the question."

"My prospects," began the suitor.

"Are without end, sir," interrupted the tea-broker. "It's the case with all of us. But they aren't the sort of asset I favour in a marriage contract. Real estate, sir; a balance at your bankers; a profitable occupation—those are the telling arguments."

He bent his heavy eyebrows on the visitor, who sat looking down and nervously roping his gloves together.

"Young gentleman," he said, "you'll do me the justice of assuming that my daughter Kate is at least as dear to me as she is to you. Only I've got a more intimate experience of her worth. Put it on the practical footing, then, that I'm not going to sell precious goods cheap. I want my equivalent for value received—my equivalent, you'll understand, which is nothing less than a guarantee of her happiness at the hands of a possible vendee. Do I see that in your offer? which, of course, at the same time, I acknowledge with all politeness. I ask you, as a mere question of business, Would you pledge the best of your credit with a bankrupt?"

"You're too hard on me, sir. You spoke of a profitable occupation. Surely the Bar is that?"

"Surely it may be—to a publican. As to your tale of briefs, now?"

The suitor blushed.

"I've some, what you may call, good connexions, sir."

"I don't dispute it."

Consciously or unconsciously, the tea-broker seemed to glance at the varnished boots again. Anyhow, he sniffed.

"Your family's all right," he said. "I don't dispute it, I say."

"With influence, moneyed influence, to back me," began the suitor, momentarily deluded into eagerness; but the other checked him.

"So, young gentleman," he said, "I'm to be your bribe to Fortune? I'm to accept you first and make you afterwards? Why, any beggar at the gate could equal that guarantee."

The suitor's hopes, bitterly abashed, fell to zero.

"I didn't quite mean it," he murmured. "You—you spoke of Kate's—Miss Huggins's happiness. I don't—with respect, sir, I don't yield to you in that matter. However unworthy I may be, she, at least, believes it to be bound up in mine. But, perhaps, she hasn't— you don't—"

"Make your mind easy. She's taken me into her confidence. I've been treated to a deal of the sort of stuff they call fairy gold—precious glittering stuff, too, in the light of gas-lamps and romance, but dust, sir, dust in the light of day and commonsense. *I* know in what her happiness has laid up to now, and I know, as a practical man, that it's not going to accommodate itself all of a sudden to buses and third-class fares."

"Really, sir, you exaggerate."

"Do I?"

"I've a small independent income."

"What return—you'll excuse me—do you make on it to the assessors?"

"None; I'm exempt—that is—moreover, I earn a little by literature."

"By what?"

"Literature—articles, and so on, in the papers."

"O, indeed! What's the most you've ever made out of it, out of anything, in a day?"

"In a single day?"

"There's no need to waste words."

"O! I couldn't tell, really."

"A hundred pounds?"

"I'm afraid not."

"Fifty?"

"I can't say as much."

"Ten?"

"No, not even that."

"What, then?"

"I once got a cheque for two-five for a short story in *The United Family*."

The tea-broker rose, the other with him.

"Good day," said the former.

"You will give me—us—no hope whatever?" pleaded the suitor desperately.

"Young man," said Mr. Huggins grimly, "you may have heard, or you may not have heard, of a neighbour of mine called Matcham. But I won't be hard on you. Come to me at any time with the assurance that you've earned by your wits as much as a hundred pounds in a single day, and I'll reconsider your case."

"Do you give your word on that?" asked the suitor dolefully.

"I give my business word," answered the tea-broker, with a sardonic chuckle. "Only, mind, I guarantee nothing in the interval."

Mr. Dalrymple gazed at him a moment, wrung his hand fervently but respectfully, and departed in the greatest depression.

"He's not a bad chap, and well connected, too," mused Mr. Huggins, standing in the middle of the room when the door was shut; "but—all that pretence, boots and things, on nothing—and then to go and plead Matcham!"

He pursed his lips, shook his head, and subsided into thought.

In the meanwhile a tragic issue was enacting in a little room off the hall.

"Yes, my dearest girl," said Archibald, "he refuses to hear another word until I can bring proof that I've scored, off my own bat, as much as a hundred pounds in a single day."

"Why," said Kate, looking up through her tears; "that shouldn't be so very difficult. Did he limit you to the means?"

"Certainly not."

"Borrow it of me, then."

"My dear, is that moral? Besides, it wouldn't be making it."

"I don't know. There's nothing I wouldn't value one of your precious letters at."

"Yes, my Kate. But don't you see how for you to give me a hundred pounds for one, would be sort of robbing Peter to pay Paul?"

"Why?"

"Why? I should borrow from you to give to you. We might as well take in one another's washing."

"Really, Archie!"

"It's a proverb, my dear, about the wives of Scilly."

"Well, I'm sure it's silly enough for anything. But I'd rather you'd waited till I was your wife."

"Now I've offended you. Good God! and I've already, I'm afraid, put my foot in it with your father. I'm a failure all round."

"Hush! It was thoughtless; but don't be agitated. What did you say to him?"

"He asked me how much I'd ever earned in a day; and I blurted out, quite forgetting, the sum I'd received from *The United Family* for 'Love's Nursling.'"

"Mr. Matcham's paper?"

She looked at him aghast.

"That was unwise—but—"

She dwelt a little, pondering on his eyes. Kate certainly covered a multitude of paternal sins. She was a very sweet homely girl, with just a fragrant genius for domesticity. Her surname was her least lovable possession, and even that greeted one with a hug. While she gazes in silence, we will slip in a parenthesis.

Mr. Huggins and Mr. Matcham—the latter proprietor-editor of *The United Family* magazine—were brother masons, near neighbours on Brixted Common, and deadly enemies in spite of everything. Their mutual hostility turned upon a question of land-grabbing. Mr. Huggins had arrogantly enclosed within posts and rails

a strip of public green, situated beyond the haw-haw which termi-
nated his front lawn on the Common side, and Mr. Matcham, a
furious democrat, had called him a thief in consequence. That had
been sufficiently offensive; but the word had carried, and had been
intended to carry, a bifurcated sting, the second point of which
touched upon an unfortunate occurrence which had lately further
complicated the relations of the two. Mr. Huggins, present master
of the local masonic lodge to which they both belonged, had, about
a week before the date of this narrative, been entrusted with the
care of some official badges (antiques, and of very considerable
value), which he had promptly gone and lost. He had carried them
home in a cab, from which he had duly conveyed them into his
house (of that he was certain); and thereafter they were not. Such
was his story, and such was nobody else's belief. The loss was serious, the scandal grave. There were whispers of unhallowed merriment at the dinner which preceded this catastrophe. There were
whispers of a man who had dined too well. The cabman who had
conveyed this man—Mr. Huggins, to be frank—home, was found
and cross-examined to no purpose—by the defaulter himself, that
is to say. But to others he told, in self-defence, a dark and, paradoxically, an illuminating tale of an inebriated fare who, deposited at the gates of his own drive, wrestled for some time unavail-
ingly with the simple latch of a swing gate, and finally, having
mastered it, tacked his way housewards by a series of cannons from
tree to tree. Then appeared an advertisement, offering a reward of
two hundred pounds for the recovery of the jewels, and no questions asked. No questions asked! Scandal should think not, indeed!
A disgraceful business altogether. He had never conveyed the
packet into his house at all. Probably he had dropped it, getting
into or out of the cab, and it had been snatched by some prowling
loafer. Possibly the cabman knew more about it than he would tell;
possibly, even, tea-broker and cabby were in collusion. The jewels
were worth an astonishing sum, which grew in immensity from day
to day. Ugly, and quite unjustified, slanders pierced to Mr.
Huggins's ears, and he recognised, or believed he recognised, in

their propagator his injurious neighbour. Judge if Mr. Dalrymple's ingenuous confession predisposed him in favour of that suitor.

Kate smiled into her lover's eyes. She was already a beautiful rebel. Unknown to her father, she had regularly and loyally taken in *The United Family* ever since the appearance of "Love's Nursling" in its pages. She referred to it now.

"Do you know," she said, "that there is a treasure-disc story running through it at this very moment?"

"No," said Archibald.

"But there is, dear; and a hundred pounds (isn't it strange?) hidden somewhere for anybody who can find the clue. Archie, it's a providence! Find the hundred pounds, and I am yours! Pa never goes back on his word."

Pa, having, in a fit of profound abstraction, forgotten the two, now suddenly awoke to his remissness, and was heard noisily approaching. The young man stared between joy and bewilderment.

"To wring it out of Matcham!" he whispered ecstatically. "It would be a double triumph! I'll do it, Kate; I'll find it, if I have to turn grave-digger!"

He bolted before a portentous cough, tip-toeing away on winged though varnished feet.

That night he set to studying those current and back numbers of *The United Family*, which enshrined the clue so far as it had got. Before another fortnight was passed, he had mastered, with the final number of the story, the momentous problem. He seemed sure of the fact. He rose from his last perusal with a sort of choking gasp. The scent appeared to lie in so ridiculously obvious a direction, that he could not but plume himself on his own facile perspicacity in detecting it. He was cleverer, after all, than he had dared to suppose himself, than any other had seemed to suppose him to be. But, at the same time, he stood aghast before a revelation his discovery embodied. For it was patent, to him at least, that the disc-voucher for the hundred pounds was hid somewhere in Mr. Huggins's illegal enclosure on Brixted Common! In a flash he understood all the fiendish ingenuity of the plan. The deadly

Matcham had designed this way of testing the right of his enemy to exclude the public from the plot in question!

It complicated matters; but it must be gone through with now, since Kate was the priceless guerdon of success. So, armed with a long-handled spud, artfully concealed in a wrapping of brown paper, he took train the next morning for Brixted, and, fervently praying that the tea-broker might already have departed for town, made his way, tingling, across the Common, uncovering his weapon as he went.

He was rather astonished to find its lonely acres unusually populated at that early hour. A scattered concourse of pedestrians streamed to a focus from every direction. They were mostly of the common sort, hurried and rude in action; and every one was furtively armed with a trowel, hoe, or other implement. Some, even, carried no more than fragments of old iron—a horseshoe for luck, the rusty blade of a table-knife, a two-pronged fork. One woman, with bibulous glazed eyes, held a shawl to her shaking mouth and an iron spoon half-concealed in the folds of it. She was a melancholy illustration of the catering to a hunger which knows no decency. One and all they moved on with a set eager purpose, spectres of a famished lust, hating each his neighbour in the race for gain—a sordid crew.

And then, in a moment, Archie gathered the clue to all this fevered rush, and stopped with a shock. The railed enclosure was black with swarming figures, which stooped and dug like rooks upon a new-ploughed field. He was not the first, it appeared, by a couple of hundred, to strike the obvious trail!

In the same instant he was aware of a sudden disturbance in the group. A stout and furious figure, flourishing a hunting-crop, had sprung into its midst, and, with maddened gesticulations, was scattering it in all directions. But it fled only to reform and hem in its devastator. The situation, literally at a blow, had become menacing.

Mr. Dalrymple's first impulse, in the immediate destruction of all his hopes and plans, was to turn and sneak away. Then a wiser and more generous policy prevailed. Here was his desired father-in-law in peril. He must go to the rescue of the old man. Besides, if he could help to clear Tom-Tiddler's ground!

In his agitation, becoming suddenly conscious of his incriminating spud, he thrust the thing in a panic up the right leg of his trousers, and stuck the end into his sock. Thus besplintered, he made anyhow for the enclosure, and, crossing the chain like a man on stilts, danced up to connect himself with the defence. That, gasping red anathema, was already, it seemed, on the verge of apoplexy.

"Ha, Dalrymple!" shouted Huggins; "I know who's work this is! What the devil, man! Are you a recruit to his ranks?"

The newcomer ranged himself alongside and panted:

"Premonition, sir—couldn't keep away—dreamt you were in danger—and Miss Huggins—come to give a hand."

"To give a hand? What's the matter with your trousers? Damned bad fit, I call 'em! Hoop there!"

He swung his crop, clearing a circle. He was evidently half off his head with fury and excitement. The mob came on.

"Clear out of this, you dashed old hass!" shouted a ringleader.

"Clear out of it? Clear out of my own?" bellowed Huggins. "It's private property, you dogs! I'll have every man jack of you impounded for trespass! I'll ruin you every one!"

"Don't listen to him!" cried a voice on the outskirts. "He'd no right to enclose it; it's common land."

Vicious, glaring, spectacled, combative as a French poodle's, the face of Matcham showed through the press; and the next moment Matcham himself skipped up.

"You hound," roared the tea-broker. "This is your doing!"

Matcham folded his arms.

"It's an honester way to make money than some I've heard of," said he.

"Corrupting the poor!" snarled Huggins.

"Better than compounding a felony," said Matcham.

Mr. Huggins gasped.

"What do you mean by that?"

"Two hundred pounds reward to catch a thief," cried Matcham. "I say, Charity begins at home."

With the word, the two respectable men were at deadly grips, while the crowd hooted and laughed. Shocked and horrified, Archie drove between, with such force as to separate them. The next instant—how, he could never tell—he himself and Matcham were reeling and wrestling together, the furious poodle face of the editor breathing fire into his own. Round they went in a sort of Walpurgis dance, the shrieking voice of the crowd their accompaniment; and then somehow—the strength of the little monster was amazing—they were by the gates of the drive, on the brink of the haw-haw where it ended, and he was flung over and down. The spud cracked as he fell, lacerating his calf. He bowled like a tumbler to the deep bottom of the ditch, where, amongst the ferns and little gorse bushes, he subsided half stunned. Presently he gathered his senses and looked about him.

When, later, he was helped out, by the butler and Mr. Huggins himself, he rose to a consciousness of a cordon of gardeners and policemen ringing the empty enclosure, and of an excluded mob beyond sullenly dispersing or lingering in baffled groups. Mr. Matcham's name had been "taken"; the field, anyhow for the time being, was won. Silently hobbling, he was assisted into the house, and deposited on a chair in the library. Mr. Huggins, near as dishevelled as himself, and infinitely redder, suddenly stood before him, his hands behind his back.

"You've caught it," he said. "Good Lord, man, nobody would take you for a gentleman to see you now. Well, I'm obliged to you, and to this evidence of what you came for."

With a quick action he brought the broken pieces of the spud from behind his back.

"You didn't find the disc?" he said, with a grin.

Archie shook his head.

"No," went on the tea-broker; "and so you're as far as ever, you see, from earning your hundred pounds in a day. O! I understand, and I say I'm obliged to you, for all you came with a different intention. But trust me to take care you don't get the chance again."

Archie rose. He saw suddenly the sweet unbidden face of his love at the door. It was all clouded with trouble and concern. He lifted his hand, and she fled to him, in the uncontrollable impulse to claim and console.

"Hey!" roared her father, starting back. "What the devil's the meaning of this, miss?"

Archie looked firmly over the head bowed upon his breast.

"Never mind the disc, sir," he said. "*I* claim the two hundred pounds reward."

Kate trembled in his arms; but he held her close

"The— What do you—?" gasped the father.

"For the lost badges, sir."

"Where are they?"

Groping in his inner breast-pocket, the young man produced a small brown-paper parcel, torn and sodden. The tea-broker, as in a dream, held out his hand for it.

"I don't understand," he began stupidly. "Where did you find—?"

"In the haw-haw—at the end, under the gate. There's two hundred pounds to me, made in a day. I shall have to ask you to reconsider my case, sir."

A thrilling pause succeeded.

"I don't remember—" began the man who had dined too well; then stopped suddenly, seemed to realise in a moment all that it meant to him both of shame and triumph, gave quite a foolish little laugh, flushed distinctly through his earlier red, and, turning, softly tip-toed from the room, leaving the two together.

Now, ultimately, adds history, Mr. Dalrymple, the public being excluded from the enclosure, rooted up the treasure-disc at his comparative leisure, which so delighted Huggins, for the final means it gave him to retort on Matcham, that he consented without further demur to a union which had never really been very remote from his wishes.

The Poison Bottle

"As well look for green peas in March as for sentiment in a Government analyst," says Sergeant Dyce in his autobiography; yet that that phenomenon may occur is proved in the personal reminiscences of the late Professor Ganthony, some extracts only from which have appeared in the public prints. From what remains we are free to select the following passages, in irrefutable testimony to the existence of that verdant spot in the constitution of the great pathologist; and it is with the purpose rather to vindicate their narrator's memory from a charge of moral insensibility, than to recapitulate the evidences in a pretty recent *cause célèbre*, that the choice is made. The allusion is to what the reader will remember as the Footover Poison-bottle case.

As curious and touching a case as any in my experience, says the Professor, was that of young Langdon. I refer to it particularly, because circumstances brought me into unwonted association with some parties to the affair, and to the knowledge, connected with it, of as strange an instance of youthful clairvoyance as might be related.

Young Harry Langdon was the heir presumptive to the Langdon baronetcy and estates, at that time enjoyed—save the irony of the term—by his great-uncle Sir Hugh Langdon, who was a childless widower and paralytic. The boy was, I understand, a particularly bright intelligent youngster of fourteen at the time of his death, which was due to poisoning by cyanide of potassium. I received officially—here follow some details which may be omitted—and

199

attended the inquest in due course, to give my evidence. It was plain enough, for all my concern in the matter; painfully plain, moreover, it appeared, from the ex-professional point of view. The boy, with his little sister Marjory, had been on a visit to Langdon Court, South Hampshire, a county famous for its lepidoptera. Naturally he had started to make a collection of butterflies—bug-hunting, in the modern vernacular; and had secured for his lethal purposes one of those squat wide-mouthed bottles—containing a deposit, to about a tenth of their depth, of inspissated cyanide of potassium—which are used by collectors to kill their insects when netted. This bottle had been found upon the poor young fellow's dressing-table, incident upon the discovery of its owner's body lying dead in an arm-chair near the fire-place. The cork was out; the stuff at the bottom showed unmistakable signs of having been prodded and raked at, and the boy's own penknife, smeared with the poison, lay beside. Circumstantially the case was clear. Moved by one of those reckless explorative appetites to which youth is subject, attracted, no doubt, by the sweet almondy or peach-stony savour of the stuff, he had dared to taste, and had paid with his life for his mad temerity. The supposition was quite plausible. Indeed it is a frequent matter for wonder with me that unconsidering youth does not more often than happens fall a victim to the thousand temptations, in the way of insidious foods and drinks, which assail it. My evidence, I say, was clear and unequivocal. The only other, of local importance, was contributed by William Brash, Sir Hugh's butler. It is necessary, before detailing this man's sworn testimony, to say a word as to the circumstances surrounding the case.

These two children, Harry and Marjory, were, it appeared, the only offspring of a widowed lady of adequate but not considerable means. The boy had been educated in virtual ignorance of his presumptive title to the baronetcy, and his fateful visit, with his little sister, to the Court, had been his first and last. It seemed that Sir Hugh, with the perversity of a sick-grained valetudinarian, had fought, until nearing his end, against the acknowledgment of his heir in the person of a remoter scion, and had only succumbed to the inevitable when that became obvious. Then, with what grace he could recover, he had sent for the children to visit him, and, from making a virtue of necessity, had come to take a delight in the bright fearless boy. The end had been at least as great a shock to him as to his household at large; to the mother it had come, of course, as a potential death-blow.

Langdon Court lies pretty sunk and secluded among the heathy environs of the New Forest. Its owner, at the period of the calamity, was living in a considerably self-restricted state, and much of the house was shut up. Visitors, the few who came, were accommodated in a wing of the building remote from the neighbourhood of the nervous and suffering invalid, and but few servants were kept. Of these few, William Brash was the principal. He had been in Sir Hugh's service some two years when I saw him. He was a slow, large man, reserved of speech and with a very quiet manner. His face was round and impassive, with close black eyebrows, and a projecting lower lip. He had extraordinarily thick hands; and, when he turned, one saw a regular tonsure, like a monk's, sunk in the crown of a very thicket of hair. It was due to an old scurvy, I believe, and not to natural baldness. It is his evidence to which I now come.

William Brash deposed to his pleasant intimacy with the deceased, who, he declared, with some hesitancy of emotion, was as handsome-spoken a young gentleman as one might wish to serve. The visit of the young lady and gentleman had extended to a fortnight when the disaster happened. During the last week of this fortnight Master Harry had developed an extraordinary interest in butterfly hunting, and, latterly, had got him, Brash, to procure him a poison-bottle, the one in question, from the local chemist in Footover. He had obtained it to command, had duly signed the book, and had handed over his purchase to the young gentleman on the evening preceding that morning of the fatal discovery. He was perfectly sure of the circumstances in their every detail. He had returned rather late, and had gone straight, by direction, to Master Harry's bedroom, where he found the boy busy in writing letters. He had placed the bottle on the dressing-table, and was about to withdraw, when Master Harry had detained him with a request for stamps, having none of his own, and it being too late to disturb his uncle. He had gone and procured the stamps desired from his own room, had returned with them to the young gentleman, and had seen him place them on his letters, which he had handed over to him, Brash, there and then, to put with the night post. They had been five in number, and had been addressed, one to his mother, and the other four, he thought, to provincial dealers in insects, of whom Master Harry, by his uncle's sanction, had more than once already bought specimens. He had then bidden the young gentleman good night, and had retired to his own part of the house, which was comparatively distant. The boy had been placed by himself, rather remote, in the west wing of the building. It was a housemaid who, coming with the hot water the next morning, had made the dreadful discovery. And so the matter ended. Incidentally it was demonstrated that the bottle still held its poison-label firmly attached, though some reference, unjustifiable, I think, was made to the inconspicuous position of the warning. The remainder of the evidence was of a piece with that quoted, and in the end the jury gave in their verdict of death by misadventure.

But before this happened, there had occurred one most curious little scene.

I suppose the minutest enquiry into cases of sudden and violent death, even where the face of the circumstances surrounding them appears plain as day, is persistently to be advocated; elsewise any suspicion of laxity in this respect would surely encourage the wrongdoer. Instances have occurred within my knowledge where a scrap of purely formal testimony, so regarded, has put an entirely new complexion upon hitherto accepted facts; and I have known more than one conviction result upon a chance insinuation offered at the eleventh hour. Nevertheless, it was, I confess, with a certain qualm that I heard the deceased's little sister called upon to give her atom of formal evidence, and a word of protesting pity was near coming to my lips when I saw the child brought forward by a servant. She stood up there before us all in her black frock, the most pathetically attractive little body one could imagine, with her solemn round face, full of fear and trouble, and the plentiful brown hair rolling down to her shoulders. The coroner, of course, designed to be very brief and gentle with her. His questions merely touched upon her knowledge of her brother's propensities in the matter of reckless experiments with forbidden things, and of any possible previous instance she might recall in which he had made himself ill by a venture of the like sort. Her answer, soft and infantine, took the court like a shock of electricity. Hal wasn't like that, she said; Hal didn't kill himself; it was Cousin Francis killed Hal.

I think for a minute a bluebottle in the pane had the silence all to himself. Then the coroner bent forward very quiet and serious.

"My dear," he said, "aren't you talking wildly? You must tell me who is Uncle Francis."

The little girl's lip came out and her lids down. She twined her fingers together. The attendant maid bent to catch her faltering whisper, and answered for her:

"She says she saw him look into her room that night when she was asleep, sir; and he had a bottle in his hand, which he shook at her, and then went on with it to Master Harry's room."

"When she was asleep?"

"I expect it was just a bad dream, sir—not that night, but since."

"I expect so too. Who is this Uncle Francis?"

But, before answering that question, the maid had to be sworn in.

So I describe her; but I had erred, it seemed, in my estimate. Miss Roper was, in fact, a sort of governess-companion in the Langdon, the visiting Langdon, household. She had not accompanied her charges at the first; but had arrived a day or two before that which was to terminate their visit, and had remained to represent the bereaved mother, hopelessly stricken down in her home, at the inquest. She presented the appearance of a sallow, dull-faced young woman, with hard steady brown eyes gleaming over dusky crescents, and with small-boned limbs. She was so austerely dressed, in a habit approaching that of a hospital nurse's, that my mistake was natural. Her accent was refined, but her speech reserved almost to lifelessness.

Her evidence amounted to little; but it was conclusive. Uncle Francis was her employer's deceased husband's half-brother. She knew little of him—certainly little to his credit; but his character, for good or bad, could be nothing to the point, inasmuch as he had emigrated to America some eighteen months before, and, to her sure knowledge, was there still. Once, on the eve of his departure, he had visited the Langdons for a few days, when, it was true, the little girl had developed against him one of those instinctive antipathies to which children are wont; and she supposed that this haunting impression was to account in the child's mind for the fancy which had overcome it under abnormal conditions of terror.

So we all thought; and there the matter ended. The verdict was delivered, with all the appropriate expressions of sympathy, the poor small body put to sleep in the family vault; and, a day or two later, the little girl was taken home by her governess.

Now circumstances, which are neither here nor there, had detained me in Footover; and, so it chanced, my arrival on the platform was coincident with that of the two travellers. I observed that the woman recognised me; but I had no thought of her taking any further interest in my presence until we entered the Basingstoke train, when I found her deliberately following me into the compartment, an empty one, which I had selected. She acknowledged my formal bow with a salutation as grave, but showed no intention to speak, until, presently, the little girl fell asleep in her arms. And then, all in a moment, she seemed to flash into an intensity of being, and, looking across, addressed me in a low hurried tone.

"Please to pardon me; the time is so short, but, to me, so opportune. I want to know so much. He died of that poison? There is no doubt whatever about that, is there?"

Professionally I am insusceptible to surprise—habitually on my guard against it. My pulses just gave a little surge and regulated themselves.

"You heard the verdict given," I answered quietly. "In my opinion it was a just one."

She seemed to gulp, putting a hand to her bonnet-strings as if to adjust them. My demeanour, I am sure, gave no token of the wonder within.

"We shall see," she said. "If there is a God of Vengeance not too jealous to make a woman His instrument, we shall see, perhaps."

I did not answer, while she struggled to control herself. Presently she tightened her arm, inexpressibly fond, about the sleeping child.

"As I love this stricken one," she said, much more quietly now, "so by many degrees of priority did I love the other. So frank, so brave, so sensible, and to commit the act of a gluttonous lunatic! Did I know him or not? He never took the poison of his own free will."

I was startled from my reserve.

"You must hold your tongue," I said sternly. "You are suggesting nothing less than murder."

"Nothing less," she answered.

"Then," I said, "I refuse to listen to you. If you have knowingly withheld any evidence—"

"None," she broke in. "But why did this child have her dream?"

At that I was as much relieved as disturbed. I believed that the poor woman's mind was unhinged by the catastrophe. I sought to humour, to mollify her.

"You yourself supplied the reason, a very plausible one, I think," I answered.

"I!" she said scornfully. "Was it my policy, do you suppose, to speak my suspicions? There are wicked powers that can be exerted from a distance—even half across the world. It has never occurred to you, I am sure, that by the removal of our darling, this man, this Uncle Francis, becomes the heir presumptive to the title and estates?"

I stopped her peremptorily.

"I will listen to no more. Lunatic nonsense—you must forgive me. I—"

The train began to slow down. She leaned forward a little.

"If," she repeated low, "He will condescend to make a woman His instrument. Mad I may be—such grief could not keep its reason—but the mad can hate. Look in the papers."

I protested; she hushed me down, ineffably sweet and tender in a moment with her waking charge. At the last, as she left the carriage, she turned her head.

"Look in the papers," she repeated, "and perhaps, presently, you will come to see."

I did, and to recognise the truth that it is better for the wrong-doer to have a score of blood-hounds on his track than one vengeful woman.

Some months had passed, and the case in question was long dismissed from my mind, when, taking up my paper one morning, my eyes were confronted with the announcement, "Footover Poison-bottle Case: Starling Sequel: Arrest on a charge of murder," in thundering headlines. I stood open-mouthed a moment, then settled myself to peruse. Before I had read a dozen lines I was already profoundly absorbed; at the finish of the first paragraph I was murmuring to myself, "This is to be my case again"; and, in fact, a communication from the police reached me within the hour.

The contemporary public knows the end; to the new generation, for which I write, a *précis* of the processes by which that end was reached may be not without interest. The inquest had excited considerable comment, and a plentitude of moralising on the inefficiency of the by-laws affecting the sale of poisons. That was all beside the mark, as the following explanation will show. It was elicited, at length, before the magistrate, under examination and cross-examination; but, for the sake of brevity, I condense it into narrative form—a simple matter in reality, since the evidence of the witness-in-chief, Miss Roper, was all that counted in the first degree. It was given with a curious deadly precision—the matter of which I can reproduce, but hardly the manner—and is to be summed up as follows:

"William Brash, arraigned before Mr. . . . on a charge of procuring the death of Henry Langdon by poison, Barbara Roper, witness for the prosecution, gave evidence:

"In the horror of the discovery we had all come into the room, the butler, the other servants and myself. After the first paralysing shock was overcome, I began quietly to take notes. The uncorked bottle stood on the dressing-table, and I looked into it. A faint odour, like almond or peach-kernels, rose to my nostrils. It occurred to me that the marks in the stuff did not tally with the shape of the penknife-blade, opened ostentatiously beside. They had a distinct, though irregular, elliptical form to my eyes, as though produced by the point of a very small scoop or spoon, and afterwards roughly effaced by a sharper instrument. I said nothing about this at the time, but was resolved to go unobtrusively about my observations. I started with two equipments for my task—an utter incredulity as to the deceased's inclination to so insane a deed; an instinctive prejudice or antipathy against the butler. They should have disqualified me, you will say. That is for the defence to prove.

"It was very shortly after—no farther than the next day—that I got upon my clue. I had occasion to go into the butler's pantry, and found William Brash there, smoking. He was to go to his master, and I remained behind. A coat of his, which I had seen him wear after hours, was hanging behind the door. I felt in its pockets and discovered in one of them a curious little instrument, a sort of smoker's combination tool, which consisted of a pipe-stopper, pick and cleaner, the three fastened together by a single pin or swivel. The last was in the form of a miniature spoon, and I put it to my nostrils. Barely, but just distinguishable, the same odour was there to be recognised—the odour of peach-stones. From that moment I knew that William Brash had murdered Harry Langdon.

"There remained the method and the motive. I had my suspicions about the latter; the former, in the meantime, was to be my practical concern. It was quite incredible—to me, at least—that the boy would have allowed the butler to persuade him into tasting a spoonful of the stuff; how, then, and how insidiously, had it been administered? I thought over all the points of the butler's sworn testimony, and decided that it was unlikely that so finished a scoundrel—granting that my theory was correct—would have lied on questions of evidence open to easy proof or disproof. No, he had told the truth, in all its essential details, and to the truth I must look for a revelation of the truth. What was negotiable therein? 'He had found the boy busy in writing letters.' As in a flash of diabolic light, the heart of the mystery was revealed to me.

"He had written five letters, had borrowed stamps for them, and had had them posted. Within a day or two, in fact, answers to four were returned. I secured, privately, the addresses of the senders; and when, having left the court, I was free to act, I visited those addresses. Not one of the senders, as I feared, had preserved the envelope containing his original communication. That was unfortunate; still, my case was clear without such confirmatory evidence. The fifth letter had been written to the boy's mother, and I knew that my employer, Mrs. Langdon, never willingly parted with a scrap of her son's writing. In that one instance the envelope had been preserved, and its testimony was sufficient. As I held it before me, in the privacy of my room, I knew that my theory was justified, and that I had hit upon the truth. The stamp was much discoloured, and it still emitted a faint scent of peach-stones. I maintain that William Brash never delivered the bottle at all to Henry Langdon living; that he probably put the boy off with some excuse of his inability to procure it, and, afterwards, going to his own room for the stamps, smeared their backs with the mixture, and, returning, handed the poisoned paper to his victim, who, passing it over his tongue, was led to encompass his own death. I maintain that the knife and bottle were placed in the position in which they were found after the consummation of the deed, that the remoteness of the room lent itself to the act, and that, according to the medical testimony, the nature of the poison, rapid and deadly in its effects, rendered the perpetration of such a horror practicable. And I maintain, finally, my firm belief that this murder was committed by William Brash not on his own initiative, but at the instance and instigation of another who shall be nameless."

It was the case, exactly as she had said it. Such intuition and deadly persistence struck every one of her hearers, I think, appalled—not least the man in the dock, who collapsed before the terrific figure of the vengeance he had evoked. There was a tremendous scene in court. Pressed as to her last statement, the witness referred to the little girl's vision. "She dreamt it," she said, "on the very night of the occurrence. I implied otherwise at the inquest; but that was for a purpose. I designed to lead those interested off the scent I was following." Cross-examined, she admitted that her antipathy to Uncle Francis, born into existence on the one and only occasion when they had met, was inexplicable according to natural laws. He had been quite debonair and courteous. She was willing to acknowledge that the association of the child's nightmare with the fact of her having ascertained that the person in question had been seen in William Brash's company, on the occasion of his final visit to the Court before emigrating, might have served to antedate her prejudice, at least in the measure of its virulence. But as to his somehow complicity in the deed she declined to alter her opinion.

And she was right again. The denouement—which was for psychologists rather than for sober analytical chemists—was a tremendous business. William Brash, in the hope, the mistaken hope, of his being accepted for King's evidence, made a full confession while awaiting his trial in prison after the magistrate's commitment. It was a very cruel plot he revealed—a plot of calculated and quite inhuman treachery. The murder and the method of it had been circumstantially planned between him and Uncle Francis, now the actual next of kin, fully eighteen months before, the early doom of the paralytic, and the probability of his having his great-nephew over to visit him, having been clearly foreseen. It was William Brash who had first persuaded the boy into starting his collection of insects. His reward for the deed was to have been more than substantial. I never took greater pleasure in helping to hang a man than I did in knotting the noose about that gross criminal neck.

Uncle Francis disappeared—absorbed into the wilds of his adopted country. I once saw a tinted photograph of him, and that was all. It showed a small, neat, red-haired man in a white waistcoat; and if ever one might imagine a weasel in human shape there was the picture of him.

A Cure for Consumption

Uncle John was very poorly; and poorly in a new way for him.
Being an ex-civil servant, Anglo-Indian, he was accustomed to regard his liver as a captious quantity, to be reckoned with on all
occasions of festivity. But this chest trouble, with its continuous
nausea and hacking cough, was something out of his experience,
and frightening because of its novelty. There was consternation in
the house, too, because Uncle John was a favourite, and had only
recently, during the Christmas Day jollifications, proved his full
claim to the title. If it had been the turkey, or the plum-pudding,
or the champagne-punch, he would have known how to meet it with
philosophy; a perpetual cough, to one of his generally sound constitution, was another matter, and one that, morally, rather
"floored" him. He stayed in bed, and meditated somewhat funere-
ally on the proverbial fatness of churchyards during green win-
ters. There had been a good deal of rain in this, and he had shown,
perhaps, some recklessness in his careless exposure of himself to
conditions of damp and sopping feet. A man, especially of his age,
had to learn not to presume upon his long immunities. He was,
secretly, considerably disturbed about his condition.

His married sister, with whom he was staying, pooh-pooh'd his
fears; but he seemed conscious of something significant in the as-
siduity of her attentions. "Saucy," his pet niece, stared at him, when
she was allowed to minister, with preternaturally solemn eyes, in
which was evident the instinctive estrangement of health from sick-
ness. The old family doctor, moreover, gave him no real comfort,

but was elusive about his state, in a pompous, fatherly, and entirely non-committal way. Altogether, Uncle John, disquieted and a little shocked, as all men must be over their first real encounter with the shadows, was beginning to turn his thoughts to the dismalest of contingencies. The thing, after all, always most difficult to teach the individual man is his excessive proneness to death.

It was the night-sweats which finally gave some direction to the doctor's genial speculations. Uncle John did not know when or how the word consumption first sounded in his mental auricula. It seemed impossible, preposterous. That he could have developed consumption, and on such ridiculously trifling provocation! Still, assuredly, there was the pain in his chest, the temperature and, above all, the incessant, worrying cough. He could force no appetite, and began to take on something the aspect of the disease professionally imposed upon him. By the end of the fourth day, dating from the first symptoms, things were beginning to look bad.

On the morning of the fifth, his sister coming to visit him, with "Saucy" obligato, proposed with some diffidence a remedy.

"You may as well try it," she said, "pending the arrival of the London specialist. These old recipes can at least do no one any harm, and at most may give real relief. They were the sum of much simple wisdom. If it was only effective in easing your cough a little! Phillida, if you giggle I shall send you out of the room."

"What old recipe?" asked the invalid querulously.

"It is called 'A good water for consumption,'" answered his sister, "and comes out of an ancient recipe book possessed by Martha Gamage. The good old creature was up nearly all the night before last preparing it for you. Come, take it, to reward her."

Uncle John made a wry face. "I don't fancy these rustic medicaments. Where did she get the book from?"

"O, it's been in her family for generations, she says. Of course, you haven't got consumption; but at least your cough can't be made worse by it. Come."

Uncle John, with a melancholy resignation, sat up in his bed. His cough was really racking him. He was given two large dessert-spoonfuls of a mucilaginous fluid from a bottle, Phillida looking on curiously and expectantly the while.

"There," said the lady. "It wasn't so bad, was it?"

The invalid shuddered, with a decidedly queer look. "No," he whispered heroically.

At that instant the mistress was called away, and Phillida, being bidden to be very careful not to upset her uncle, was left alone with the invalid. She opened upon him with a gleeful precipitancy, producing something from behind her back. "Uncle John! I've got it!"

"Got what?"

"The book that that—that was taken from—what mother gave you. Shall I read it to you?"

"What do you mean? Yes, go ahead."

And Phillida began to read hurriedly:— "'A good water for consumption. Take a peck of garden snails'" (she glanced tentatively at the patient), "'wash them in beer, put them in an oven, and let them stay till they've done crying. Then, with a knife and fork, prick the green from them, and beat the snails, shells and all, in a stone mortar. Then take a quart of green earthworms'" (she looked up, the wings of her little nose quivering: "There were simply millions of them in the garden that night," she said), "'slice them through the middle, and straw them with salt. Then wash them and beat them, the pot being first put into the still with two handfuls of angelico, a quart of rosemary flowers, then the snails and worms'"— she broke off, and hurriedly removing the basin from the washhand-stand, put it on the floor, and shoved it with her foot towards the bed. Then she backed. "There's lots to come," she said.

"Thank you," said Uncle John, after an interval, "I think not; I think that does me, I'm obliged to you."

He was leaning over. He uttered a sudden exclamation, and sank back upon his pillows. "Sixpence, by Jove!" he said.

The young lady gave a shriek, dropped the book, and clapped her hands.

"There!" she cried, "I knew you'd swallowed it in the pudding. And now all the money's accounted for."

An Apostolic Catspaw

Simon Patrick episcopus, expository theologian, practical divine, and, since the nonjuring clearance of 1690, Bishop of Ely, came rolling in his great strap-hung coach towards the gates of his townhouse in Holborn. It was not the Holborn of to-day, by any means. The cluster of streets encroaching on the episcopal preserves, and dating from but a few years back, though already a lusty earnest of the life to come, still left to Ely Place something of its pleasant aspect of rural isolation. If the palace no longer stood, as in Tudor times, in the midst of "vineyards, meadows, kitchen-garden and orchard," there was yet enough grass and timber about its shorn splendours to dispute very rustically the increasing impositions of the town. Indeed, it resisted those so stubbornly that almost into our own times there survived some fragments of the ancient buildings, to testify to the enduring nature of the struggle carried on in that district between *rus* and *urbs*.

Grave, kindly, human—if a little pompous, as befitted his office—Bishop Patrick stood well for that period of moral transition when the Church, free, and finally, from a degrading coercion, was beginning to look to its own unfettered responsibilities. He was a scrupulous pastor, a voluminous pamphleteer, he loved nothing better than to meet and defeat a waverer on his own grounds of schism. And no doubt that weakness of his was well known to an irreverent scamp who here appears upon the scene.

The Bishop's coach, turning into Hatton Garden—one of the then newly constituted streets—found itself held up for a few minutes by the press of the throng, and the Bishop, in order to ascertain the cause of the stoppage, put his venerable head, bonnetted in a wig like a fat puff-ball, out of the window. Beyond the ordinary congestion of traffic there appeared to be nothing to account for the delay, unless it might be the local interest concentrated on a little group of men at altercation hard by. These men were three in number, two of them rough and ill-kempt fellows of a dubious aspect, the third, of a disputative cast, being a rather overdressed macaroni, displaying, through a wide-flung waistcoat, a lavish bosom of lace, and wearing, tilted back on his head, a rich three-cornered hat with feathered edges. This was in fact, though quite unknown to the Bishop, no less a person than Mr. Joseph Haines, playwright and comedian, one-time keeper of a droll-booth at Bartholomew Fair, Pepys's "incomparable dancer," and in general popular scapegrace and daredevil wag. He was very red and voluble, appearing to expostulate with the others in a manner marked by much vehement emphasis and gesticulation, while the two stood stolidly listening but unconvinced.

"Bustle about, bustle about!" cried the coachman from his box. "Way for his Lordship of Ely there!" "Way for his Lordship of Ely!" bawled the footman over the coach roof.

The voluble disputant turned sharply round, took in the situation, re-faced his recalcitrants, appeared to persuade them to something, and came hurriedly towards the carriage, the others following pretty closely at his heels.

"My lord," he said, putting his head in at the window; "my lord"—in a confidential undertone. "I presume upon your lordship's well-known disposition to proffer a request. Here are two poor fellows of my acquaintance, more waverers than sinners, who are so tormented between truth and disbelief, so torn by scruples and racked by despair, that, if nothing intervenes, they are like to make an end of themselves. I have wrestled with them to no purpose; but if your lordship—"

It was to touch the pious soul on his tenderest, and perhaps vainest nerve. Certainly there seemed something in the face addressed to him not all compatible with the godly purposes the lips conveyed. Yet who was he to judge of a Christian by his exterior? He looked very kindly towards the two hovering in the background:—

"Very well," he said, and called to the pair of doubters:

"You men, come to me at ten o'clock to-morrow morning and I will satisfy you."

The fellows pulled a forelock apiece to his lordship, the coach rolled on, and Mr. Haines, turning triumphant, swept off his hat with ironical unction.

"You saw and heard, bully-huffs?" said he. "So God and my cousin quit ye"; and with that he swaggered away.

Punctual to their appointment, the men came to be shown in to his lordship on the following day. He had his pamphlets "Parable of the Pilgrim," "The Friendly Debate" and another, on the table before him. He was a busy man, and he lost no time over preliminaries. "Now, my friends," said he, "what are your difficulties, your scruples of conscience? State them as clearly and briefly as you may."

The fellows gaped, and one of them pulled a paper from his hat.

"Scruples be blowed!" he said. "This here's the writ, and this here the amount of debt and costs—suit of Sampson and Lilly—that your lordship engaged to pay on behalf of your cousin."

"My cousin!" exclaimed the astounded Bishop: "what cousin?"

"What cousin?" said the man. "Why Joe Haines, to be sure—him that we'd arrested yesterday for a debt of twenty odd pound, when your lordship came by and offered to settle the bill."

"*I* offered?"

"Didn't your lordship say, 'Call to-morrow at ten o'clock and I'll satisfy ye'?"

"I never meant it—not in that way!"

"Zounds, then! In what way? Sure your lordship's not going back on your word, and the gentleman your own cousin!"

"He is not. I don't know him from Adam. I had never to my knowledge seen him in my life before."

"Never seen him—not Count Joe? Phew!" The bailiffs—bandogs in popular parlance—looked at one another in dismay. "Another of his tricks, Jimmy," says one— "He's been and sharped us again." Then he turned on the cleric: "'There's my cousin,' he says to us— 'the Bishop of Ely. Let me but speak to him, and I lay he'll go bail for me.'"

The Bishop's hand dropped rigid on the third pamphlet lying before him— "The Christian Sacrifice" it was entitled.

"Well," he said, with a sigh. "It is an unscrupulous rogue; but if it appeared that my word was pledged before witnesses—sooner than innocently propagate a scandal—"

He rose, and went reluctantly towards a locked armory in the wall.

COX'S PATENT

Mr. Gaster, manager of the Barstock branch of the Counties Deposit Bank, sat in his official snuggery one dusky November evening. It was past four o'clock and closing time, the last of the staff had departed, and the Bank porter was in the act of securing the doors, when the sound of hurried voices accosting the man became audible to the manager in his den.

Probably some belated customer appealing uselessly to the inflexible Williams. Mr. Gaster sat tight, impatiently awaiting the intruder's withdrawal. He was a bachelor; he lived on the premises, and a cosy fire and an attractive novel before dinner appealed to him irresistibly from the upper storey. In person he was small, with a somewhat droll face, thin staring hair, and red eyebrows that came close together. They met now in a rather petulant frown.

"Do, for goodness' sake, clear out," he muttered to himself.

But the colloquy continued, and, driven beyond patience, the manager rose, opened his door and looked out. There were two men in altercation with the porter at the half-closed entrance. Beyond in the street throbbed the lungs and shook the lights of a motor-car. "What is it, Williams?" called the manager.

"They say they must see you, sir," answered the porter, half turning. "I tell them it's past closing time and agen the rules."

"Who are they?"

"One's a police-officer, sir."

Mr. Gaster stepped to the door. "Well?" he said.

217

"Can't we see you private, sir?" protested one of the strangers—he in uniform. "We don't want to raise a scandal."

"Scandal about what?"

"Marston's the name, sir. Your head cashier, isn't he?"

"Well; he's away on a holiday."

"He is," said the stranger emphatically; "on a holiday—a rare one."

"Come into my room, will you? Williams; wait there and keep
the door on the latch for a little."

Mr. Gaster led the way to his sanctum, and the visitors followed.
Motioning them in, he closed the door and turned to regard the
two. The one who had spoken stood square and upright, patently
the expressionless official, spotless and self-possessed—by his trim
silvered cap and beltless jacket an inspector; the other, a tall, bent,
rather gasping weed of a man, in a long tight-waisted brown coat,
was, as Mr. Gaster learnt, a plain-clothes detective.

"Who are you?" demanded the manager.

"Inspector Jarvis, sir, of the Southsea police. This here's P.-C.
Billiken. We've got your gentleman under observation at Southsea."

"Mr. Marston?"

"Mr. Marston."

"He's stopping there, is he? And why have you got him under
observation, inspector?"

"For suspicions of our own, sir, aggravated by a chance discovery."

"What's that? I understand nothing of your implication at
present."

"Why, sir, when you see a young Bank gentleman going it on
his holiday, putting up at the best hotel in the place, flinging his
money about in every direction, and spending seemingly at the rate
of five thousand a year, you begin nat'rally to ask yourself questions. That's what the manager of the 'Portland' did, and the failure of a satisfactory answer worried him. He came to me, bringing
with him a piece of evidence that one of the maids had found in
the gentleman's room tucked among his collars."

"What was that?"

The inspector produced from his breast a folded canvas bag, which, on examination, was seen to be imprinted with the Bank mark and number.

"Did that or did that not come from here?" he demanded.

"It looks like it," said the manager. There was a note of keen distress in his voice, apparent for the first time.

"You recognise it for the Bank's property?"

"Yes."

"It is such a bag as is used to contain money—gold?"

"Yes."

"Had Mr. Marston free access to the strong room?"

"I see what you mean. For all practical purposes—yes."

"Ah!" The inspector drew himself up from the hips, like a man relieved. "It give us the clue, that did. I thought I'd run over and make sure. Now, sir, the rest lies with you. Take my word for it, where the place of that ought to be you'll find a hole—possibly a row of holes."

"It's easily proved. You had better come with me and look."

He turned stiffly, obviously in part to command the emotion with which this ugly revelation of a crime had overcome him. "I hope you are mistaken, inspector," he said, a little hoarsely. "It is a terrible charge—a terrible charge. And I had such complete faith in the man."

He took some keys from a safe in the wall, and silently motioned the two men to follow him. As they obeyed, the inspector just glanced at the detective and the detective at the inspector.

The manager, leaving his room by the back, led the way across a little lobby to a flight of iron stairs, which descended thence to the basement. At the bottom he unlocked a massive iron door, which, being opened, admitted them into a little close compartment, a mere four-square cell hewed out of fireproof cement, having the chilled steel door of the strong-room sunk in its further side. Switching on the electric light, he then closed and secured the first door, before proceeding to unlock and swing open the second, when the great maw of the strong-room yawned upon the visitors like the mouth of some cold subterranean monster. Mr. Gaster, leaving the key in the lock, stepped in.

It was a wonderful place, eloquent of a profound and impregnable security; solitude fast-locked in an eternal mausoleum; sunk out of human reach like a treasure barque foundered in fathomless waters, and hugging its massed riches in a silence that no voice of man, no throb of life's pulses could penetrate. There were stacks of strong-boxes here, arranged on grilles, each box classified and docketed, the property, on deposit, of some customer of the Bank. There were safes within the safe, and, beyond all, a night of impenetrable darkness.

The manager, inserting a key into a hole in the wall, disclosed a recess loaded shelf above shelf with canvas bags such as that produced by the inspector; only these bulged, and were fat with inviolate opulence. He ran his eyes along the orderly rows. "No sign of despoliation here," he said—and, with the word, felt himself caught from behind in a staggering grip. He recognised the truth on the instant, and after the first shock did not even struggle.

"Right you are," said the voice of the weedy stranger, speaking, and for the first time, into his ear. "I've got him, Jemmy, tight as a trivet. Bale out the swag while I hold on."

The pseudo-inspector needed no urging. He cleared the safe of its treasure, bag by bag, throwing each as he removed it upon the floor of the cemented cell.

"How many can we carry, Tim?" said he. "We've got to guy the porter, mind you."

"Trust to my blessed coat-skirts. I've got the strength of a dozen porters in me."

Mr. Gaster, resigned to his hopeless position, fully endorsed the statement. The man's strength, for all his slack appearance, struck him as infernal. He felt as limp as a mouse in a cat's jaws.

"Nip his weasand there if he squeals," said Jemmy.

"I'm not going to squeal," said the manager. "Nobody could hear me if I screamed my lungs hoarse. What are you going to do to me?"

"No harm, if you keep quiet," said Jemmy. "How about the flimsies, Tim?"

"Leave 'em alone, boy. I'm all for real property, and we've got our bellyful. Now, mister, by your leave?"

The bags were all out, scattered upon the cell floor. Gaster, reading a sudden determined purpose in the eyes turned upon him, struggled in the deadly grasp.

"Good God!" he cried, "you are never going to do such a diabolical thing?"

"Aren't we, though!" said the weedy man. "Where's the harm. The porter won't be long in smelling a rat; and there's plenty cubic feet of air for you to draw on in the meantime. Come, you little devil!"

Actually they were going to shut and lock him into the strong-room. The cruelty of the deed roused the manager to frenzy. He fought and maddened in the merciless grip. It was all of no avail. In a moment he was thrust in and the key turned upon him.

"Phew!" said Tim, giving a little dry whistle. "What a spitfire!" He looked gloatingly upon the heaped bags and began to unfasten his coat. It was accommodated within the skirts with a number of ingeniously contrived pockets, so calculated and placed as to give little hint of the weighty secrets they might contain. "Now for the loading, Jemmy."

It took the two a considerable time to dispose to their satisfaction as much of the swag as they could safely carry; but at length the task was completed.

"Now, sonnie," said the uniformed criminal, "you go first, and I follow, pretending, as I come, to speak back to the gentleman. Savvy?"

"Go on, Jemmy. I wasn't pupped yesterday."

"Where's the keys, then? O! in the lock."

He took the little bunch from the strong-room door, and stepped across to the door of the cell, whose wards he manipulated for some time without result.

"What," he said, "the hell's the matter with the thing?"

"O, here! let me try," said the other impatiently. "It needs a little coaxing, that's all."

But he too had to desist after some minutes of barren prodding and twisting.

"There must be some trick in the blamed thing," he said. "I've tried every blessed key on the bunch, and—"

"We shall have to ask him."

"Ask— Hullo, Jemmy. I've got it!"

"Got it open?"

"No. There must be a second bunch, that's it, and he's taken it in there with him."

He came erect. The two rogues stood grinning at one another.

"To think," said Jemmy, "of the cust little sharp hoping to gammon us like that!"

"We must have the things off him."

"No question of it. Unlock the strong-room again, my boy."

The tall man took a hurried step, drove in the key, swung open the door.

"Here, you, Gaster!" he called into the depths. "Come out of that. We want you."

No answer whatever was vouchsafed.

"He's skulking," said Jemmy. "Or—God o' mercy, he can't have died of fright!"

There was an electric switch just within the cavern. He hastily snapped it on, and the gloom sprang into light. Together they plunged in.

Not a sign, not a sound of the captive anywhere. He had vanished utterly.

Suddenly Tim uttered a stifled roar:

"Here's another door in the wall!"

It was placed further in at right angles to the first—placed handy for any such emergency as this. They had boxed up the manager, with the means to his own escape lying ready in his pocket. And he had got them securely trapped between two impassable exits.

"Goosed us, by thunder," whispered Tim. They stared at each other in blank dismay. Here, with all the treasures of the Bank opened to their choice, they were worse than condemned paupers. They could only stand and curse one another's insanity, waiting for the end.

It came soon enough. As, in a last frantic effort to falsify their own convictions, they were striving feverishly once more to force the outer lock, the door was swept open upon them and there on the stairs thronged quite a posse of constables. The manager was waiting for his prisoners in the office above, when they were brought in to him handcuffed. He rose with a chuckle and a bow.

"Cox's patent, gentlemen," he said. "It was most considerate of you to have left me in possession of the second bunch of keys. Really I calculated on that, you know, when I decided to lure you into the trap. Your story was extremely convincing; your possession of the canvas bag a real surprise; your scheme altogether very elaborately and cleverly worked out; only, unfortunately for its success, Mr. Marston himself returned to his work this morning—from Broadstairs; and we happened to have tallied together our stock of gold. Cox's patent, gentlemen. Don't forget. It's full of surprises. You will find your chauffeur outside waiting to take you—and himself—to the station."

Deus Ex Machina

"It is simply amazing," ejaculated Strype, lowering his morning paper, like a window, for a breath of fresh air— "*Sim*-ply amazing!" He was of a gaunt, cavernous constitution, bony, prematurely bald, and almost as fleshless as a ladder.

Pouncey, seated at the breakfast table, just glanced at the speaker, and back to his scrambled eggs. A cherubic man he, with a tiny mouth which he fed lusciously, like a crab. This was at Welcome's boarding-house, where the two were long acquaintances.

"This ineradicable belief of man in his creative power!" continued Strype, desperately apostrophising space, his paper held down to his knees.

"I came across a lovely instance of that yesterday," said Pouncey.

"Surely," said Strype, with a glassy eye fixed on the invisible, "the world, until our incredible age, has never known so preposterous a misuse of a term."

"Don't let it affect your health," said Pouncey. "What I was going to say—"

"Pro-creative, if you like," said Strype. "That was a reasonable and sufficient word for our ancestors. It is too impersonal for us—too impersonal for these days of individualism run mad—when we confidently discuss the origin of life, and challenge the Almighty on his own ground."

"What I was going to say—"

"We have dispensed, in our insane arrogance, with the prefix altogether: we create. The poet creates, the novelist creates, the

224

artist, the *modiste*, the actor—he, of all performing apes, the most imitative and insufferable."

"It was this way—"

"Does any one of the gibbering maniacs who use this term so loosely and so flagrantly consider for a moment its meaning and significance? To create is to beget out of nothing."

"Well, that's to say an empty head; and very modest of the novelist to admit it. What I was going to say—"

"To create is the sole province of the One, of the Omnipotent. It is a term single to Him and totally inapplicable to any creature deriving, in spirit and substance, from the work of His hands. Put any one of you scientists, who talk so glibly and so smugly of the near-discovered secret of the principle of life, into an air-pump—"

"There's not one of 'em would go in—not even into a vacuum-cleaner. But what I was going to say—"

"Let him create there. Let him first produce out of Nothingness his life-jelly, or whatever the precious rubbish is called, and then out of Nothingness impregnate it. Stuff!—pernicious, outrageous and impossible stuff! He knows he couldn't do it: he knows that every one of his experiments is based upon given and existing facts, and dependent upon certain laws of chemical combinations, which he accepts as if he himself originated them. Given your materials, you can apply them; but, if the faculty of creation were man's, he should be able to produce actually new materials, and not be dependent on those to whose uses, or possible uses, he was born. His capacity is not to create, but to discover—to ring some new change upon the myriad conceivable changes that matter presents to him."

"Yes, that's true. But to mention my instance—"

"Your poet create—your novelist—bah! He takes what he finds about him, either in character, nature, or idiosyncrasy—there's plenty of choice in a world where no two are, or ever have been, in facsimile—makes a blend after his individual taste, and presents a figure. He has not created it: he has produced a new result out of a novel combination, that is all. And as to your actor"—Strype lifted his *Daily Mail* in his left hand, and smacked it violently with the knuckles of his right— "Listen to this, if you please: 'Mr. Lawrence Theobald, who created the part of Dewbury in *Playful Fanny'"*— he paused, looking towards the other with a grin of fury— "Created!" he whispered hoarsely— "created!"

"Of course," said Pouncey emolliently, helping himself to marmalade, "your play: you wrote it. It was you who created Dewbury."

"These fools would never admit it," said Strype. "It is always the monkey actor who gets the credit for the feat."

"I know. It's infamous. What I was going to say—"

"Well, what?"

"Only *à propos*—what was it? 'the ineradicable belief of man in his creative power.' It extends, it seems, to grocers. I found one out in it yesterday."

"Found one out? How do you mean?"

"Why, I was buying sardines, and a lady came into the shop to give an order. 'By the way,' said she, 'two of those eggs you sent yesterday were bad.' 'Indeed, madam,' answered the man; 'then we'll make them good.'"

"Well?"

"That's all."

"Have you really been interrupting me all this time to—" Strype got up, paused, looked as if about to do something dangerous and stalked rigidly out of the room.

Pouncey, his eyes agape, his cheek bulged motionless on a piece of toast, watched him go.

"I didn't know," he murmured, "I really didn't know that when he talked about the Almighty he meant himself."

Gun Practice

Picture to yourself a waste of troubled sea, grey-green as ploughed stubble, and sown all over with white bosses like scattered stones. The wind is southerly and vicious, the sky stoops torn and low. Away there over the long Bill of Portland stretches a tiny streak, whose ashen under-shadows half obscure, half reveal, a populous city of battleships, as unsubstantial in seeming as lightning-charged clouds. But long ago there was one which, detaching itself from the mists, forged slowly into definite being, and now rests inert, preparing for gun practice, some three miles off the coast of Lulworth where we stand.

To the north you can see the target, in charge of an Admiralty tug. Laboriously the little vessel hauls the floating mark to its ground, moors it in position at a range of some 2,000 yards or so, and casts off. You know the moment by the sudden increase in its speed, patent even at this distance. You can see it pitch and roll, wallowing like a porpoise as it tears away, hidden sometimes for seconds, in a manner to bring your heart into your mouth, then emerging, a blink of sunlight firing its copper funnel, so that it looks like a flaring buoy. It is in a flurry to escape.

Snap! As you look, a light winks from the watching monster, and over the stubble-field rise in succession three little puffs of white dust. Not till the third has sprung up does the slam reach your ears, and by then the engulfed shot is wobbling down to its everlasting rest on the ocean floor.

227

All that you can see or imagine; but what you cannot see or imagine is the tragedy that has occurred between the casting-off from the target and the firing of the first gun. During those hurried minutes a man has fallen overboard, unnoticed, from the tug, and his loss has never been observed until all hope of recovering him from that trackless welter is seen to be a vain thing. The poor fellow has perforce to be abandoned to his fate.

Years after I had the story from this man's own lips. He was one of the strangest looking souls I have ever seen, perfectly colourless, and with his skin all over fine crackles like china. He was young, and yet his hair was white. If a child screamed or a boy whistled near him he would involuntarily duck his head. But his manner was quite quiet, and his voice low.

"It was blowing stirfish when it happened, with a nasty sea. A gust took me under the oilies as I was bending down and, the tug heeling at that moment, lifted me clean over the side like an umbrella. There was one that noticed me with the tail of his eye, and thought it just a tarpaulin flapping. I went down, sir, and the screw thrashed at me, and missed. I had my sea-boots on, and what with them and the oilies I believed I was done. Somehow I came to the top, where I kicked and struggled free of all. But by then, at the rate she was going, and in that wind and sea, the tug was out of hail, even if I'd had a voice to hail her with. I swam after, desperate-like, but she ran away, 20 yards to my one, and it was evident that those aboard hadn't missed me. My God, thought I, it's all over, and I stopped, treading water. Then I looked back and saw the target. With luck I might reach it—and what then? But it was a chance anyway and my only one.

"I wasn't a fanciful man—not then. I reached the target, pretty nigh spent, and clung on to the raft with both hands, gasping to get back my heart. And then suddenly the truth burst upon me. Not that patched triangle of canvas, but I, was the devil's mark for the guns pointing at us a mile and a half away.

"In the first shock of the thought I was for scrambling up on the raft, in the hopes that they might see me and stay their hands. I was clinging to its further side, and I had already got my right knee and elbow hitched over, when I saw a flash in front, and down I went again with a choke. It was a 4-incher, and its last ricochet sent it skipping, with a scream like an engine-whistle, 20 ft. over the target. Safe for that once; and I thanked God for the report that followed. There's no thunder for the ears of the man struck and killed by lightning. Well, now I was in for it—the 4-inchers, eight of them in all, as many Hotchkiss quick-firers, and the Maxims. I knew the armament, and I had to swallow the lot. Likely you can imagine what I haven't the gift to describe. For as long as I could I hung by my hands to the raft, my head no more than above water; but I knew that couldn't last for ever. The time would come when my strength would be all gone, and I should have none left for emergencies. So, while I could do it, I hooked my elbows over the raft and, lying as low as I could, watched the shells coming. Yes, sir, you may wonder at it, but I watched them; and I felt in my forehead, as each flew down, the sort of crawling one gets there when a pointing finger's slowly moved towards it. It was a queer sensation; and a queer sight to see those specks coming out of the flash, and growing from leap to leap—and then over, with a screech and a flop. I felt it then, all alone with the flying devils, and my poor soft body their butt; but I didn't feel a thousandth part of what I felt afterwards when it was finished. The raft ducked and rose like a gull; and the gunners made bad practice, for which I was the only one thankful. But at last it had to be neck or nothing with me. I could hold on no longer; and I had only just strength left to get aboard, where I flopped down and lay like a log. And it was at that moment that there came a hell's crash overhead, and the water leapt all round as if a shoal of mackerel had passed. They had fired a charge of shrapnel, and 'My God,' says I; 'but that does me!'"

But the shot was already out of the muzzle as he climbed from the water, and they had seen him in the act. Then the tug signalled and bore down. He took it coolly, they said, at the time. It was during the long subsequent reaction that the man bleached in that astonishing way. But to one with imagination enough to read between the lines of his unaffected narrative it is perhaps not so astonishing.

JOY-HOMICIDE

High up in the building Valmy sat writing his weekly "turn-over" for a paper to which he contributed. He had a good subject, "Joy-Homicide" (vide the "Joy-rides" of transatlantic motor Thugs), suggested by a recent crime, whose mystery and apparent motivelessness appeared likely to place it within the category, already uncomfortably extended, of insoluble murder problems. An errand boy, of thirteen or fourteen years of age, had been found done to death on one of the seats of the Victoria Embankment, his neck broken and his face smashed to a pulp. The night preceding the discovery of the body had been frosty and foggy, and no clue of any sort existed. The boy had not been a good boy; he had played truant; he had more than once slept abroad: he became absolved, a piteous lamb, an excusable wastrel, in the horrible tragedy of his end. And there seemed no motive whatever for the deed; it was just for the time being a penniless waif, worth nobody's evil attentions. One single *pièce de conviction* was alone to be sought—a green leathern watch-guard, with a silver token-pig attached, which the mother swore to have seen on her boy the day he left her for ever. It had a key at each end for its sole safe-keeping; and it had disappeared. Scarcely an adequate instigation to a crime so foul; yet, such as it was, its tracing was the only hope of the authorities. But it had not been traced.

Valmy entered into his subject with relish; and also with some vague feeling of exultation. It was not only that it was one which gave scope to his enjoyingly analytical and inductive habit of mind;

230

he thought what a gratifying thing it would be if in the process of postulating his theories he should actually hit upon the spoor of the criminal. He would rejoice could he be instrumental in bringing that scoundrel to justice, even though he could do no more than adumbrate the type of mind to be sought for in the connection of unprovoked homicide. It was a beastly crime, under whatever impulse committed, and the kindly, shepherding instinct in him craved for retaliation on the wolf who could so vent his damnable ferocity on a weakling of the human flock.

Killing for joy! That was surely a suggestive theme—an unworked vein. And yet it was a quite plausible hypothesis. For what bloodshed and self-mutilations was not religious exaltation responsible? Excess of joy, like other excesses, was wont to manifest itself grotesquely, indecently, indicating, as it were, an over-oxygenised condition of the moral constitution. Women especially, when intensely exhilarated, would do things, commit hilarious violences, of which they were normally incapable—slap, rend, and shriek with laughter. It was the *joie de vivre*, uncultivated and unrestrained, which moved trippers of the hooligan type to the wanton destruction of trees, turf, and so forth. But a step further was needed, to find them smashing heads and limbs in an uproarious self-abandonment.

He dotted down a few such headings, preparatory to elaborating them into a consecutive thesis. He wrote with a certain difficulty; his hands felt a bit stiff—from rheumatism or something—had been curiously so for days past. What a jerry-built structure was a man, even one like himself boasting great bones and muscles, always to be going wrong in his joists and jambs, and ready to drop to pieces if a brick fell out. He paused a moment, stretched himself and yawned. Certainly his profession was a test of a man's full capacities—at least as he used it for his sins and virtues. It served him for the enormous exercise of body and intellect his sanity required. He might overdo the thing at times—did, he knew, taught by reactions, exhaustions, periods of infernal apathy when he seemed conscious of organic existence as only a torturing immurement in matter. But generally it satisfied the insatiable "go" in him, the craving for movement, variety, sensation, emotion—all things, in fact, which made life living and potential. He was perpetually losing himself in the crowd of his own interests, which was the blest and only state for a soul of his overwhelming nervous virility. Penalties? Well, they were hardly worth considering in the sum of gratifications. He took up his pen again.

Joy-homicide! He could almost understand it—from a psychologic point of view. Men had died from joy: why should they not kill from joy, since joy was thus proved kin to death? Better to kill than, when lifted to the threshold of Nirvana, risk the least recall from that moral supremity. The gods were gods by sacrifice; the lambs must die to vindicate them. He thought suddenly of a picture which had always appealed vividly to his imagination, Titian's "Bacchus and Ariadne," the divine rapture, with its madcap Satyr flourishing a ghastly severed joint. There was the thing epitomised—the delirium, the ecstasy, the bloody holocaust. What was it a limb of? An innocent steer—a once glad young life? Poor beast—poor boy! Joy? Of course, overprojected, it flashed into the opposite pole of rage, bestial and insensate. He had known it to do so in himself more than once, jarred by some extrinsic influence— in himself, a cultured and reasonable creature. There must be something in us all of epilepsy, that mysterious, undiagnosable condition, with its mad ebullitions, its blank stationary intervals, its intensified emotions. One should be careful never to venture one's nerves beyond the reasonable limits; never to over-step the border-line between the normal and the forbidden. To do so meant strange lapses of memory, strange things done and forgotten, but recorded in secret places.

Those opposite poles—the meeting of the extremes in a flash and stunning shock. Joy transcendent—it might be evoked by any recent ecstasy—love, music, the soft intricacies of dancing feet. And yet a sound, a touch, could shatter its perfection, like a drop of grit falling on a lightly sailing bubble. A cough, a sniff, often repeated, would be enough. How he hated a sniffer!

Valmy sat up abruptly, leaned back in his chair, and felt instinctively for his handkerchief. It was not in his pocket. Never mind; there would likely be one in the overcoat hanging on the door-peg. He got up, lifting that shambling-jointed, huge frame of his, as if it were a burden a little in excess of his will-power, and walked to the door. Feeling vainly in one pocket after the other, his fingers caught in something which seemed to communicate a galvanic shock to their tips. One moment he paused, then resolutely drew the thing out. It was a green leathern watch-guard, dangling a tiny silver pig, and carrying a key at each end.

He may have stood a full minute, absolutely motionless, his eyes fixed in an unwinking stare upon the token in his hand. Then very softly he dropped it and walked to the window. It was wide open. Sixty feet below lay the pavement. He put his hands above his head like a bather, and dived out.

Once Too Often

"The Goose that goes too often to the kitchen
ends on the spit."—*Danish Proverb.*

I

Two men, one middle-aged, the other scarce more than a
shrewdly precocious boy, sat breakfasting late together in the
coffee-room of a second-rate hotel at Southampton. Of dingy reputation, the hotel in question happened to be convenient for afflicted
passengers landing from the Channel boats; hence, no doubt, its
chance selection by the elder gentleman, whose sojourn there had
already run into a second day.

This person was large both in body and in presumptive benevolence. His formal dress was that of an English clergyman, serene
and orthodox; his face, with its minute-pupilled and somewhat
blind-looking oyster-grey eyes, was massively blunt-featured, his
smile was perpetual and his manner smooth. His companion, who
had only joined him that morning, and whom he addressed, and
pretty constantly and ostentatiously, as Lord Burnside, was suggested, rather than built, on a small cockney plan. He looked as if
he knew most things, including a capacity for taking care of himself. The table at which the two sat in the dark eating-room was
chosen as being remote from other feeding company; the iterated
title was exploited for the benefit of the dirty waiter alone, who,
being sufficiently impressed by it, communicated, as expected, his

knowledge to the management, and thereby evoked some hovering curiosity in the background.

"Take or leave, Barry, my boy," said the clergyman, the Reverend William Wardroper by name. He was leaning easily across the table; he could impart to the deadliest matter the most casual manner possible, smiling and taking abstracted note of his surroundings while his lips were calculating their every damning phrase. He beamed now at a casual breakfaster, while his fingers trifled with a spoon. "It is just the opportunity of our lives, that is all," he said. "Substitute self-confidence for indecision, and the risk is really not worth the counting. There is positively a providence in it all. *Encore l'Audace*: remember Danton's phrase."

"He was scragged, nevertheless, wasn't he?" said the young man coolly, and he drained his cup. Mr. Barry Smith had been quite reasonably educated. It was not the fault of his training that he lived most of his life in the local booking-office of a London terminus, a machine rather than a man, clipping and flinging out vouchers, himself no more than a voice and an indistinct presence. But he was fond of reading in his midnight hours.

"The knife, my boy," answered the clergyman; "not the rope. A distinction with all the difference in the world. But you must make up your mind."

"Give me the objections again, governor."

"There are none."

"The points, then."

"Listen now. Roger—"

"Ugh! That gives one a nasty turn. There was another Roger I've heard of mixed up in a like business."

"Your risk is next to nothing. I take the bulk of it, you understand. Roger Beck, I say, was a complete nonentity. For years he and his mother had been mere continental wastrels, known to nobody—least of all in their potential connections—poor, unattached, spending their lives in wandering from place to place, and never settling anywhere. It was in Switzerland that I came across them, and, worming myself into their confidence—"

"Trust you for a proper serpent, old man."

"Don't interrupt me again, please. Easily, I say, I acquired with them a sort of confidential position—adviser and travelling tutor in one. The boy was ill-educated; the mother a fond dotard. She never supposed but that impassable barriers separated her lout from the title. It was the realisation of her mistake, I conclude, that killed her."

"That was at Chamonix?"

"Above Chamonix, on the Montenvert. It was late autumn, and the little deserted hotel was preparing to close. I found her sitting dead, with the English newspaper which had informed her of her mistake slipping off her lap. I spotted the tell-tale paragraph, and I kept it to myself."

"Well?"

"The boy—now, unknown to himself, you understand, Lord Burnside—was completely in my hands; ready to do anything I advised. I counselled England; the woman was buried in Chamonix; and then, in order to the restoration of his health and nerves, I despatched my pupil on foot, by way of the Glacier des Bois, to Martigny and the Rhone valley, thence to go on home by rail. I myself was just to settle up our affairs and follow, which I have done."

"A guide went with him."

"To be sure. That Mer de Glace, or Glacier des Bois, is a ticklish place, full of deadly crevasses, four or five hundred feet deep some of them, and very lonely at this time of the year. I trust they got safely over it. But I shall know soon. Terray was to telephone me within a day or so of my arrival here. He knows my address."

"Terray—the guide?"

"A rogue of a fellow," said the clergyman; "a loafer in Chamonix and a half-English alien. I found out something about him that made him fear me more than a little."

The young man was rolling a cigarette, which crackled stickily in his fingers. His face was almost as white as the paper.

"He was to come on to England, too, was he?" he muttered. "A dangerous witness."

"Of what?" said his companion blankly. "If you said a possible murderer, now, I could understand. But he would think twice, wouldn't he, before double-knotting the noose about his own neck?"

Mr. Barry Smith put his cigarette to his lips with a sickly air of bravado; but his fingers shook.

"What next?" he said, in a difficult voice.

The clergyman smiled ineffably. With his elbow leaned on the table, he examined his fingernails with critical nicety.

"I ascertained the name of the lawyers," he said, "and wrote to them before crossing, informing them of my position, of the facts, and stating that I proposed to convey the heir to his inheritance in the course of a few days. Their reply was formal and satisfactory, and I now await no more than Terray's communication to respond to it. That given, and given reassuringly, the rest lies with you."

"I know it does," said the young man, with some desperate sullenness in his tone.

The clergyman lowered his arm, and caressed the other's sleeve lightly with his finger-tips.

"My dear child," he said, in the softest, most ingratiatory voice; "it is for you to choose. Observe, I put no pressure upon you whatever. I might have selected a more competent agent, only that the natural affections prevailed with me. Consider well, however, before you decide, your equipment for the task before you. You have a retentive memory, I know, a fund of cool assurance, and sufficient manners and education to play the part. That you have not more you must attribute not to any parental neglect, but to the chequered nature of a career whose designs for your good have always been greater than its capacities. There, however, you come certainly into line with the character you are proposed to represent. He was no more refined, no better informed than yourself." (It was significant how naturally he fell into the past tense.) "For the rest, circumstances have prepared the ground for us in a way, provided we move with merely reasonable caution, to make a slip impossible. Trust in me. Have you ever known your friend to fail?

You, of all people, should have faith, I think, in my methods. I have given you proof often enough of their efficacy."

"Often enough is the father to once too often," said Mr. Barry Smith, with sententious bitterness.

"Let us suggest rather the grandfather," said the clergyman smoothly. "You never knew your grandfather, I think, Lord Burnside. Ah, waiter! What is it?"

"You're wanted at the telephone, sir," said the man.

Mr. Wardroper rose and, smiling genially, followed his conductor, at dignified pace, out of the room to the secluded instrument. Once secure there in isolation, he put the receiver to his ear.

"Yes; my name is Wardroper," he said. "Who is it?"

"Are you alone?" came the answer.

"Yes, alone. Are you?"

"Yes. I am Terray."

"What Terray?"

"The guide, sir."

"Where do you speak from?"

"London, sir."

"You have something to tell me?"

"It is this. You are safe to go ahead."

The clergyman returned to the coffee-room and to his company. If his glassy eyes shut in any terrific secret, there was only one there capable of interpreting the dim shadow that moved behind them.

"*L'audace, encore de l'audace, toujours de l'audace,*" he said softly as he reseated himself. "Have you decided, Barry, my boy?"

"Well, if we're to be broke, we must be broke, I suppose," answered the young man, with dogged resignation. "Curse the moral of it all. It's a prize worth risking something to get, anyhow. Let's hear my instructions."

"I shall want you to be an attentive pupil, Barry. You have got to cram, you understand. I think I mastered most of the essential facts during the time I tutored Master Roger. Now, turn your mind's ear this way, if you please."

For an hour they conversed low together. It was like the prolonged murmur from a confessional, discussing what inaudible
infamy, in a Catholic church. At the end the clergyman rose.

"We can be in London by two o'clock," he said; then added
softly, as the other got to his feet: "*L'audace*, my boy, *l'audace*,
l'audace. Every move has been calculated; every surprise foreseen
and provided against. Provisioned as you are, the ordeal of the lawyers will prove a mere bagatelle; and, once accepted, self-confidence will carry us on triumphantly. Only—*audacity*. Remember
it is neck or nothing with us."

"A beastly way of putting it," said Mr. Smith. He felt instinctively at his collar, as if his neck-stud worried him, and cleared his
throat. "Well, come on," he said.

II

Let it be confessed at once, without any misleading of the truth,
that William Wardroper was a congenitally wicked man. He did
not lead the double life, he would have told you; he merely frankly
and cynically exploited his profession, a paid and profitable profession like any other, for purposes of self-interest and self-indul-
gence. If that were wrong, the fault lay in the system, not in its
adherents. The Church never pretended to be anything but an exclusive way to office and the coveted emoluments of office; its
morality was exactly on a par with that of "dirty" politics, with
which, after all, it was closely associated.

Wardroper was one of those intellectual human abnormalities
by whom all knowledge—because, it seems, of its easy acquire-
ment—is applied contemptuously to worthless ends. He had been
a double first class at Oxford; a shrewd debater; a deadly contro-
versialist. Yet from the first there had always seemed something
wrong about him, indefinable, yet surely communicated to the seis-
mograph of the normal conscience. He had no soul, in the spiritual acceptance of the term; he was not so much immoral as moral-
less. And that atmosphere, rather than any definite suspicion of

heterodoxy, had kept him persistently unattached and poor. So handicapped, the natural evil in him had not hesitated to turn his "profession" to whatever material profit it could command, and he had descended by inevitable gradations to the mere clerical adventurer, using his pseudo-sacred calling for a cloak to cover his depravities. He was a profligate by temperament; his appetites made him a criminal; chance, in the matter of the Burnside succession, put into his hands the opportunity to become a gigantic criminal. The magnitude of the stakes involved appealed to the most daring in him.

Such men have, as a rule, a much greater fondness for the fruits of their vices than of their rare virtues. Mr. Barry Smith had had reasonable cause until now to congratulate himself on the fact. His cockney career had consistently owed as much as it was worth to the influences of a parent, who disdained ever to make a secret from his offspring of their relationship, or to withhold from that offspring's ears a narration of the principles which, in practice, served to keep them both going. Only it was a different thing to Master Barry when he found himself called upon to take an active personal share in the exploiting of those principles in one very tremendous direction. However, being the true son of his father, he ended, as we have seen, by consenting. In a question of "neck or nothing," as it had been disagreeably expressed to him, any informal cutting of his duties had appeared a matter of the smallest moment, and he had left the booking-office, as he knew, never to return to it.

At the hour named the two men entered Messrs. Sherrard and Stormont's offices in Norfolk Street, Strand. Mr. Smith, for all his vamped-up assurance, was looking peaked and glum; Mr. Wardroper was humming a blithe little air as they entered the glazed partition occupied by the commissionaire whose business it was to take down the names of visiting clients on little slips of paper, and convey the same into this or the other of the inner sanctums. The man came back almost at once, and ushered the gentlemen into a hushed apartment, lofty, gloomy, and severely legal in its appointments. A tall, calm-looking gentleman, of virile middle-age, just raised his body an inch or two from the chair in which he sat before a substantial desk and, with that apology for a salutation, sank down again and immovably conned his visitors.

"Mr.?" ventured the clergyman, with a smile.

"Stormont," answered the gentleman. He just bent to glance officially at the slip of paper and looked up again. "And you?"

"Wardroper," said the clergyman; "and"—he signified his companion— "my pupil, Lord Burnside."

"Exactly," said the gentleman. He seemed quite to brisk up. "We received and answered your communication, I think, Mr. Wardroper. Pray be seated."

"That is so, Mr. Stormont."

"There are one or two formalities to be gone through with—certificates, identification, and so forth. You will understand that?"

"Assuredly. I am prepared, for my part, to satisfy all inquiries."

"Just so. As for instance, how there come to be two claimants for the title at one time?"

It all happened in a moment. The shock was proportionate to the occasion. Mr. Wardroper, risen in an instant to his feet, was conscious of the snaps of cold steel about his wrists, and turned to find himself in the custody of a burly inspector of police. A supplementary constable had timely performed the same neat and rapid office for his offspring.

The inspector spoke: "Charge of conspiracy and attempting to procure murder," and shut his mouth.

"Attempting!" The comment was out before the astounded criminal could stay it, or realise its significance.

"It's my duty to warn you," began the inspector.

"O, I know, I know!" said the clergyman, with a little genial impatience. He had quite recovered himself. "Mr. Sherrard, I presume?" he said, addressing a stout and satisfied gentleman, who stood in the background, beaming through a pair of spectacles. "This is amazing treatment, my good sirs, for one of my cloth. I trust you will not live to repent it."

"Done with the neatest privacy and despatch, Sherrard," said his partner. "I congratulate you. And now we need not delay bringing in our witness."

At a sign from him a pale, skimp young man came into the room. Wardroper gasped.

"Let me re-introduce to you," said Stormont, "our Lord Burnside—formerly your pupil, Mr. Roger Beck."

The clergyman's lips, the clergyman's staring eyes, shaped their own inarticulate message. But still the mechanical smile never left his face.

"Hullo, Roger, my boy!" he shook out at length. It sounded somehow like an appalling blasphemy.

"Tell him, if you please," said Mr. Stormont, "and get it done with."

The young man came forward. One could understand from his physical meanness, from his common tone, tainted with a queer little foreign accent, how it had ever occurred to that other to replace him by so vulgar a substitute.

"We were crossing the glacier," he said; "we were skirting a narrow, deep crevasse, when he, that Terray, lifted and threw me in. At least he tried to; but my alpenstock caught across, and there I hung by my hands. And as I hung, he told me all about it—the lord I had become, the plot to do me out of my title and my life. He enjoyed telling it me, the devil; he laughed at my tears and entreaties. 'When you have relished it to the dregs,' he said, 'I shall just kick this, so, and down you will drop to eternity. And for me, I shall go on to England and be paid my price—the first price, that is, which is to be.' He was leaning over and gloating at me, when there came a sudden wind up from the abyss, cold as death and blinding with ice, and he staggered and fell in."

"The glacier-blast," put in Stormont, nodding his head like one who had climbed mountains, and knew.

"I heard him scream as he fell," continued the young man. "It was like an express engine, faint and fainter. Then I was mad, all alone there. I don't know how I got out. I got my knee somehow upon the alpenstock, and then my foot. My nails burst, and only I knew I was lying safe above, and presently the cold revived me. Then, saying no word to anybody, sick only that he might still follow and kill me, I came on to England, and sought out the late lord's solicitors."

He ceased. "There is little essential to add," said Stormont. "The clue once in our hands, with your letter"—he addressed the clergyman— "to confirm it, we had simply to await your arrival and thereafter shadow your movements. You have been watched, sir, at every point, since you landed. The telephone message from the supposed guide was spoken by the inspector here. Do you wish any more information?"

Still the same ghastly smile and mute lips.

"It was, to do you full credit," continued the lawyer, "infamously well planned. The utter obscurity attaching to the life of our client; his own ignorance of his succession; the absence of any witnesses capable of testifying to the truth. I won't say, had it not been for that strange providence, but that one of the cunningest frauds of our time might have been successfully perpetrated. You can take that negative comfort to your doom."

Mr. Wardroper, rallying ineffably from his stupor, waved his large hand.

"Surely it is not spoken yet, sir," he said. "I see nothing in all this but the inadmissible evidence of hearsay to associate me with any conspiracy or evil design whatever."

He was interrupted by Mr. Barry Smith, who had sat collapsed hitherto in the chair into which he had sunk.

"Conspiracy," he snarled, lifting his head. "I wish I'd never answered to your summons; I wish I'd never agreed to play my lord to your bloody-handed piping. Trust in you, indeed, you old devil and dotard! You may get out of it as you can. I've had enough of your infallible methods, and I'm going to tell the truth!"

Mr. Wardroper appeared to stagger a little. He closed his eyes and re-opened them, and wonderful to relate they were wet.

"You to turn King's evidence, Barry, my boy!" he said.

"There," said the lawyer, "that will do. Take them away, inspector."

PROVIDENCE

Have you ever heard of the Gorlestone Tunnel murder? Probably not, since it belongs to your father's generation, and many more notable railway mysteries have interposed themselves between then and now. But of one thing I am quite certain, that any shadowy recollection of it which may exist in your minds will not be associated with the name of Mr. Trillet Boomby. It could not fail to be, could it, supposing that extraordinary name had figured in any way in the case? As a matter of fact, it did not: at the same time, as a matter of fact, the case owed its ultimate issue entirely to the unconscious intervention of Mr. Trillet Boomby, always working, be it understood, under Providence.

Now, circumstance is like an endless revolving band, the world its fly-wheel, the driving force somewhere up in the blue yonder. If you would think to trace the genesis of any particular "providence," so called, by reversing the wheel and hunting backwards, you would reach of course in time the primal protoplast from which everything derives. That is true enough; still, in the case of these special "providences," it is possible sometimes to detach and isolate, for the purpose of proving and illustrating them, a special group of coincidences, which date from a more or less definite point in the train of events. That point, to be sure, is an insecure one, and of loose interpretation: you may trace back, for instance, the fly that choked the pope to the maggot that was the fly, to the carrion that bred the maggot, to the huntsman who made the carrion; or you may continue, through the family history of the huntsman himself, to the particular circumstances which led him on a particular day to kill a particular beast, which bred a particular insect, which a particular accident at a particular moment deposited in the papal wine-cup. For all essential purposes, however, we may elect to date Mr. Trillet Boomby's association with the Gorlestone murder case from the moment when he slipped on the pavement outside the Lowther Arcade (it existed in those days), and sat down rather hard.

There was a piece of orange-peel—but let that pass. The main point is that it was outside the Lowther Arcade that Providence brought Mr. Boomby to this abrupt stop. He got up, unnecessarily ashamed—it was no fault of his—and instantly sought refuge from his confusion in the Arcade itself. It occurred to him to try to look natural, so he pretended that he had come to buy a toy. The pretence, as it happened, was both an inspiration and a reproof, for he had actually been on his way, when he collapsed, to Waterloo Station, thence to journey on a week-end visit to the father of his godson, who lived a half-mile outside Swithunminster on the Ramsley road. Some earnest of his spiritual relationship would be expected of him by Johnny, and undoubtedly not less by Johnny's parents on Johnny's behalf. They were all very religious people.

"Uncle" Trillet thought of a clockwork engine. The stall at which he applied happened to be out of the article. He thought, with diminishing inventiveness and without success, of a few other things. Finally, time pressing, he was inveigled by the astute young lady into purchasing, what she had mentally imposed upon him from the first, a flying top—the very latest thing in toys. You pressed a grooved metal rod, or centre-bit, into a miniature propeller, which, violently set revolving thereby, rose into the air and whirred away in eccentric flight—a weapon of destruction to delight any boy. With the packet under his arm, Mr. Trillet Boomby hurried off to catch his train.

Now, I ask you to consider the absolute irrelation of two nevertheless converging forces. I doubt if Uncle Boomby, a kindly-natured man, had even read about the Gorlestone case. Certainly it never for one moment occurred to him, as he drove past the grim prison on the Ramsley road, that lying immured within its walls lay the young seaman convicted, though on circumstantial evidence, of a very brutal murder, and condemned to suffer for his crime on the morrow. The visitor drove past and on, beaming benevolence, and was only a little dashed, on reaching his destination, to receive a message to the effect that his host and hostess were temporarily called away, but that Johnny would do the honours in their absence.

Johnny, in fact, was nothing loth, and presently godfather and godson were out in the garden, the latter excitedly eager to test the new purchase. Once, twice, thrice he essayed the trick, and on the fourth attempt let fly with vigour. And at that moment!

At that moment the prisoner lay in his place, Mr. Trillet Boomby stood in his, and a strong, thickset man, carpet-bag in hand, was walking up the hill from the station towards the prison. Dusk was already falling, and!

The propeller spun, rose, hovered a moment, and whizzed away with a little buzzing song. It made straight for the wall overlooking the road, and hit a cat that was dozing on top (rotating and edge-on, it had almost the cutting force of a knife). The cat, bouncing up with a screech, and leaping anywhere, landed full among a tray of plaster images an Italian hawker was bearing past on his head below. The Italian cursed and jumped, the tray, with its ruin of casts, went crashing into the road, and so startled a horse drawing a cart-full of washing that the beast bolted incontinent, and went tearing down the hill, leaving its pedestrian master gaping and hooting in the rear. A little below the prison the cart smashed on a lamp-post, and vomited its load all over a toiling cyclist, who, being overturned from his machine, was shot with considerable force into the middle of the thickset man with the carpet-bag, who in his turn went down with a broken thigh. And so the end, prepared for outside the Lowther Arcade, was fulfilled.

For the thickset man, do you see, was the public executioner, arriving overnight in preparation for his job; and, since he was *hors de combat*, and no other could be obtained immediately to fill his place, the execution had to be postponed for twenty-four hours, late during which interval, some startling new evidence having come to light, a reprieve arrived for the condemned man, who was ultimately pronounced innocent and discharged.

So the gods will sometimes make a practical joke of even their mercies, as the orange-peel witnesseth. But to the day of his death Mr. Trillet Boomby remained ignorant of the part he had played in averting a tragedy. Indeed, certain ominous sounds following the flight of the cat had made him rather shy of revealing himself. And in any case there was a second propeller in the box.

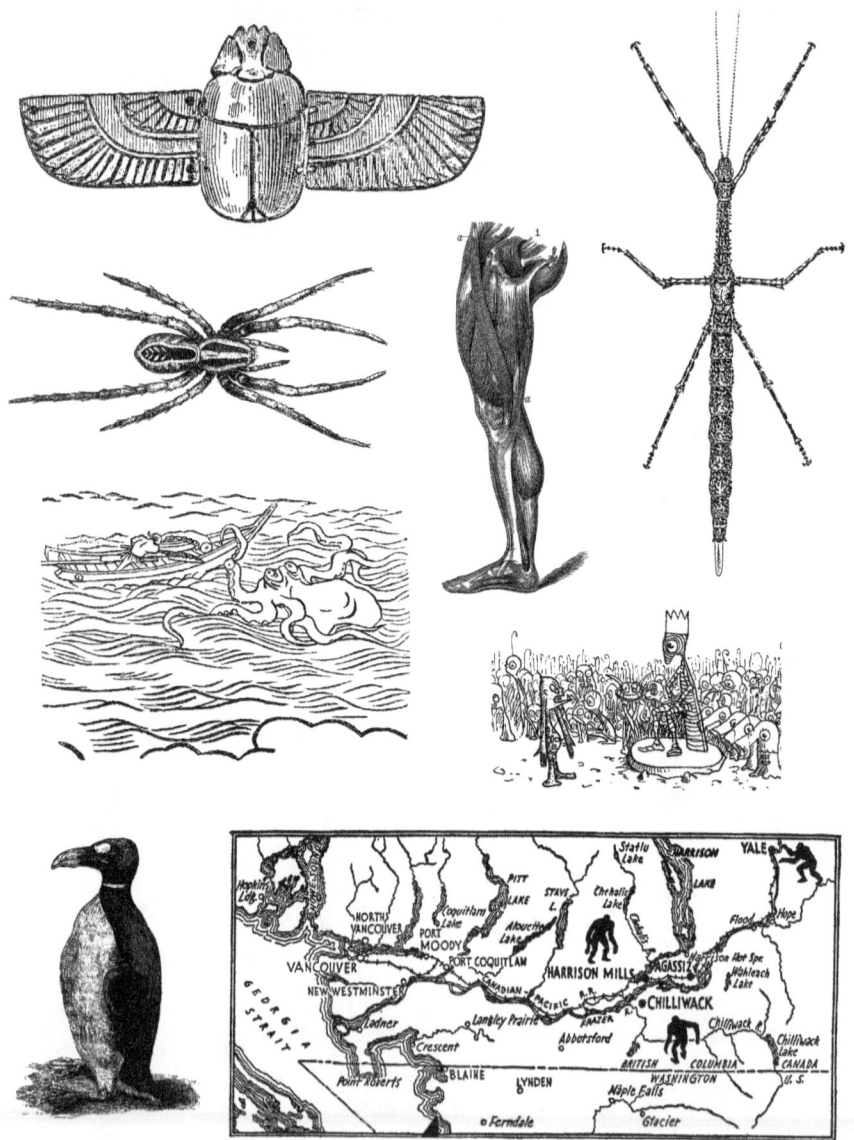

COACHWHIP PUBLICATIONS

COACHWHIPBOOKS.COM

DANCING SHADOWS

TALES OF THE SUPERNATURAL
BY BERNARD CAPES

Dancing Shadows
ISBN 1-61646-093-8

Ancient Haunts:
Stoneground Ghost Tales / Tedious Brief Tales
ISBN 1-61646-005-9

Strange Haunts:
F. Marion Crawford & H. B. Marriott Watson
ISBN 1-61646-091-1

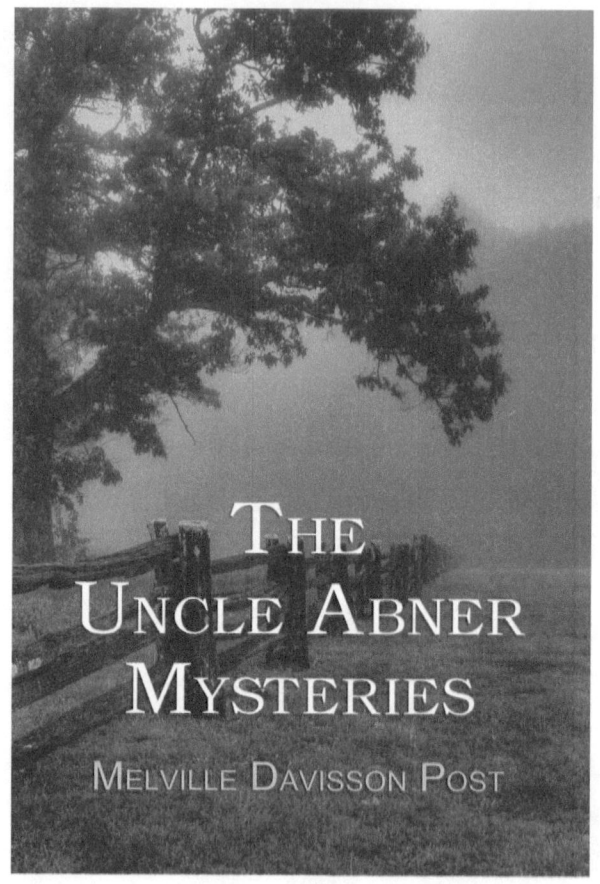

THE
UNCLE ABNER
MYSTERIES
MELVILLE DAVISSON POST

The Uncle Abner Mysteries
ISBN 1-61646-016-4

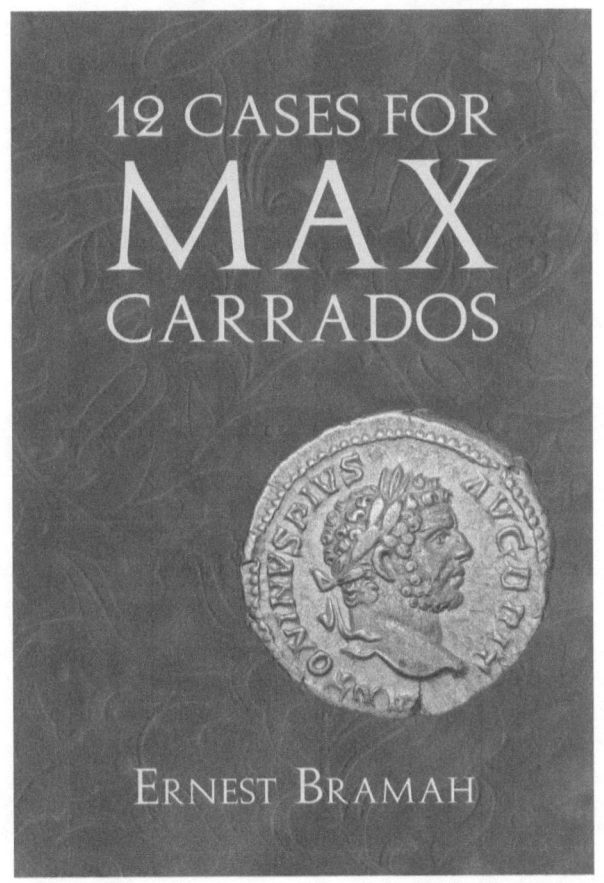

12 Cases for Max Carrados

ISBN 1-61646-018-0